PRAISE FOR

Corpse Pose

"Sure to leave readers breathless."
—Madelyn Alt, author of *Where There's a Witch*

"Diana Killian has outdone herself . . . *Corpse Pose* has it all,
from a well-written plot and sharp prose to wit and humor
that had me rolling with laughter . . . Fun, fun, fun!"
—Michele Scott, author of the Wine Lover's Mysteries

"[A] fresh, solid, and most importantly, entertaining, kick-
off to her new yoga-themed series."
—ReviewingTheEvidence.com

"A tight, well-written story."
—*Gumshoe Review*

"A funny and fun cozy mystery."
—*Affaire de Coeur*

D0805218

Berkley Prime Crime titles by Diana Killian

CORPSE POSE

DIAL OM FOR MURDER

Dial Om for Murder

Diana Killian

BERKLEY PRIME CRIME, NEW YORK

THE BERKLEY PUBLISHING GROUP
Published by the Penguin Group
Penguin Group (USA) Inc.
375 Hudson Street, New York, New York 10014, USA
Penguin Group (Canada), 90 Eglinton Avenue East, Suite 700, Toronto, Ontario M4P 2Y3, Canada
(a division of Pearson Penguin Canada Inc.)
Penguin Books Ltd., 80 Strand, London WC2R 0RL, England
Penguin Group Ireland, 25 St. Stephen's Green, Dublin 2, Ireland (a division of Penguin Books Ltd.)
Penguin Group (Australia), 250 Camberwell Road, Camberwell, Victoria 3124, Australia
(a division of Pearson Australia Group Pty. Ltd.)
Penguin Books India Pvt. Ltd., 11 Community Centre, Panchsheel Park, New Delhi—110 017, India
Penguin Group (NZ), 67 Apollo Drive, Rosedale, North Shore 0632, New Zealand
(a division of Pearson New Zealand Ltd.)
Penguin Books (South Africa) (Pty.) Ltd., 24 Sturdee Avenue, Rosebank, Johannesburg 2196,
South Africa

Penguin Books Ltd., Registered Offices: 80 Strand, London WC2R 0RL, England

This is a work of fiction. Names, characters, places, and incidents either are the product of the author's imagination or are used fictitiously, and any resemblance to actual persons, living or dead, business establishments, events, or locales is entirely coincidental. The publisher does not have any control over and does not assume any responsibility for author or third-party websites or their content.

PUBLISHER'S NOTE: The recipes contained in this book are to be followed exactly as written. The publisher is not responsible for your specific health or allergy needs that may require medical supervision. The publisher is not responsible for any adverse reactions to the recipes contained in this book.

DIAL OM FOR MURDER

A Berkley Prime Crime Book / published by arrangement with the author

PRINTING HISTORY
Berkley Prime Crime mass-market edition / November 2009

Copyright © 2009 by Diane Browne.
Cover illustration by Swan Park.
Cover design by Lesley Worrell.
Interior text design by Laura K. Corless.

ISBN: 978-0-425-22705-3

BERKLEY® PRIME CRIME
Berkley Prime Crime Books are published by The Berkley Publishing Group,
a division of Penguin Group (USA) Inc.,
375 Hudson Street, New York, New York 10014.
BERKLEY® PRIME CRIME and the PRIME CRIME logos are trademarks of Penguin Group (USA) Inc.

PRINTED IN THE UNITED STATES OF AMERICA

10 9 8 7 6 5 4 3 2 1

To Candace, Dorothy, Lynn, and Tanya.
With thanks and affection.

Acknowledgments

I'd like to thank my husband, Kevin Burton Smith, for his love, support, and hot dinners. I'd also like to thank my terrific editor at Berkley Prime Crime, Sandy Harding, for her keen eye and superhuman patience.

One

❦

"There's a call for you on line four."

A.J. Alexander, momentarily distracted from sorting through potential candidates for a receptionist position, tore her attention from the MySpace page on the laptop screen before her. It was not easy to do given the pounding beat of "Get Freaky" by Play-N-Skillz, and the video clip of eighteen-year-old Tabitha Lowe's tattooed and undulating body. Very lithe, Miss Lowe, but did she really think a prospective employer was going to be impressed by comments like "Partying with my posse" under the Interests section? Granted the list of Things to Do in an Elevator was pretty amusing. A.J. particularly liked number five: *Crack open your purse, and while peering inside ask, "Got enough air in there?"* Even so, it seemed clear Ms. Lowe was not going to fit the corporate profile—even a corporate profile as flexible as Sacred Balance Studio's.

"Who is it, Suze?" she asked the plastic face of the intercom, clicking out of MySpace. She had a stack of resumes to get through before this afternoon, and so far the hunt was not going well. Sacred Balance Studio was currently short one receptionist now that Suze MacDougal had been promoted to teaching beginning yoga courses.

"Nicole Manning," Suze's voice crackled back.

A.J. ran a hand through her chin-length chestnut bob. Conversations with Nicole didn't tend to be quick or easy. But Nicole was one of their two local celebrity clients, and she expected to be catered to. A.J. sighed. "Okay. Put her through—and, hey, why are *you* answering the phones?"

"Charlayne called in sick again, so Lily told me to cover and said she'd have someone take my classes."

A.J. squashed the flare of irritation at Lily's highhandedness. Lily Martin was A.J.'s co-manager, and she was always butting heads with A.J. It made sense for Suze to man the phones. She was the only instructor with receptionist experience, and these days the Sacred Balance phones were pretty busy. But A.J. knew Lily would have tagged Suze for that duty anyway because she disagreed with A.J.'s decision to promote Suze. That was just one of many of A.J.'s decisions that Lily disagreed with.

Suze knew it, too, and there had been a trace of resentment in her tone.

A.J. said, "Thanks so much for jumping in, Suze. It's such a relief to know I can always rely on you."

And she meant every word. Sounding mollified, Suze said, "No prob. Here's Nicole. . . ."

"Oh my *God*," Nicole breathed before A.J. could do more than open her mouth. "A.J., I don't know *what* I would have done if you weren't there!"

"Hey, Nicole!" A.J. said brightly, hoping to stave off with small talk whatever crisis this was, because obviously Nicole was, as Tabitha and her posse would say, "crisied out."

"This is like *such* an emergency," Nicole said. "And, I mean, I *so* hate to even ask, but you are my *last* hope, A.J."

A.J. tried to imagine what this emergency service could possibly be. Donate a kidney? Carry letters of transit across enemy lines? Give Nicole three free months' membership at Sacred Balance?

She said cautiously, "Well, I mean, if there's something I can do . . ."

Nicole hadn't stopped long enough to hear that. "If you say no, I don't know what I'm going to do. Seriously."

A.J. could picture the text message now: *Srsly?*

"What is it you need?" she inquired.

"I left my cell phone at the studio."

"*Oh.*" That was easy enough. A.J. relaxed and moved Tabitha Lowe's resume to the don't-call-us-we'll-call-you pile. "I can bring it to the party this afternoon."

Nicole gave a nervous laugh. "Well, *no*! I mean, I sort of need it *now*. That's why this is an emergency. I'm expecting a really important call. From my *producer.*" The fact that she hastened to add that bit of unnecessary detail struck A.J.

"Won't your producer just call you at home if he can't reach you on your cell?" A.J. wasn't sure why she was bothering to argue, because she already knew she was going to have to run Nicole's cell phone out to her. It was a simple enough request, and they were too short-staffed to spare anyone else, so A.J. would have to make the trip to Nicole's luxurious ten-bedroom colonial home—and it wasn't the end of the world. She could use a break from reading misspelled resumes and investigating indiscreet blogs at LiveJournal and MySpace.

"They—I—I just can't take that chance," Nicole faltered. "Anyway, no one calls me at home. Everyone uses my cell. And that phone is *expensive*, A.J. It's a Nokia Gold Edition. It's worth, like, three-thousand bucks."

"Are you kidding me?"

"No, I'm not kidding you! Will you do it? Will you bring me my phone right *now*?" Nicole couldn't quite curb the impatience in her tone.

Was there some reason Nicole couldn't get her cute little gluteus maximus down to the studio and pick up her over-priced cell phone herself? Why didn't she send Bryn Tierney, her long-suffering personal assistant? A.J. opened her mouth, but her gaze fell on the photo of Aunt Di on her desk. Just a little over eight months ago, Diantha Mason, a legendary yoga instructor and lifestyle guru, had bequeathed her beloved Sacred Balance Studio to A.J., and she took that trust seriously. As she studied Aunt Di's enigmatic photograph-smile, she quashed her irritation at Nicole's arrogance. Nicole didn't mean any harm, really; she was just oblivious and totally self-centered. A few years in Hollywood could do that to a person.

"Do you know where you left your phone?" she asked.

"At the studio!"

"*Where* at the studio?" A.J. hung onto her temper with an effort.

"Oh. I'm not sure. Maybe the shower."

"The shower!" She closed her eyes. Granted, for three thousand dollars, Nicole's cell phone ought to, at the very least, be waterproof.

"Not *in* the shower, but that's the last place I remember seeing it. It rang when I was blow-drying my hair. I picked it up and I must have set it down on the counter."

Maybe it was time for some kind of crack down on cell phone use during classes? The use of phones and pagers was gently discouraged during sessions, but maybe A.J. needed to take this one to the mat. And take it to the mat she would have to, because anything that offended big-name clients like Nicole or Barbie Siragusa was going to send her co-manager Lily skidding right off the eightfold path and on a collision course with A.J.

"Okay, I'll have a look for it. If it's not there—"

"If it's not *there*?" shrieked Nicole, and A.J. held the phone away from her ear. "Why wouldn't it be there?"

"It probably is. I just meant—"

"No, you're right!" Nicole exclaimed. "That bitch Barbie probably took it!"

"Whoa!" A.J. said. "I never said anything like that. I'm sure your phone is right where you left it. I'll just run upstairs and find it and bring it out to you."

"Oh, A.J., if Barbie took my phone, I'll kill her. I'm not kidding. That would just be *so* typical of her. And don't let her tell you that it's an accident or a mistake, because she is out to *ruin* me."

"No, no. Really," A.J. soothed. "I'm sure your phone is right where you left it. Let me go check."

"Call me back *immediately*!"

"I will." A.J. made more reassuring noises, cutting off Nicole's threats and promises and entreaties, and hung up.

A three-thousand-dollar cell phone was floating—maybe literally—somewhere on the premises. Terrific. Leaving her office, she started down the hall to the front lobby.

As she passed Lily Martin's office, Lily called peremptorily through the half-open door, "A.J., I want to talk to you!"

A.J. bit back her instant aggressive response. Although she owned Sacred Balance, per the terms of her Aunt Diantha's will, Lily was A.J.'s co-manager—for as long as they both could bear it. Lately A.J. had come to think that her pain threshold had been breached.

"What did you need?" She forced a smile and pushed wide the door to Lily's office.

Lily sat at her desk, clicking away at her laptop. She looked up, unsmiling, a petite, forty-something woman with a razor-sharp black bob and severe eyebrows. Her nod at the chair in front of her desk was not so much in invitation as command.

And though A.J. told herself again and again that she needed to make a greater effort to understand Lily, her reflex was one of resistance.

"I'm on my way over to Nicole's," she said. "Can it wait?"

"I suppose it'll have to if you're taking off early."

A.J. managed to hold on to that pleasant smile—mostly because she knew that would irritate Lily more than giving into her own ire. "Actually, I'm just playing errand girl. Nicole left her cell phone here. I'll talk to you when I get back."

The severe brows raised. Maybe that *had* sounded more like a threat than a promise, but oh well. A.J. summoned another one of those artificial smiles and continued to the front lobby. Suze, looking actively unhappy, was busy on the phone. Her blonde hair stuck up in agitated tufts reminiscent of Crackle, one of the elves on the Rice Krispies box.

A.J. passed the cubbies, the gift shop, and went briskly up the two flights of stairs to the locker room and showers. The smell of steam and shampoo reached her as she walked through the doorway on the women's side. Several stalls were occupied, and she could hear a couple of clients chatting—loudly—over the rush of water.

"It's just that yoga isn't very sexy."

"Are you kidding me? Have you ever seen a Rodney Yee DVD?"

A third voice said, "Oh, I think it's improved my sex life. It's put me in touch with my body, with my feelings. And I feel sexy when I feel good about myself."

"Now Jazzercise was sexy."

"*Jazzercise?*"

Another woman was blow-drying her hair in front of the long mirror. On the granite counter next to her gym bag was a gold cell phone. Literally gold. Like 24K.

A.J. reached for the phone, and the woman blow-drying her hair said, "It's been ringing and ringing."

"Thanks," A.J. answered, starting back downstairs.

Who the heck spent three thousand dollars on a cell phone? Even a candy-bar form cell with e-mail, camera, Bluetooth, MP3, high-speed data GPRS, and video. Not that she didn't understand about status symbols. And not that she couldn't afford a gold-plated cell phone if she wanted one. Along with the yoga studio, A.J. had inherited close to eighteen million dollars in various properties and subsidiaries from her aunt. She had her own addiction to Veblen goods, but somehow a Hermès Birkin bag or a Patek Philippe watch didn't seem so wasteful. She would receive a lifetime of wear from those items. What would a three-thousand-dollar cell phone give Nicole other than an equally horrendous phone bill—and a radiated brain? Although in Nicole's case, who would know the difference?

As A.J. reached the second level, she found herself surrounded by a number of pregnant students filing cautiously down the stairs, indicating that Denise Farber's Prenatal Pilates session must have just ended. Nicole's phone began to ring.

It went through her mind to answer it—Nicole had said the call was urgent—but she heard her name. A.J. stopped on the stairs and the sea of swollen bellies parted around her.

Barbie Siragusa stood on the landing above, and A.J. started back toward her. Barbie was her other celebrity client, the wife of Jersey mob boss Sam "Big Bopper" Siragusa, now on year five of a fifteen-year prison stretch.

"What did you need, Barbie?" A.J. asked, reaching the other woman.

Barbie was fifty-one and strikingly beautiful in a sharp-featured, hard-as-polymer way. From the crown of her raven-haired extensions to the tips of her spray-tanned toes, Mrs. Big Bopper made the most of her assets.

Voice held steady with an effort, Barbie said, "Just so you know, I don't appreciate the disrespect, A.J."

"Uh . . ." began A.J.

Barbie's skinny frame was vibrating with tension as she glared down from the landing. "Refusing to let my film crew into the studio. You think I don't know who's behind that?"

"I'm behind that," A.J. replied quietly, only too aware of the curious looks they were getting from the women moving around and past them. "I offered to let you film after hours."

"After hours is not reality!"

"I'm sorry, I don't think it's appropriate or fair to the other students to allow a film crew to disrupt—"

"No one was disrupting anything!" yelled Barbie. "They were just going to film me in my class. It's a reality show. They have to film everything."

"It's just a couple of hours out of your day," A.J. pointed out, striving to sound reasonable.

"It's my *reality*!"

Now this was almost touching. Someone who actually believed in the legitimacy of reality TV. A.J. said, "But it's also the reality of everyone else in the class and the studio. The other students and the instructors."

Barbie stared at A.J. as though she were insane. "It's *TV*," she said. "Everyone wants to be on TV. Everyone wants to be on my show—except that bitch Nicole Manning."

Okay, now they were getting to the heart of the matter. A.J. glanced automatically at the cell phone she held as it began to ring again—another direct dial from Crazy Land, no doubt.

"Nicole had nothing to do with my decision not to allow a film crew inside Sacred Balance." She added hopefully, "Why don't we take this to my office and discuss it there?"

"Are you going to reconsider your decision?"

"Probably not, but we can—"

Barbie made an eloquent hand gesture—kind of a cross between Queen Victoria and a Palermo cab driver. "Don't waste my time. This is all about Nicole Manning. She openly mocks me in that crap show of hers. That whole Bambi Marciano shtick. Who do you think that's supposed to be? That's me! Now she's trying to ruin my own show because we get better ratings than hers ever did. She's a jealous, frustrated—"

"Wait." A.J. stopped her. "We can't discuss this here. Really. I know you're upset. Let's go down to my office and talk about it."

Barbie ignored her, sweeping past as she headed down the stairs. "There's nothing to say," she threw over her shoulder. "Nicole Manning is dead to me. *Dead.* That's my reality!"

Two

⊰⊱

"**Wow,**" said Suze when A.J. reached the bottom level. "We could hear that all the way down here. She is *mad*. She nearly ran over a couple of yummy mummies in the parking lot."

A.J. sighed. "And it seemed like it was going to be such a great day this morning. Birds were singing. The sun was shining."

"It's still shining."

"That's merely an illusion."

Suze grinned. "Are you seeing Jake this evening?"

A.J. nodded. And despite everything, she couldn't help smiling as she met Suze's bright blue gaze. A.J. had started dating Detective Jake Oberlin eight months ago—not long after she moved to the small northwestern New Jersey township of Stillbrook. It was very casual. A.J. was in no hurry to get involved following the disastrous end of her ten-year marriage. At least, that's what she kept telling herself. And luckily—sort of—Jake seemed to agree.

Suze leaned on the reception desk, munching yogurt-covered almonds. "Well, if it helps, I think it would be kind of cool to be on TV."

"It doesn't help," A.J. retorted. Heading for her office, she called back, "Don't forget, the camera adds ten pounds."

"Ugh." Suze wasn't speaking on her own behalf. She was thinking, correctly, of the effect appearing fat on national TV would have on the morale of so many of the female patrons of Sacred Balance.

A.J. sat down at her desk and dialed Nicole as requested. The phone was busy on the other end. Didn't Nicole have call waiting? A.J. dialed again. Another busy signal. A.J. hung up. She took a couple of slow, long breaths and focused on the calming play of the water over stones in the fountain sitting in the corner.

Yeah. Nice try, but she was basically getting more and more irritated as the moments passed. She dialed again, and again reached the annoying buzz of the busy signal. It wouldn't be so aggravating if Nicole hadn't specifically ordered A.J. to call her.

But whatever the reason, no one was answering the call, and A.J. finally gave up, grabbing her keys and purse.

"I'll be back in an hour," she called to Suze who—on the phone again—waggled her fingers in good-bye.

It was a blue and blazing May afternoon. Heat shimmered off the road and sunlight seemed to gild everything in gold as A.J. drove along the country lane. She began to relax a little, the stress from the scene with Barbie fading as the miles passed. Not so long ago she would have zipped down the road aggravated with every tractor and trailer that got in her way, but today she was content to drive the speed limit, enjoying the scenery which last year would have been no more real to her than images flashing past on the Travel Channel.

Now she not only noticed, but she even appreciated the graceful stone spire of a distant church, the gold and green crazy quilt of fallow and fertile farm land, the distant blue glitter of lakes and rivers behind trees. Despite its unfortunate reputation, New Jersey had its scenic spots, and the Skylands were some of the nicest. Rough and rural, a contrast of quaint villages, farms, and wild parkland, the "Great Northwest" of the Garden State was a far cry from A.J.'s former life in Manhattan.

In her final letter, Aunt Diantha had written: *Darling Girl, the blessings that I would bestow upon you are a joyful spirit and a heart at peace.* A.J. didn't know if she had actually achieved a joyful spirit and a heart at peace, but she realized that she now looked forward to each day, and that she was coming to terms with the past—and that was a lot right there. Far too many people never even had that much.

Though she had to admit, it was easier to hold onto this mildly nostalgic sense of peace and harmony with her mother safely out of the country on an Egyptian cruise, and Andy, A.J.'s ex, in New York, where she never had to see him or deal with his troubling desire to remain friends.

A few minutes outside of Blairstown she pulled off the main road and drove past white-fenced pastures until she came at last to the mansion Nicole Manning had purchased during the five-year run of the popular TV series *Family Business*.

A catering van was parked next to a florist's minivan in the drive. Blue-jeaned minions carried elaborate arrangements of roses, eucalyptus, and delphiniums in large crystal vases up the steps of the three-storied white colonial. A.J.

parked and got out of her Volvo, following the florists though the double doors of the mansion.

A young woman with short red hair and freckles pushed through the line of people, planting a six-inch, crimson wedge-shaped heel into A.J.'s foot in her haste to exit.

"Ouch!" said A.J., staggering and bumping into the person next to her.

"Well, excuuuse *you*," said one of the florists who had narrowly missed dropping her plumy arrangement.

The red-haired young woman's eyes met A.J.'s briefly, and A.J. was startled to read something like terror in the wide blue gaze. The next moment the woman was out the door and down the steps, sprinting across the gravel toward the back of the house.

"Well!" said the florist, meeting A.J.'s eyes and then glaring after the fleeing woman. "How rude!"

A.J. shrugged. A few minutes of Nicole's company tended to have the same effect on her.

"Right this way!" chirped Bryn Tierney, Nicole's PA. "Only forty-five minutes to show time!" She was a slim, efficient young woman with very long blonde hair, which she habitually tied back in a French braid. Bryn beckoned the florists toward the dining room. Catching sight of A.J., who held up the gold Nokia phone like a cop flashing a badge, she said, "Oh, thank goodness! Nikki is going crazy. Just go on through to her office."

A.J. was still trying to equate the idea of Nicole with "office" as Bryn pointed to the left. A.J. nodded, peeling off from the floral contingent and following what appeared to be a genuine antique Axminster carpet down the long hallway to the door that stood partially open.

She knocked on the door, but there was no answer. From inside the room, pop music played loudly, showcasing the

talents and tonsils of some female artist. A.J. tried to think
who. Lately, she felt a little removed from what was happening in the rest of the world, and she wasn't entirely sure
that was a good thing. Who *was* that singing? Britney
Spears? Beyoncé? No. Shakira.

Relieved that her pop culture skills were still relatively
sharp, A.J. knocked louder.

Shakira continued to belt out "Hips Don't Lie" at the top
of her lungs.

Pushing wide the door, A.J. called, "Nicole? I have your
phone."

At first glance she thought the room was empty. No one
sat at the fragile, decorative-looking desk, although A.J.
noted that the receiver of the white and gold princess phone
was lying off its hook as though someone had stepped away
in the middle of a call.

That must explain the busy signal.

But even as the thought registered, chill recognition
prickled down her spine. There was something . . . not
right . . .

"Hello?" she called, raising her voice to be heard over
the music.

Gigantic photographic images of Nicole in various film
roles beamed and twinkled from the walls of what was
otherwise an elegant room. A.J. had a quick impression
of traditional yellow and white striped wallpaper, a book-
shelf which seemed to be filled with books matched for
size and color, and perfectly coordinated furnishings that
were either genuine Empire antiques or very expensive re-
productions.

A.J. walked into the room. "Nicole?"

She stopped. A tall window looked out over the flowering garden. Sunshine poured into the room and sparkled off

what A.J. at first took to be shards of smashed glass on the parquet floor. Then she made out what appeared to be the crystal head of an animal of some kind. A bear or a monkey—no, a koala. The crystal koala head sat in a puddle of water—was, in fact, melting into a puddle. Ice. An ice sculpture.

A.J. was still trying to make sense of this when her gaze sharpened, picking out two motionless feet in blue high heels extending from behind the long primrose-colored sofa. Something about the graceless slant of those limbs alerted A.J.

She rushed forward even as, belatedly, her brain began to connect the dots: the deafening music, the phone off the hook, the broken ice sculpture . . .

Eyes half-open, Nicole lay sprawled behind the sofa, a mess of blue silk and water and blood. Her upswept blonde hair was matted with dark stickiness. She was utterly still. A.J. had never seen anything as still and silent as Nicole Manning crumpled on the floor, and she stopped herself from kneeling beside the fallen woman. Nicole's gray waxy pallor and the dreadful, ominous lack of movement told her it was already too late. Had been too late for some little while.

She took a step back, sucking in a breath as she narrowly avoided the carved ice body of the broken koala bear—tinged pink. For a moment reality shuddered, and A.J. wondered if she was going to do something totally uncharacteristic like . . . faint.

Someone spoke behind her—voice raised to be heard over the pounding music.

"Nicole, the caterers want to know . . ." Bryn Tierney's voice died. "What's going on?" she asked, approaching A.J. at the edge of the blue oriental carpet. "What's wrong?"

A.J.'s lips parted but there was no need to try and find a gentle way of breaking the news. Reaching her side, Bryn stared down at Nicole's body. She turned to A.J., eyes cartoon-sized. Her mouth worked, and she began to scream. . . .

Three

"Okay, let's just run over your statement."

Emergency vehicles and police cars crowded the drive—along with a couple of news vans. Crime scene specialists moved across the grass talking and nodding. For these people it was . . . business as usual. A.J. tore her gaze away from the window that looked onto Nicole Manning's front lawn and met Detective Jake Oberlin's eyes.

"I'm not sure what more I can add," she said. What she wanted to say was *Not again! How about a little sensitivity here? Do you have any idea how horrible it is to stumble on a murder scene?* But of course she didn't say that—and, besides, he *did* know.

Tall, dark, and official, Detective Oberlin had broad shoulders, piercing green eyes, and zero sense of humor when it came to his job. Today his job was Nicole Manning's murder. Still, as his eyes met A.J.'s, there was something almost sympathetic in his gaze, as though he understood exactly the sick mix of shock and horror she felt. Nonetheless, his voice was brisk, and it was clear to A.J. that her sort-of boyfriend, Detective Jake Oberlin, was not pleased to see her involved even peripherally in his homicide case. And she sympathized, because she wasn't exactly thrilled herself.

"I want to make sure we haven't missed anything," he said, and A.J. sighed.

She had never felt more tired. The initial surge of adrenaline that had kept her moving after the ghastly discovery of Nicole's body had gradually drained away, leaving her feeling more than a little shaky. She had been at Nicole's house for nearly three hours. First they had waited for emergency services and the police who had taken initial statements. Then they had waited for a homicide detective to show up—which had turned out to be Jake. Jake had taken a more complete statement, and now he was verifying every little detail with her. Which made sense, of course, but A.J. desperately wanted to go home, to leave this scene of violence and tragedy.

Jake stared down at the paper he held. His long, dark eyelashes threw shadow crescents on his tanned cheeks. The eyelashes were disarming because A.J. had never met a man more aggressively male than Jake.

He raised those strikingly green eyes to hers. "So you got a call from Nicole at exactly what time?"

"About one-thirty."

Jake opened his mouth, and A.J. said, "I didn't look at the clock, but I'm pretty sure it was close to one-thirty because I was thinking I'd have time to get through another two or three resumes before going home to change for the party."

"Cutting it a little fine, weren't you?" he remarked. "According to Manning's PA, the party was supposed to start at three."

Was he going to lecture *her* on social etiquette? He didn't even *like* parties.

She retorted, "I think it was more of an open house. They were planning on a buffet rather than a sit down meal. And anyway, I planned on being there by three-twenty, which is well within the fashionably late no harm, no foul margin."

"Right. So Manning calls and tells you she's left a three-thousand-dollar cell phone in the bathroom, and can you bring it to her immediately because she's expecting an important call from her producer?"

"Yes."

"And the producer's name is?"

"She didn't say. I didn't ask."

He made a check mark on his notes. "You run upstairs, you find the cell phone right where Manning described, you run downstairs and try phoning Manning—"

Jake broke off as A.J. moved uncomfortably. "What?"

"It's probably nothing."

"See, this is why we go over the statements. *What* is probably nothing?"

A.J. really did not want to bring up her conversation—that was one word for it—with Barbie. It wasn't as though Barbie had actually threatened Nicole. Saying someone was dead to you wasn't the same as saying you were going to kill them. But Barbie and Nicole had had a contentious relationship, and, worse luck, that discussion had taken place on a crowded staircase in front of easily a dozen witnesses. Important client or not, A.J. was going to have to mention Barbie's name to the police.

She replied, "On my way downstairs I bumped into Barbie Siragusa." The glint in Jake's eyes gave her pause. "Barbie mentioned how unhappy she was that I had decided not to allow any filming of her reality show, *Barbie's Dream Life* inside Sacred Balance Studio."

"*Barbie's Dream Life*?" Jake repeated slowly. His mouth twitched with a hint of grim amusement. "Do they have an episode where Barbie visits the Big Bopper in the dreamy new federal "supermax" facility in Florence, Colorado?"

"I'm not a regular viewer," she admitted primly. It was only too easy to picture just such an episode. "Anyway, Barbie seemed to believe that my decision was influenced by Nicole."

"Was it?"

"No. Not at all. I mean, it's not a secret that Nicole was scornful of Barbie's . . . um . . . work. But I didn't want a film crew inside the studio because it would be disruptive. I can just imagine what Aunt Di would have thought of that idea. Anyway, I tried to explain to Barbie, but I don't think she really believed me. . . ." A.J. trailed off as a sudden thought hit her.

Barbie had seemed to be part of the group leaving the neonatal Pilates session. Not one of her usual choices. Was that because Barbie had missed her regular Pilates class or could Mrs. Siragusa possibly be pregnant? Maybe A.J. needed to tune into *Barbie's Dream Life* more often.

"And?" Jake inquired.

A.J. snapped back to the present. "And I invited her to come down to my office, but she declined and left the studio." At about eighty miles per hour.

"What are you not telling me?" Jake said in a resigned tone that indicated he knew that no one ever told him everything.

A.J. made a face. "Well, before Barbie left she said that Nicole was dead to her." Hurriedly, she added, "She didn't say she was going to kill her."

Jake considered this without comment. Then he returned to his notes. "Okay. Let's talk about this woman you saw leaving the house when you arrived. The woman who bumped into you."

"Shorter than me." A.J., who was tall and lanky, gestured to her nose. "Petite. Spiky red hair, freckles. She was wearing a Kay Unger embroidered blouse, Billy Wildcat jeans, and red platform shoes with six and a half inch heels."

Silence.

Jake said, "You can recall what she was wearing down to her six and a half inch heels but you didn't notice her eye color?"

"Blue, I think."

He nodded skeptically. "Had you ever seen her before?"

"Maybe." A.J. added apologetically, "She did seem vaguely familiar, but I'm not sure I've actually met her. I couldn't place her. Granted, I only saw her for an instant."

Another nod. Another note.

Into A.J.'s mind popped the image of wide blue eyes in a pert, freckled face. Yes, she'd seen that look before . . . like on the face of someone destined to be an alien hors d'oeuvre—or serial killer victim number two.

"She might be an actress," she said slowly.

Jake's eyes narrowed thoughtfully, then he went back to looking noncommittal. It was a little annoying. She understood that he had a job to do, and that it was crucial to keep a professional distance, but . . . still. Irksome.

"So the redhead runs out the door and Bryn Tierney, the PA, tells you Nicole is in her office. You walk in and . . . describe again for me . . ."

A.J. described again walking into the room: the pounding music, the smashed ice sculpture, the phone off the hook—

She broke off her narrative. Through the window she could see several uniformed men wheeling a gurney across the drive to the waiting vehicle marked *Coroner*. On the gurney was a black body bag.

Following her gaze, Jake glanced at the window. He cleared his throat. "You said you tried calling Nicole before you left the studio."

A.J. blinked and turned back to him. "Right," she said. She was relieved that he was picking up this point. No one else had seemed to think it was significant. "The line was busy—now I realize that it was because the phone was off the hook. At the time it didn't make sense to me because Nicole had specifically told me to call her right back, and I knew she was frantic about her phone."

"And this mysterious phone call she was waiting for."

"I don't know if the phone call was mysterious. She said it was her producer."

"Why wouldn't her producer call her house number?"

A.J. had no answer for that; she had wondered the same thing.

Jake asked, "When did you try calling?"

She did some mental calculations. "Probably between one forty-five and one fifty. I left right after that." He was watching her closely, confirming her own suspicions. She said, "Of course Nicole could really have been speaking on the telephone part of that time. Either way I'd have got a busy signal. There's no way of knowing for sure when she put the phone down."

Even assuming she had put it down voluntarily.

"It's possible," Jake said noncommittally. But as his eyes met A.J.'s eyes, she knew with a sick feeling in the pit of stomach that Nicole had probably been dead by the time she left the studio.

Four

"Okay," Jake said, as his cell phone began to ring. "I'll follow up with you on a couple of points, but you can go."

A.J. rose and hesitated. "I'm guessing dinner is off?"

He grimaced, and for a moment the hard, professional mask slipped. "Yeah. Sorry. There's no way I'll get free tonight. This is high-profile stuff." His voice dropped. "I'll call you, okay?"

A.J. found that tentative "okay?" revealing. She had the impression, though Jake had never come right out and said so, that he was used to women not showing much understanding of his work schedule.

"Okay," she said, and offered a cautious smile.

He smiled—fleetingly—in return, and pulled out his cell phone. She turned away.

"Oh, and A.J.?"

She glanced back, and Jake admitted, "That was sharp thinking—using your cell phone to take pictures of the position of the murder weapon."

And she actually blushed! As though he had paid her the rarest of compliments. Granted, compliments from Jake *were* pretty rare. Unlike Andy, A.J.'s ex, Jake was not much given to flowery sentiments. That wasn't necessarily a bad thing; it just took some getting used to. Andy had been a wonderful communicator—in all but one thing—Jake, not so much.

"It must have been all those Trixie Belden books I read as a kid," she offered. She had been prepared for much harsher words since it had been her suggestion to Bryn that they freeze the mostly melted lumps of ice—all that remained of the ice sculpture someone had used to smash Nicole over the head. She had yet to hear what the forensics people thought of her method of preserving the murder weapon.

Jake raised his brows, clearly having no idea who Trixie Belden was, and answered his cell.

As A.J. left the dining room where the police had set up base, she heard his crisp, "The boyfriend? Good. Let him through. I want to talk to Mr. Young."

An attractive, bearded blond man of about forty was walking across the lawn toward the house as A.J. started down the wide porch steps. She recognized J.W. Young, Nicole's live-in boyfriend. Young was a director—mostly documentaries and programs for public television—and he collected Civil War memorabilia. That was the extent of what A.J. knew about him, although they had met a couple of times. She watched as he made his way through the police and troopers, while from down the drive and behind the yellow police line, media photographers snapped pictures.

Gray-faced and grim, Young passed A.J. without seeing her.

"Oh, J.W.!" cried Bryn from inside the house.

A.J. glanced back in time to see Young framed on the porch with his arms around Nicole's sobbing PA. Not that A.J. blamed them. She could relate to the need for a hug about then, but down the road the photographers were clicking away frantically, zoom lenses focused unsparingly on their target.

As a former freelance marketing consultant it was second nature to A.J. to consider image, and she had a feeling the likeness of Young and Bryn locked in an embrace might not look quite so platonic on the cover of *The National Enquirer* or other supermarket tabloids. She could imagine the headlines now: *TV Mob Wife Gets the Business in Hollywood Love Triangle.* Right next to the ever-popular space alien babies and amazing pet rescues.

Young gently freed himself from Bryn's embrace and seemed belatedly to notice the photo op they had provided. He slammed the white front door shut with a resounding bang. The cameras continued to snap away.

A.J. proceeded to her car, backing carefully down the drive, avoiding all the crime scene personnel and vehicles, the florist and catering vans. Everyone on the premises had been held for questioning, and she realized that she was lucky to be one of the first permitted to leave. Apparently dating a cop did have a perk or two attached to it, though she'd just as soon not require a Leaving the Crime Scene Early pass too often.

A few yards farther down the drive she had to negotiate her way through a gauntlet of reporters shouting questions and photographers peering inside her car, flashbulbs popping. Beyond the reporters and the photographers, sightseers had begun to gather.

It was a relief to reach the main highway. A.J. drove without thought, now completely oblivious to the beauty of the

scenery around her. It still seemed unreal that Nicole was
dead—that someone had taken a section of the ice sculpture
from the buffet table and whacked her over the head with it.
And this in a house full of people.

So *many* people. Caterers, florists, the household staff.
Nicole's killer was either crazy or had coldly counted on
all those extra bodies to provide some needed camouflage.
Either way someone had surely seen something that would
set the police on the right trail. It could only be a short time
before an arrest was made.

A.J. thought again of the red-haired woman who had
bumped into her as she rushed from the house. Talk about
suspicious behavior. Still, there were all kinds of reasons a
young woman might be observed running around as though
her hair were on fire—A.J. had done her share of that when
she had worked freelance.

And how glad she was that those days were over, even if
now and then she did wind up trying to balance a normal
life with the occasional murder investigation.

Glancing at the clock in the Volvo dashboard, she decided there was little point in returning to the studio. It was
nearly five o'clock and Lily would likely be gone for the
day. Of course she could always call and make sure—even
ask the other woman to wait—but the idea of another con-
frontation with Lily was more than A.J. could handle. There
had been enough bloodshed for one afternoon.

Not for the first time she wondered at the terms of her
aunt's will. Diantha Mason had been a wonderful woman—
one of a kind—but she had been as stubborn as she was in-
novative, and a perfect example of that stubbornness was
tying up A.J. and Lily in a business partnership that was
probably destined to end—at best—in an ugly lawsuit.

Perhaps the stubbornness was genetic, though, because

A.J. wasn't about to give up Sacred Balance, despite the fact that if someone had told her a year ago she'd be living in rural New Jersey running a yoga studio she'd have checked the bushes for the Candid Camera.

On impulse she turned off the exit and drove into the small town of Stillbrook, past the graveyard where Aunt Di rested with her one great love, the naturalist and photographer, Gus Eriksson.

Stillbrook was the kind of village one might expect to find along the California coast. While it wasn't precisely an artist's colony, there was a strong arts and crafts element to the town. In addition to the art galleries and bookstores, there were little bakeries and specialty shops. Several museums were within twenty minutes driving time, and the Mauch Chunk Opera House was less than an hour away. In the center of town, cute historic buildings circled an old-fashioned village green with a large pond and a bronze statue of a WWI soldier and mule.

A.J. loved all these things about Stillbrook, but she also loved the fact that there was a Starbucks, and a conveniently located Kentucky Fried Chicken—not too far from an equally conveniently located Taco Bell. Not that she didn't try to eat sensibly most of the time—that was part of the commitment to her new life—but nothing triggered her fast food cravings like stress, and today had topped the charts.

First things first. A.J. stopped first by the market to pick up a movie. The woman behind the counter greeted her cordially, recommended the *Sex and the City* DVD, and asked if she'd heard the terrible news about Nicole.

A.J. paid for her DVD rental and admitted she had.

The woman peered over her thick, black-framed glasses at A.J. "Mob hit," she said wisely.

A.J. started to say she couldn't picture a mob enforcer using an ice sculpture to knock someone off, but then it occurred to her that the method of Nicole's death might not be public knowledge. Jake hadn't told her to keep it to herself, but perhaps he had thought that too obvious to need mentioning.

She said cautiously, "You mean because she was in *Family Business*?" Not that the popular cable TV show was exactly the stuff of hard-hitting crime exposé.

"That *and* . . ." the woman leaned across the counter. Reluctantly, A.J. bent forward to hear this revelation. "Barbie Siragusa had a vendetta against her."

"A *vendetta*?"

"It means blood feud."

"I . . . right. But why?" A.J. remembered something Barbie had said at the studio that morning. "Because she thought Nicole was making fun of her in *Family Business*?"

The woman shrugged mysteriously.

A.J. decided this had gone far enough. Not that she didn't enjoy a little juicy gossip as much as the next person, but this was verging on slander. She said, "Well, that is certainly an idea."

"Yep," the woman said, and handed A.J. her change.

The theory at KFC was that a demented fan had done Nicole in.

"You read about that kind of thing all the time," an earnest ponytailed teen informed A.J. while they waited in line.

"I guess so," A.J. said. Stranger things had happened; there were people out there who would sell their souls for Neil Diamond tickets. And while Nicole had never struck her as the type to inspire a cult following, anything was possible in this crazy world—especially in New Jersey.

"I bet the police will find all kinds of crazy letters from fans and stalkers," the girl told her knowledgeably.

"I saw that on an episode of *Law and Order*," the gangly youth at the cash register put in. "She should have hired a bodyguard. The police can't do anything until the guy tries something, and by then . . ." He snapped his fingers. It had a final sound to it.

The girl in line behind A.J. shivered in pleasurable horror. In fact, all of Stillbrook seemed in a state of titillated shock. A.J. realized it had probably been the same after Aunt Di's death, but at that time she had been living the drama herself and had been unaware of public scrutiny.

"Did you ever hear anything about Nicole being stalked?" she couldn't help asking.

The two teens looked blank.

"You usually hear about it *after* something like this happens," the boy told her, and A.J. supposed there was some truth in that.

She ordered the weekly special: fried chicken, mashed potatoes, coleslaw, biscuit, and a soft drink, paid for her dinner, and headed out to Deer Hollow Farm determined to put all thoughts of death and violence out of her mind.

Not that this was easily done—Nicole's death had opened some scarcely healed wounds.

A.J. had been living at the farm since her aunt's death eight months earlier, and during that time she had come to love Deer Hollow. As she drove down the dirt track that evening, dust turning gold in the sunset, the car fragrant with meadow-sweet scents—and fried chicken—she was thinking of how very happy she was to be coming home.

Deer Hollow had been in the Eriksson family for generations, and although Diantha Mason had lived there many years, in most ways the 1920s farmhouse reflected the taste and attitudes of its previous owners rather than the famous yoga-guru. That was because, uncharacteristically, Diantha had submerged her own strong personality and preferences beneath those of her predecessors. She had left the house virtually untouched, and it retained all the original charming features such as gleaming wood floors, decorative moldings, and floor-to-ceiling stone fireplaces.

It had fallen on A.J. to renovate the less charming kitchen, replacing much of the old plumbing, adding new appliances and cherrywood cabinetry, which she had done following a small fire the previous fall. She had also installed a heated garage next to the house, and a breezy stone patio where, in warm weather, she did her morning yoga. The patio was also nice for dining al fresco, and she and Jake had already enjoyed a couple of summery evening meals beneath the flowering vines.

She rounded the bend in the dirt track and the house stood before her, white clapboard and gray stones surrounded by perennial flower gardens and fruit trees.

An unfamiliar blue sedan was parked in the front yard.

"Oh hell," A.J. said. She was not in the mood for company, let alone someone offering to steam clean her carpets or save her soul—or vice versa. Of all the terrible timing! Five minutes later and she probably would have missed this caller.

But as she pulled up beside the sedan, she realized the occupant was not moving. In fact, the front seat had been tipped back in the reclining position and the driver appeared to be sleeping.

A.J. peered at him through the lightly tinted glass, and the hair on the back of her neck stood up.

She knew him.

In fact, once upon a time, and not that long ago, she used to be married to him. Andy Belleson, her ex-husband, was sleeping in her front yard.

Five

❧

A.J. tapped on the window and Andy jerked upright and blinked sleepily at her through the tinted windows.

"What are you doing here?" she demanded.

He opened the car door, and A.J. backed up as he climbed stiffly out.

"Hey," Andy said. "I thought you were trying to get away from working late." He moved to hug her.

She accepted it gracelessly. They had grown friendlier since Diantha's death and A.J.'s move to Back of Beyond, but things were still not entirely easy between them. Not on A.J.'s end anyway, and she wasn't sure that they ever could be, despite Andy's desire to remain close.

He was smiling, though there was something not right in his face. She realized that it wasn't a trick of the dying light—there was a bruise on his left cheekbone—and found herself unable to tear her gaze away. People always said they looked enough alike to be brother and sister, both tall and slim and chestnut-haired. A.J.'s eyes were brown and Andy's blue, but they could still pass for kissing kin. And, in one sense, they had been kissing kin, if a decade of marriage counted for anything. They would still have been married if Andy had not discovered that he was gay.

Of course that wasn't fair. Andy hadn't *discovered* he was gay, he had just finally admitted it.

And that was the part that was hard to forgive, even while understanding that the last thing Andy had wanted was to hurt her. Or to hurt anyone. Which was one reason A.J.'s stomach did an unpleasant flip as she took in the bruise on his face. That hadn't happened shaving.

"How's . . . Nick?" she asked, trying for casual.

"Good," Andy said quickly. Too quickly? "He's out of town. Business." He shrugged. Nick Grant, Andy's new "partner," was an FBI agent, and he traveled a lot. Something that did not make Andy happy.

A.J. asked, "And how *is* business? Your business, I mean."

It used to be *their* business, but A.J. had sold her half of their partnership back to Andy after she had decided to accept Aunt Diantha's gift of a new beginning.

"Business is good. Business has never been better." And apparently this was not a source of joy, either.

"What happened to you?" A.J. questioned, abruptly out of polite conversation.

He laughed awkwardly. "I fell."

Fell? A.J.'s internal alarm bells were ringing. But she was distracted by a familiar yowl. Peering into the back seat of the car, she spotted a pet carrier. A well-known, thuggish feline face was smooshed against the mesh.

"Lula Mae?" She stared at Andy and he smiled that not-quite-right smile again.

"I thought you'd like to see her again."

"Well, yeah, but . . ."

"And she misses you."

She reached in and hauled the carrier out. Lula Mae was small, sleek, and black. She had huge green eyes and a broad vocabulary for a cat—which she demonstrated long and loudly as A.J. lifted her out of the carrier.

"Oh, I've missed you, too," A.J. told her, kissing Lula Mae's nose. To Andy, she said, "I don't know how Monster is going to feel about this."

A.J. had inherited Monster, an aging golden lab, from Aunt Diantha.

"She can take him," Andy said confidently. "My money's all on Lula Mae, but maybe you better keep her in the carrier till you know for sure."

Andy and Monster did not enjoy the warmest of relations, and Andy bearing cats was probably going to be even less popular, confirming all Monster's deepest suspicions.

Lula Mae objected vociferously to being crammed back into her container. Andy took the carrier; A.J. retrieved her fast food dinner out of her car and led the way to the house. She could hardly fail to notice that Andy was limping as he followed her up the porch steps.

"How did you fall?" she asked.

"I just . . . did."

He was so obviously lying she couldn't seem to wrap her mind around it. She stared at him, and Andy said, "I wanted to ask a favor."

They weren't exactly on favor-asking terms. Well, that wasn't quite true. Andy had expressed willingness to do A.J. any favor whenever she liked. A.J. was the one not yet truly at ease with the tentative truce between them.

She replied warily, "What's that?"

"I was wondering if I could stay up here for a few days."

"*Here?* With me?"

He nodded.

"No."

He didn't say anything, and she said, "Why?"

"I just need a little time to . . ."

She opened the door. Monster stood on the threshold wagging his tail. His dismay at seeing Andy was almost human. The tail stopped midwag and his ears flattened, his muzzle drawing back to show a little bit of his teeth. He said something uncomplimentary.

"Monster, no!" she said sharply.

She turned. Inside the carrier, Lula Mae was loudly offering her opinion of a dog with the manners of Monster. Andy had put a hand out to the door frame to brace himself from an anticipated onslaught from Monster. That gesture caught A.J.'s heart when she least wanted it to. Maybe there were aspects she didn't know or understand about Andy, but she knew him well enough to gather that something was seriously wrong.

"What on earth—?" she began.

But Monster was already extending a curious nose at the window of the carrier. Lula Mae hissed with all the attitude of a full-sized cobra. Monster wagged his tail.

"Oh, Monster," A.J. murmured. He just had a knack for falling for the wrong critters. But then Monster didn't know he was a dog.

"His ass is grass," commented Andy. "My little girl is going to whup him from here to eternity." He seemed to have recovered his equilibrium, and A.J. pretended not to have noticed that odd moment when he reached for support.

"Monster, you goof," A.J. said. She dragged him away from the carrier and Andy brought Lula Mae inside, following A.J. into the kitchen. Because she needed to say something—he had thrown her for a loop with his request—

she babbled, "This has been a terrible day. Nicole Manning is dead. She was murdered. I found the body."

"*The* Nicole Manning?"

Had Nicole achieved "The" status? Apparently she had. And of course Andy said all the right things. Andy always said all the right things. He listened with appropriate alarm as A.J. told him about being summoned to Nicole's home and her reliving of those terrible moments when she had walked into Nicole's office; he asked intelligent questions. He expressed shock and sympathy. And before long A.J. had told him everything and was offering to split her fried chicken, mashed potatoes, and coleslaw.

He grinned. "I notice you don't offer your biscuit."

"Keep your hands off my biscuits."

He opened his mouth, but let it go, and A.J. was abruptly recalled to the situation between them. And reading her correctly, as he always did, Andy said seriously, "I'm not that hungry, but thanks."

She studied him, frowning. It struck her that he didn't look well: tired, pale—and he'd lost weight. He reminded her of the way she'd looked eight months ago when her life was unraveling around her. Although, being Andy, he hadn't hacked his hair to pieces in defiance. He was still perfectly groomed. It was hard to picture a situation where Andy would not be perfectly groomed. Even in bed—well, perhaps better not to go there.

"What's going on, Andy?" she asked. "Something is obviously wrong."

He met her eyes. "It's nothing. It's just what I said. I need a few days to . . . work through some things. Clear my head. And I miss you. You're my best friend."

"Andy . . ." She sighed. "I don't know if I'm ready to be best friends with you."

He said stubbornly, "I stayed here after Di's funeral."

"I know, but . . ."

But what? But it was just so much easier to deal with the old pain by ignoring it? Forgetting it? Andy's presence meant having to actively work at forgiving him, and that was hard. Forgetting was much easier than forgiving—forgiving was an on-going process that had to continue past the dramatic declarations of apology and absolution.

Real forgiveness meant allowing Andy to continue to be a part of her life, and A.J. wasn't sure she had spiritually evolved to that extent. And she wasn't sure all the yoga and tofu in the world could change that.

She chewed her fried chicken slowly. She couldn't see his face as he fiddled with the door to the pet carrier. He lifted Lula Mae out and cradled her against his chest. Lula Mae put up with the cuddles for about three seconds and then wriggled free to investigate this strange new world. Monster immediately rose from his rug and came to investigate Lula Mae—whereupon the cat did her impersonation of a Halloween decoration. Monster retreated, looking wounded.

"Do the police have any leads?" Andy asked, and A.J. was jerked back to awareness.

"I have no idea. It's probably too soon."

"It's never too soon," Andy scoffed. "The husband or the boyfriend is always the primary suspect, right? Who was she living with these days—that director?" Before Andy had married a G-Man, he and A.J. had watched a lot of television—especially crime shows.

"J.W. Young. But he wasn't there," A.J. said.

"You *think* he wasn't there."

"True, but the house was full of people: servants, caterers, florists . . . me. Someone would have noticed if he'd been hanging around."

"Not if he didn't want them to notice him. Who knows the house and everybody's routines better than him?"

A.J. said, "I'm trying not to take it personally that you are absolutely convinced that the husband would be the most likely person to want his wife dead."

Andy grinned. "Boyfriend. Hey, I don't make the TV shows, I just watch them. Anyway, my personal choice for prime suspect would be this red-haired woman with the scary taste in footwear. The one who you said looked familiar?"

"She did look familiar," A.J. agreed thoughtfully.

"Could she be one of your students?"

A.J. shook her head, preoccupied with slathering honey over a biscuit. "I don't have so many students that I wouldn't recognize them on the street."

"Are you still teaching dog yoga?"

"Doga. Yes, and don't you dare laugh at me. I'm also teaching the Itsy Bitsy Yoga."

"I'm afraid to ask."

"Yoga for babies."

Andy snickered. "You don't even like babies."

"I like babies! I just wasn't sure . . ." A.J. stopped. This was veering into deep and dangerous water. "Anyway, I don't have time to do a lot of teaching—which is pretty much a relief to everyone involved, me in particular. There's a lot to do on the business and administrative end."

There was a brief silence.

"So are you thinking of looking into it?"

Her thoughts still in the past, A.J. asked blankly, "Looking into what? Having babies?"

Andy reddened. "The murder."

The bear-shaped honey bottle made a rude sound as she clutched it. "You're joking, right?"

But Andy did not appear to be joking. He said as though it were the most reasonable thing in the world, "You solved the last one. You're the one who figured out who killed Diantha."

"That was just a fluke," A.J. told him. "And no way would I want to go through that again. The only reason I got involved at all was—"

"Yo . . ." Andy said.

"Momma," A.J. said with him.

They grinned at each other. "How *is* Elysia?" Andy asked. "Is she having a good time in Egypt?"

"The cradle of civilization has been well and truly rocked. This morning she sent back a slew of digital photos of herself riding in jeeps and on camels and in hot air balloons."

"Hot air balloons?"

"Apparently the very best views of Luxor are from hot air balloons."

A shadow seemed to cross Andy's face. But before A.J. could question him—assuming she could decide what to say—he said, "Now Elysia would have no hesitation diving into this murder."

"Don't even say it," A.J. pleaded. "I can hear it now." She mimicked her mother's BBC English accent. "I remember when Twiggy was a guest on *221B Baker Street* and we had to solve the *gruesome* murder of a Scottish poacher. . . ."

Andy was laughing, and for a minute it was just like old times. A.J. did a little communing with her better angel, and said, "Listen, Andy, if you want to stay a few days, I guess it's all right."

His face lightened. "Thanks. You're a sweetheart."

But not his. A.J. smiled ruefully.

* * *

The guest room door was closed.

A.J. noted it with relief, then padded into the kitchen to feed Monster and Lula Mae.

Andy had retired early the evening before and was apparently still sleeping, which was fine with A.J. She wasn't at all sure about the wisdom of her decision to let him stay. It was done and she needed to make the best of it, but she hoped Andy would give her plenty of space. His being there was stirring up a lot of memories she'd have been happier to leave as sentimental sediment. Not that they weren't good memories. That was the trouble.

In A.J.'s old life Sunday mornings had meant freshly brewed coffee, hot croissants from the bakery around the corner, a stack of magazines and newspapers, and that perfect blend of chat and comfortable silences shared with Andy. Or, alternatively, omelets and brioche at Savann or Elmo or some other trendy eatery in Manhattan.

For the first few months after she'd inherited Aunt Diantha's yoga and fitness empire, business had taken over A.J.'s life, and she had regularly worked days, nights, and weekends from dawn to dusk. She had told herself that this was necessary and all part of her learning curve, but eventually her mother's nag—er—gentle remonstrance, and the knowledge that Aunt Di had never intended her to become a workaholic, had encouraged her to keep regular and sensible business hours. She had faced the truth that allowing Sacred Balance to become her entire life would simply be a way of hiding from the world.

Plus hanging around Lily that much was making her nuts.

She turned the radio in the kitchen on softly and listened to the news while she readied the ingredients for summer squash pancakes. Predictably, Nicole's murder was the lead story on the local station, although there didn't seem to be a lot to report so far. Naturally this did not stop the media from rehashing the little information there was.

Even so, there were only so many ways to say that the thirty-five-year-old actress had been slain in her home by an unknown assailant while preparations for her birthday party were underway.

With grim humor, remembering Andy's comments the night before, A.J. heard that at the time of the attack, Nicole's boyfriend, director J.W. Young, had been flying back from Mexico where he had been filming a documentary on the 2006 protests in Oaxaca by the local teachers union. So much for Andy's theory.

According to the radio, the New Jersey native and star of the hit TV series *Family Business* appeared to have been struck repeatedly with a koala ice sculpture. Ironically, Nicole had been very active in koala preservation, and so on and so on.

There was discussion of Nicole's role in *Family Business* as street-smart matriarch Bambi Marciano, and some vague allusions were made to real-life mob missus Barbie Siragusa. It sounded to A.J. like Barbie might not have been completely off base in her suspicion that the Bambi Marciano character was based on her. Well, wasn't imitation the sincerest form of flattery? Surely it wasn't sufficient motive for murder?

Not that anyone was suggesting that Barbie was a suspect. In fact, there seemed to be a distinct lack of suspects—although there was some passing reference to a possible falling out between Nicole and her fan club.

There were a couple of interviews with Hollywood bigwigs who tried to find nice ways of saying that Nicole was a mostly adequate actress. Huge talent or not, her violent death ensured her place in the Hollywood pantheon.

After the commercials there was a very brief snippet of an interview with Jake, and hearing his voice over the radio gave A.J. a pleasant little jolt while she laid strips of turkey bacon in the cast iron frying pan that had well served generations of Eriksson women.

But Jake had little in the way of news to report either. In fact, "The investigation is ongoing" seemed to size it up.

Poor Nicole. A.J. felt a little guilty because she had not liked her more.

She was thinking about this as she poured granola in two dishes and orange juice into goblets. Her negative opinion of Nicole didn't change her fate, but it seemed to add insult to injury. It wasn't a logical reaction.

A.J. glanced down the hallway. The guest room door was still firmly closed. That was unusual. Andy was by nature an early riser—as was A.J., although these days her mornings were spent doing her sun salutations or taking a quick walk in the meadow or woods with Monster rather than watching *Today* and gulping coffee as she did her hair. She still spared a few minutes for reading over breakfast, but the breakfast only sporadically included Pop Tarts or Captain Crunch, and her current reading was *Yoga Journal* or *Yoga + Joyful Living* rather than the *Wall Street Journal*.

Switching off the radio, she fetched her yoga mat and went out on the flagstone patio to perform her sun salutation.

Sun Salutes, a series of flowing poses or asanas, were designed to wake up and energize the body through the integration of body, mind, and breath. Traditionally the sun salutation would be performed at dawn facing the rising sun, but part of the beauty of yoga was how adaptable it was to real life. And while A.J. certainly didn't object to the spiritual aspects of yoga, she was finding that, for her, the immediate payoff was the physical benefits of an early-morning stretch combined with the calming focus provided by having to concentrate on each move.

Between trying to eat more healthily and incorporating more walks and yoga in her life, A.J. was feeling better than she had in years. Her back was mostly pain-free, and she felt much more capable of handling the little curves life continued to throw her way . . . like finding a murdered client or having her ex-husband drop in unexpectedly.

Spreading her mat on the flagstones, she sat down facing the sun. For a moment she breathed quietly, eyes closed, simply taking in the peace of the warm, sunny morning . . . the trill of a bird, the scent of the flowering vine overhead, the feel of the breeze on her skin. She deliberately put aside her tension, the buildup of anxiety normal with modern life. She clamped down on her straying thoughts: Had she covered the pancake mix? What would Elysia say if she knew Andy was staying with A.J.? What would Jake think? Had she paid the electric bill for the studio? None of that mattered now.

Rising, she went smoothly through the twelve-step sequence, starting by planting feet hips-width apart, palms together in the prayer position, fingertips brushing the center of her chest over her heart.

A.J. drew a deep breath into her lungs, opened her palms, and swung her arms back over her head, arching her back and gazing up at the vines twining through the pergola slats. She exhaled, bending forward from the hips and slightly bending her knees as she placed her hands on the floor. She made an effort to bring her head as close as possible to her legs—but it was still not easy even after months of practice.

As she inhaled, she bent her left leg, sliding her right foot back into a lunge.

The main thing was to move with slow deliberation, not pushing, not forcing. A.J. concentrated on each breath, inhaling on the open positions.

Exhaling, she slid her left foot into position beside the right and held the position, continuing to breathe—that was the real challenge, remembering to breathe steadily and evenly, matching the length of her inhalations with her exhalations.

Lowering herself from the pushup position, she rested knees, chest, and chin on her mat.

Discharge your tension into the earth. . . . She could almost hear Aunt Di's cool voice instructing her.

The morning sun was releasing the warm scent of flowers and earth.

A.J. inhaled, using her arms to push up into the cobra position. She pictured the arc of her body as she closed her mouth and tilted her chin up.

Curling her toes under, she exhaled and pushed into downward dog, feeling the stretch through her arms and the back of her legs. She slid her left foot forward so that it was parallel with the right. She rested her head in a forward bend as close to her knees as she could manage without straining.

Straightening, she swept her arms above her head, arched her back and gazed up at the wooden timbers. She could see a spider weaving a silvery web across the leaves of the vine. Once she would have reached instantly for a broom.

Actually she still felt like reaching for a broom.

Baby steps, right?

Returning inside, she showered quickly, and finding the guestroom door still closed, tapped softly.

There was no response.

She knocked again. Waited.

Nothing.

"Andy?" she called.

No response. Lula Mae twined around her ankles and meowed plaintively.

A.J. eased the door open.

The guestroom was empty. The bed had not been slept in.

Six

❧

A quick glance out the front window verified that Andy's blue sedan was still sitting in the front yard. So . . . ?

With increasing trepidation, A.J. went through the house. "Hello? Andy?"

She walked quickly from room to room. There was no sign of Andy, although his car keys were still lying on the kitchen counter.

She stepped outside and walked down to the meadow, shading her eyes as she scanned the waves of shimmering green—it was already getting hot.

To her relief she spotted Andy at the far end of the meadow. He waved to her and started back, and A.J. felt a little foolish for her brief bout of panic. What did she think had happened? The elves stole him away during the night?

"Everything okay?" she asked as Andy reached her.

Either his walk or the early morning sun had put needed color back in his face. He was smiling and seemed more like himself.

"Sure. I just thought I'd take advantage of the peace and quiet."

When was the last time Andy had professed a desire for peace and quiet? But then A.J. hadn't realized how much she needed space to breathe until she had started her new life.

They went inside and A.J. fixed summer squash pancakes while Andy drank orange juice and stroked Lula Mae, who had uncharacteristically curled in his lap, boneless and somnolent with an excess of sunshine.

The radio news announcer babbled while A.J. poured pancake batter—she wasn't really listening until Andy sat up straight and said, "Oh, *hell* no!"

"What?"

"Didn't you hear that? That thing about Nicole falling out with her fan club?"

"I know. It's hard to picture Nicole getting on the bad side of a lot of teenage boys."

Andy's wide blue eyes grew even wider. "What are you talking about?"

"Well, who else would be in Nicole's fan club? She wasn't exactly Meryl Streep."

"A.J., *we* started that fan club. Don't you remember?"

"Say what?"

He said, "Back when Nicole was our client. We set up an Internet fan club for her. She'd just done that horror flick . . . I forget what it was called. The thing about the demon bride. Anyway, she had all these creepy kids join up."

"They weren't just kids," A.J. said, her memory belatedly kicking in. "What was her name? The one who took over as fan club president?"

"Lydia Thorne. What a freak. I almost felt sorry for Nicole—with friends like that . . ."

Studying his dismayed expression, A.J. said bracingly, "It's nothing to do with us. I mean, even if Lydia did something—and that's pretty farfetched, right?—how many presidents of fan clubs actually—"

"You saw the movie *Selena*," Andy interrupted, and A.J. fell silent.

After a moment she recovered. "First off, we don't know that Lydia or the fan club is implicated. The fact that Nicole had a falling out with her fan club could be just a rumor. Secondly, even if Nicole did have some kind of break with the fan club, that doesn't have anything to do with us—you. Nicole dispensed with our services years ago—not long after she got the role in *Family Business*."

When Nicole had been hired to play Bambi Marciano, she had decided that she needed a more high-profile company to handle her promotion. It had stung a little, but mostly it had been a relief; Nicole was high maintenance.

"But *we* set up the fan club. *We* put Lydia Thorne in place as president of that fan club. If Lydia did have something to do with Nicole's death, and word gets out . . ."

Meeting Andy's stricken gaze, A.J. said, "I guess I could ask Jake if there's any truth to the rumor. I don't know that he'll tell me. He's not exactly chatty about his work."

"Ask him," Andy said. "If the fan club is implicated, I've got some damage control to do."

A.J. thought Andy was taking their—his—responsibility in this too seriously, but she had seen the media in action often enough to know that sometimes the most innocent things could be exaggerated into full-blown scandal. Their connection to Nicole's fan club was well in the past, but they had, in theory at least, vetted and approved Lydia to take over the fan club—which did give Lydia limited access to Nicole. A case could be made that they had not done everything in their power to protect a client.

They continued to listen to the radio during breakfast, but there seemed no additional news. After breakfast Andy got out his laptop and A.J. phoned Jake. He didn't answer, but he did call back within a few hours.

"Hey. Sorry, I was in the middle of something. I was thinking of dropping by a little later."

"Great!"

"Well, no." Jake sounded awkward. "I can't stay. We're working round the clock on this one. But I wanted to get your phone back to you."

"Oh. Right." A.J. tried not to let her disappointment show in her voice. It irritated her that she even felt disappointment. She enjoyed time spent with Jake, but she did *not* want to get serious about anyone for a long time to come.

Right?

She said, "I heard on the news that there might be a connection to Nicole's fan club?"

"A.J., you know I can't discuss a homicide investigation with you." That weary note brought color to A.J.'s face.

She said shortly, "I only mention it because Andy and I set up Nicole's fan club."

Dead silence.

"What are you talking about?"

A.J. explained exactly what she was talking about. When she finished, Jake said, "Let me get this straight. A couple of freelance marketing consultants set up a bogus fan club for the Manning woman?"

"It wasn't a *bogus* fan club," A.J. said, getting exasperated despite her good intentions. "We set up an Internet fan club, but the people who joined were genuine fans. Mostly boys between the ages of fourteen to sixteen. There was nothing fake about it. We just organized it. Once it was up and running we handed it—with Nicole's blessing—over to a woman named Lydia Thorne."

"What kind of a background check did you do on the Thorne woman?"

"I don't remember. Andy could tell you. I don't think it was anything too extreme. It's not like we were giving her access to Nicole's bank account or home address. The company that took over Nicole's promotion might have done their own checking—it was Nicole's official fan club, after all."

"It was up until six months ago," Jake said grimly. "But apparently Nicole's organization revoked 'official' status after the Thorne woman began writing hostile reviews of Nicole's work and posting them all over the Internet."

"Yikes."

"That's one word for it," Jake said. "And after Nicole's people put Lydia out to pasture, things really got nasty. She began sending Nicole hate mail—sometimes using her own name, sometimes posting anonymously. Only it wasn't really anonymous because she was using the same IP address with the different hotmail accounts."

A.J. felt a little sick.

"I'll need to talk to Belleson," Jake said into her silence.

"You can talk to him when you drop my phone off. Andy's staying here for a couple of days."

"Belleson is staying with you?" Even though A.J. wasn't crazy about Andy staying with her, the displeasure in Jake's voice put her back up. And it didn't help when he added, "I didn't realize you two were on slumber-party terms again."

"I guess it depends on how you define 'slumber party,'" she said shortly. "He's a friend and he's visiting for a few days."

"Then I guess I'll have a word with him later today."

"I'll tell him," A.J. said, and that was pretty much that.

Jake rang off and A.J. went to find Andy. He was still glued to his laptop. "Look at this. I ran a search on Lydia Thorne. She's posted review after review of Nicole's work on the net."

"Jake said she posted a lot of hostile reviews of Nicole's movies. Nicole's people took away the fan club's 'official' status."

"'Hostile' doesn't begin to cover it," Andy said. "Listen to this. 'Manning sleepwalks her way through the role of Karen. Someone should have given her a NoDoz—not to mention the audience.' And that's one of the positive reviews. Not only that, this is for one of Nicole's earliest films."

"So?"

"Well, Lydia had already reviewed this—glowingly. She'd reviewed all Nicole's movies, remember? That was partly how she came to our attention. She adored Nicole and she adored her work. But from what I can see, it looks like she went back and revised her initial reviews."

"Something happened between Lydia and Nicole."

"Safe to say." Andy studied A.J. speculatively.

"What?"

"I was just thinking . . . You could phone her. I might still have her number somewhere, unless she changed it."

A.J. recoiled. "Why would I want to call her?"

"It would be good to know if she's involved. If she is, I need to start doing damage control. Pronto."

"Lydia Thorne isn't going to tell me if she's involved in Nicole's death."

Andy gnawed his lip. "But you might get a feel for whether she's telling the truth," he said. "You always had good instincts about people."

"I did?"

"Yes." Meeting the irony in her gaze, he said stubbornly, "Yes, you did."

A.J. shook her head. "I'm not calling Lydia. Sorry. If you want to call her, be my guest."

"I'm not the sleuth of the family," Andy protested.

Was that a lame attempt at buttering her up? He'd apparently switched to margarine since their divorce. "Note to Andy: I'm not getting involved in another murder investigation."

"Ellie would."

"Then go stay with my mother," A.J. returned pleasantly.

"She's in Egypt."

"Exactly."

All the same, A.J. enjoyed her Sunday. Most of the day was spent reading and chatting; Andy had taken care not to impose. He had gone for two long walks accompanied by Monster—who, according to Andy, did not exactly "accompany" him so much as *track* him.

The only real disturbance came in the form of two telephone calls from local TV stations wanting to interview A.J. She had declined politely but firmly. She was less polite with a national newspaper offering to pay her for an exclusive recounting of discovering Nicole's body—and the photos off her cell phone.

"How would they even know about those?" she demanded of Andy.

"There are no secrets in this life," Andy said. "There are only delayed revelations."

"Speaking as a former messenger."

"Ouch."

Reluctantly, she'd laughed.

In the evening Andy fried crispy vegetable wontons and grilled skewers of chicken *satay*, which they dipped in a light cilantro pesto as they finally settled down to watch the DVD of *Sex and the City* that A.J. had rented the day before. They drank ruby slipper cocktails and critiqued the movie with merciless pleasure, keeping each other laughing—just like old times. Maybe too much so.

Around eight o'clock Jake finally showed up to return

A.J.'s cell phone, the Stillbrook Police Department having safely downloaded the pictures she had taken of the murder scene.

A.J. showed him into the den where Andy had put the movie on hold. Jake sat down, eyeing the cocktails glasses on the coffee table with a raised eyebrow.

"Don't worry, neither of us is driving anywhere tonight," A.J. said—and both Andy and Jake stared at her.

She wasn't exactly baiting Jake—well, maybe come to think of it, she was. Where did Jake get off judging her and her friendship with Andy? It wasn't as though they were a couple. Not exactly. They went out once a week or so, but Jake had not pushed for anything more—which A.J. told herself she was glad about because she wasn't ready for anything heavier than the most relaxed and casual of relationships.

From the local gossip A.J. had picked up, Jake had enjoyed a fairly active social life—given the limitations of his work schedule—and she wasn't sure he didn't still date other women. They certainly had never discussed keeping things exclusive.

So it was a little annoying when Andy scowled at her and turned to Jake, asking graciously, "What'll you have to drink, Jake?"

That was just Andy's good manners, but A.J. could see it had the wrong effect on Jake—Andy probably appearing to be a little too much at home.

"I'm still on the clock," he said.

"Oh, right," Andy said. "Have you had a break in the case yet?"

It was almost entertaining to watch Jake struggle with the desire to squelch Andy. Andy wasn't easy to squelch, which was one reason he was so good at his job. People had trouble saying no to him.

"Too soon to say," Jake clipped. "However, I do want to ask you a few questions." He proceeded to quiz them—Andy mostly—about the fan club. Taking them back to the beginning of their brief working relationship with Nicole, he focused mostly on how they had selected Lydia to be the fan club president.

"It wasn't rocket science. She worshipped Nicole," Andy said. "And we were looking for someone willing to take the thing over as soon as possible. Nicole really got into the concept of having a fan club, and she had all kinds of plans—none of which we had time to carry out. We were the idea people. But someone like Lydia who was willing to moderate a discussion list and handle contests and just generally act as head cheerleader was perfect."

A.J. selected a fried wonton. It crunched noisily as she bit into it. Jake's gaze moved to hers. Neither looked away. "How did you pick her?" he asked Andy.

"Sorry? Oh, Lydia. She was the first person to join the fan club. She mentioned right off the bat that she'd written reviews of all Nicole's work, and sure enough, there they were. Rave reviews. Any place you could post as a fan, Lydia had posted."

"And this fan club was an Internet group?"

"Mostly," A.J. put in. "I think some of the members got together for premieres and the occasional meal. I think it had social club aspects for a lot of them."

"It was national or local?"

"National, but the largest concentration of fans was here in Jersey. A few people knew each other offline and socialized in real life."

"Socialized . . . based on being big fans of Nicole Manning?"

A.J. said, "You have to understand about fandom. It's its own world. People come together based on passion for stamp collecting or bird watching or the Jonas Brothers or the Harry Potter books or Japanese manga—you name it, but they often form genuine friendships beyond the object of their interest."

"I'll take your word for it."

"My mother has a small but fanatical cult following," A.J. informed him. "As one example."

"You don't have to convince me that your mother would attract a bunch of nuts." Jake was grinning, but almost instantly he was back to business. "Did either of you ever meet Lydia?"

Both A.J. and Andy shook their heads.

"And what kind of background check did you do?"

A.J. looked at Andy. Andy shook his head. "I think we ran a credit check." He added earnestly, "The thing you have to understand is that Nicole corresponded with Lydia directly. In the early days of her career, she used to post to her message boards and discussion list. She was active online, and she communicated with her fans. She and Lydia connected. I mean, their relationship continued offline."

"You mean they developed an actual real-life friendship?" Jake inquired.

Again, A.J. let Andy answer. "I don't know about real-life friendship—I guess it developed into a kind of friendship. I can tell you that Nicole was all in favor of Lydia being president of her fan club. I can also tell you that A.J. and I didn't have a lot to do with Nicole after that point simply because she decided she needed a bigger and more prestigious firm to handle promoting her career."

"And how did you feel about that?"

Jake couldn't honestly think Andy was a suspect—let alone A.J. It just had to be his cop reflex kicking in.

A.J. said, "It was a relief." Andy started to protest, but she overrode him. "Come on, Andy. She was totally self-absorbed—to the point of egomaniacal. We worked our tails off for her, and the minute her career started to take off, she dumped us." She turned to Jake. "It was a relief, though. She put the tense in high maintenance."

Jake nodded thoughtfully. "Okay. So basically, you two hired this Lydia Thorne to head Nicole's fan club—and Nicole was all in favor of the idea. Is that pretty much it?"

Andy and A.J. nodded uncomfortably in unison— Raggedy Ann and Andy, judging by Jake's expression. A.J. said, "You suspect Lydia Thorne? Is that it?"

"Well, I guess we would if such a person existed," Jake said a little sardonically. "The fact is, there is no such person as Lydia Thorne. There never was."

Seven

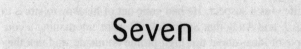

Even when you loved your day job, Mondays were . . . Mondays.

And when A.J.'s alarm went off at five thirty, she moaned and hit snooze. Two snooze slaps later, she dragged herself out of bed and into the shower.

Judging by the closed bedroom door, Andy was still sleeping. That was uncharacteristic of Andy, but depression could do that, and A.J. was sure Andy was depressed, although he certainly hadn't said anything to that effect—in fact, he had been unusually uncommunicative about himself.

She left a note for him in the kitchen, fed the critters—who seemed to have achieved an uneasy truce over the weekend—and left for work. On the drive she listened to the radio. The local station was still talking about Nicole's murder, but it didn't sound to A.J. like the police were sharing their theories on the case with the media.

Jake had definitely been closemouthed last night, although it was obvious to A.J. that he was looking hard and long at Lydia Thorne—whoever she might be in real life—as a suspect. He had gone out of his way to stress to A.J. and Andy that Stillbrook PD were entertaining a couple of ideas about this high-profile homicide, and that they had more than one suspect, but as Andy had said after Jake departed, that could just be Jake trying to keep A.J. and Andy from jumping to obvious conclusions.

"Not exactly a barrel of laughs, is he?" Andy asked as they had listened to the sounds of Jake's SUV dying away in the summer night.

A.J. said defensively, "Murder isn't funny. Anyway, he has a great sense of humor once he relaxes."

"So he does occasionally relax?"

A.J. made a face. Jake was pretty serious, but that wasn't a bad thing necessarily. The only thing that bothered her was the feeling that maybe Jake didn't trust her. Not in a serious thought-she-might-be-capable-of-murder way, but just on general principles. She figured it was a cop thing. She *hoped* it was a cop thing.

The parking lot behind Sacred Balance was empty as A.J. pulled into her space. Unlocking the glass front door of the studio, she stepped inside and disarmed the alarm. She turned on the full-spectrum lighting, and the iconic black and white posters of women doing yoga were sharply illuminated. Beneath each poster was the slogan that embodied Diantha's philosophy for the studio and her students: *It Could Happen.*

One of the posters was of a very young Diantha, circa 1960. She looked like one of those sleek English fashion models from an early Beatles film. A.J. smiled at the poster. She loved arriving at the studio before anyone else got in, loved the quiet and the peace of the place before the activities of the day began.

Not that she didn't love the energy and focus of Sacred Balance when it was buzzing like a spiritual hive, but in the cool quiet of the morning she fancied she could feel her aunt's presence. It was comforting. It helped her believe that she was up to the challenge of fulfilling Diantha's legacy.

In her office, A.J. started the small indoor fountain, switched on the hot plate for tea, and turned on her laptop. She checked her e-mail while the hot water brewed and the fountain softly played over the polished stones. Elysia had sent photos of diving and snorkeling in the Red Sea—and of herself enjoying various shipboard activities.

Shuffleboard? Did people outside of Agatha Christie novels really play shuffleboard on cruise ships? Apparently so. Elysia appeared to play with gusto.

Faintly smiling, A.J. studied the digital images of her mother. She was mildly surprised to realize that she missed her. During the past few months they had grown close for the first time in A.J.'s life. The vacation seemed to be doing Elysia good. She looked radiant in a variety of summery ensembles that showed off her new golden tan.

Who had taken all these photos of her?

A.J. thoughtfully considered the image of a very handsome, very tall, very *young* Egyptian man beaming down on Elysia in two of the photographs. *Hmmmmm.*

A.J. sincerely hoped her mother would not be bringing home a new daddy for her—especially not a daddy young enough to be her brother.

There was no message with the photos, but then Elysia had never been one for letter-writing.

A.J. sipped her tea and started on the resumes she hadn't finished checking Saturday—it seemed a very long time ago now.

She found it astonishing the things job candidates put into their resumes. One young man included his complete medical history. One young woman submitted a resume on colored paper with animal stickers in each corner.

A.J. sighed and kept reading. After all, she wasn't looking for nuclear physicists, just a conscientious, reliable, reasonably intelligent person to answer phones and open mail.

Outside her office she could hear the other instructors arriving—shortly followed by the first of the day's students.

"Morning, A.J.!" Simon Crider, who taught the sunrise yoga course, poked his head in. Simon was a very trim, very fit sixty-something. Handsome and pleasant, he apparently provided the incentive to drag over twenty women out of bed at the crack of dawn, for his classes were always packed. "I heard about Nicole," he said. "Unbelievable. Have the police said whether they're closing in on a suspect?"

"Not that I've heard."

They chatted briefly. Simon wandered away, and Denise Farber, their Pilates instructor, looked in. "A.J., you poor thing! How are you holding up?"

"Good. How was your weekend?"

"A lot quieter than yours. Any word on who killed Nicole?"

"I haven't heard anything."

"What does Jake say?"

A.J. made a face. "Jake makes the Sphinx look chatty."

Denise chuckled, they visited for a bit, and she went on to her office.

A.J. heard Lily walk by, unlock her office, and go inside.

More students arrived. A.J. could hear cheerful voices in the front lobby. Another day at Sacred Balance was beginning. She looked at the photograph of her aunt and smiled.

Four minutes before her Yoga for Tweens course was due to begin, Suze rushed into A.J.'s office. "*Oh my gosh*, A.J.! I can't believe Nicole is dead. What does Jake say?"

A.J. looked up from a magazine article on using yoga for pain relief in such hard-to-treat conditions as carpal tunnel, back pain, and even asthma. If only it cured tardiness. She said, "They're working on it."

"No way!"

"Seriously, Suze, he doesn't discuss his cases with me."

Suze's blue eyes went saucer wide with disbelief. "After you cracked his last homicide for him?"

"I didn't crack his last homicide," A.J. objected. She really wished people would stop saying that. "I just had insider's knowledge. The last thing I would ever want would be to be involved in another murder investigation."

"But you already are," Suze said cheerfully. "You found the body. You took pictures of the murder weapon before it melted. Didn't you see today's paper? They referred to you as our local Miss Marple."

A.J. stared at her, aghast. "Tell me you're kidding. They didn't. Really. They didn't, did they?"

"Sure they did! Well, you *did* find the body. What's wrong with being compared to Miss Marple? I think it's kind of cool."

"Sure! Who wouldn't want to be compared to a ninety-year-old busybody with support hose and sensible shoes?"

Suze giggled. "Hey, she always gets her man!" Then she checked her watch, exclaimed at the time, and backed out of A.J.'s office.

A.J. dropped her head in her hands. This was the last kind of publicity she wanted for herself or the studio. And instinctively she knew it wasn't going to do wonders for her relationship with Jake, either.

She waited until the first classes of the day were in session before she went down to Lily's office and tapped on the door.

"Come in."

A.J. pushed open the door and Lily looked up from her laptop without pleasure. "Yes?"

Somehow Lily always made her feel defensive. It didn't matter what kind of pep talk A.J. gave herself before approaching the other woman, Lily managed to push all A.J.'s buttons with the uncanny accuracy of a crazy person in an elevator.

"You wanted to talk on Saturday?"

"Right," Lily said, as though it was so insignificant it had skipped her mind. "Have a seat."

A.J. pulled a seat out in front of Lily's desk. She started to fold her arms, remembered that such body language might imply she was closed off to Lily, and tried to find a comfortable way to sit without actually relaxing—because one thing she always felt was the need to keep her guard up with Lily.

Lily said, "I've been thinking—and before you instantly shoot down my idea, just hear me out."

Could there be a more annoying start to a discussion? A.J. smiled—she hoped—and said, "Shoot."

"I think Diantha has been gone long enough that it's time to reconsider our direction. Our mission, if you will."

As every single molecule of A.J. objected to each and every word of that statement, she was very proud of herself for her calm, "All right."

"We don't have to start remodeling right away, but one of the most symbolic changes we could make is our slogan. That's fundamental. It's our philosophy."

"You don't like our philosophy?" A.J. inquired politely.

Lily's expression grew cold. "I was here when 'our' philosophy evolved. I was part of that process with Diantha, so don't you dare take that tone with me."

"I'm asking a question."

"You're making a judgment."

A.J. took a deep breath. She recollected a quote from an ancient samurai text, *A Book of Five Rings*, one of Andy's favorite business strategy books:

In strategy, timing is all.

"Go on," she invited. She could see her calm response caught Lily by surprise. That alone recommended it for future use.

"I think it's time for a new slogan. A new direction. A new focus. Frankly, I always thought 'It Could Happen' was . . . corny."

"I disagree," A.J. shot back. So much for timing. "I think it's optimistic, promising—which is what I think Sacred Balance is all about. It's about opening your life to the possibility of amazing chances and terrific surprises."

Lily's mouth curled. "I know your background was marketing, A.J., but you don't have to sell me on Sacred Balance. And I think we're about a lot more than fluffy, sentimental platitudes. Yoga is serious. Yoga is not a trend or a fashion. Yoga is not for everyone."

Now there was a slogan: *Yoga Is for Nazis!*

A.J. said mildly, "You've obviously given this some thought. Did you have a new slogan in mind?"

Lily smiled. "I've been jotting down ideas as they come to me. I was thinking of something along the lines of 'The Time Is Now.' Or 'The Time Is Right.'"

A.J. said dryly, "How about 'The Time Is Right Now'?"

"Nnn." Lily wrinkled her nose, dismissing that one. "I think 'Now Is the Time' is quite good."

"'Now Is the Hour'?" suggested A.J., tongue in cheek.

Lily said grudgingly, "That's not bad."

Oh boy. That was enough fun for one morning. A.J. said, "Lily, let me think about it. I have to be honest; I hadn't given any thought to changing our philosophical direction."

"I'm sure you hadn't. I know you're still . . . getting up to speed. I'll jot the possibilities down and e-mail them to you."

"Great!" A.J. said brightly, rising. "I'll look forward to those. Talk to you later."

She returned hastily to her office and tried deep breathing exercises until she was feeling lightheaded. Probably more lightheaded than calm, but it was a start. She choked down a cup of green tea and reminded herself that it was probably just as difficult for Lily to make concessions for her as it was for her to make concessions for Lily. She told herself that Lily probably had no idea how obnoxious her behavior was. She told herself this several times. Then she got back to work.

The morning passed quickly as mornings at Sacred Balance always did.

Andy arrived around eleven thirty, and Suze showed him into A.J.'s office.

"Wow," he said a little grudgingly. "I guess I understand why you decided to give up freelancing. This is really nice."

"It is," A.J. agreed. "I still have to pinch myself some mornings. I loved the first years we were in business together. I loved the challenge of building our client base and landing big accounts, but . . ."

"You burnt out," Andy said.

"It's such a cliché, but I think I did. It didn't . . . feed my soul."

Andy didn't say anything. His expression puzzled A.J. Even more than she, he had thrived on the stress, the challenge, the risk of running their own business. Now she wondered if somewhere along the line that had changed for him as well. He did look better today. More relaxed and rested. Perhaps the weekend in the country had done him some good—although he was still limping very slightly.

"Are we still on for lunch?" he asked.

"Sure. Why don't I give you the grand tour first?"

Andy affirmed, positive and accommodating as ever, and A.J. gave him a quick guided tour through the three-story building. He made all the right noises and approving faces—until they reached the top level.

"Showers on the third floor," he commented. "That is so Diantha. She's the only person I ever met who believed willpower could defeat gravity."

A.J. knew what Andy meant, and it *was* a little unusual to have showers on the third floor.

"You have to admit, it is beautiful up here," she pointed out. "All these windows looking down over the trees. Just clouds and sunlight and water. It's a lovely experience showering here."

"It's the flying squirrels you have to convince, not me."

A.J. grinned, because Andy's reaction was very much what her own had initially been.

They finished the grand tour, and A.J. directed Andy into town and the Happy Cow Steak House, which was one of Stillbrook's nicer places to dine. They had a brief wait in the lobby and Andy scrutinized the waitresses dressed like French maids, the bordello-crimson furnishings, and the sentimental Victorian paintings while the dimple that indicated private amusement creased his cheek.

"How perfect," he murmured, once they had been seated and were glancing over the menus. "They even have a meat bar."

"I know what you're thinking," A.J. said. "But there are

trendy places in New York and London and Tel Aviv that offer meat bars."

"But do they offer elk sausage with Madeira wine? Or appetizers made from smoked alligator?"

A.J. tried not to laugh. "They do a really nice filet mignon here," she informed him. "That's all I know. I'm trying to eat less red meat."

"You could try the ostrich burgers," Andy said. "I hear it's the new white meat."

A.J. laughed, but then her gaze fell on a petite red-haired woman sitting by herself at a table across the room. She sucked in a breath.

"Got a look at the prices, did you?" Andy inquired, his own gaze fastened on the red-bound menus.

"Don't turn around," A.J. said sotto voce. "I think I just recognized the woman sitting on her own at the table near the window."

Andy's elegant brows rose. He stared at the long mirror hanging on the wall opposite. "The one with the short red hair?"

"In the DKNY flutter-sleeve top," A.J. agreed.

"What about her?"

"Does she look familiar to you?"

Andy narrowed his eyes thoughtfully. "Maybe. Why?"

A.J. reached for her purse and cell phone. "I'm almost positive that's the woman I saw running away from Nicole's house right before I found Nicole's body."

Eight

"**What** are you doing?" Andy asked her, still watching the woman reflected in the mirror across the room.

"Calling Jake."

Andy was shaking his head. "She's already paid the bill. She's leaving."

Glancing up, A.J. saw that he was right. The woman was gathering her belongings.

A.J. bit her lip. An idea occurred. She said, "I'm going to stall her for a couple of seconds. Can you go outside and see what car she gets into and try to get the license plate number?"

"You're going to stall her *how*?"

"Just . . . leave it to me," A.J. said rising.

She started walking toward the entrance. As she passed the woman who was now on her feet and also moving to the lobby, she stopped.

"Oh! Aren't you . . . ?" A.J. paused as though trying to rack her brain for a name.

The woman hesitated, looking doubtful, and Andy, with a muttered apology, squeezed past the two of them and went out through the lobby and the front door.

Good old Andy, A.J. thought with genuine affection. Aloud, she said, "You were in . . . that movie, right? I can't think of the name of it."

The woman smiled a sickly smile. She was several inches shorter than A.J. Cute rather than pretty, with very short red hair and freckles so perfectly placed that they could have been painted on.

"I . . . um . . . I've been in a few things," she admitted.

"Lydia Thorne!" A.J. said triumphantly. "That's it, isn't it?"

The woman shook her head. "Jane Peters."

"Right, right. Can I get your autograph?" A.J. looked around as though seeking something the woman could write her name on.

"I . . ." Jane Peters took a step toward the restaurant entrance. "I really have to . . ."

"It'll just take a second!" A.J. now had her purse open and was giving every appearance of ransacking the contents. "I'm *so* excited to meet a real movie star!"

"We're in the way here," Jane objected, continuing to sidle toward the door.

"No, no. Here you go!" A.J. grabbed a back page out of her day planner. "Just sign any-old-where."

Jane Peters looked at her as though she thought A.J. herself might be missing a crucial page or two, but she scrawled a hasty signature and thrust the sheet back at A.J. "There you go. Thank you!"

"Thank *you*!" A.J. called.

Jane had already turned away and was making for the front door.

A.J. went to the table by the window and picked up the leather sleeve with the restaurant receipt. As she'd hoped, there was a credit card slip. The imprint read *Jane Peters*.

The name meant nothing to her. Jane Peters hadn't so much as blinked at the mention of Lydia Thorne, so it seemed unlikely that it was one of her aliases, but who was she and what had she been doing at Nicole's the afternoon she was killed?

She leaned over, trying to see out the window, and spotted Andy walking back from the parking lot. She waved to him, but the window glass was tinted and he did not see her.

Returning to their table, she met the curious glances of one or two other dining patrons and picked up her cell phone once more, dialing Jake.

As usual, she got his voice mail.

"It's A.J.," she said crisply—if quietly—into her phone. "I've just spotted the woman I saw leaving Nicole's. Her name is Jane Peters . . ."

Andy dropped into the chair across from her. He said, "She's driving a black Saturn VUE, Jersey license plate JAA 00B."

A.J. repeated this information faithfully to Jake's voice mail and rang off.

"How can he possibly resist you?" Andy inquired. "You're like the girl of his dreams."

"His nightmares," A.J. retorted. "It's like I'm a magnet for murder."

"That should be a plus. Doesn't he care about career advancement?"

"Ha." She picked up her menu. "I must say Nick seems to have trained you very well."

Andy's smile dimmed. "Yeah," he said, and picked up his own menu.

"One thing I think we can rule out," A.J. said. "I don't

think Jane Peters is the mysterious Lydia Thorne. She didn't bat an eyelash when I suggested that was her name."

"You're good," Andy approved. "That thought hadn't occurred to me."

"I'm cynical. It's the first thing I thought of," A.J. said. "Having an online persona isn't in itself sinister, but whoever Lydia Thorne really is, her feelings about Nicole—good or bad—weren't normal."

"I don't know—"

"She was obsessed with Nicole."

"You said yourself that's kind of what fandom is. And Nicole obviously didn't get the wrong vibe from Lydia. They were friends for years, right?"

A.J. laid her menu aside. "That's because Nicole was totally absorbed in Nicole. So it probably seemed normal to her that Lydia was, too. But those negative reviews you showed me—those are creepy. They weren't about Nicole's work, they were about Nicole—and Lydia's feelings for her—and I'm telling you that level of hostility isn't normal."

"We could try calling her," Andy suggested.

"What is your fascination with calling this Thorne woman?"

"It seems like a logical step. If nothing else it might eliminate her, right? And we could rest easy."

"I'm resting fine as it is." Mostly, anyway.

Andy ignored that. "I checked my day planner this morning. I do still have a number for her. It might not be good, but . . ."

"You should have immediately handed that number over to Jake. Why didn't you?"

Andy raised his brows at A.J.'s tone. "Because he'll have her number from Nicole's files, right? He's got access to all

Nicole's information, and, if anything, Nicole's information will be more up-to-date than mine."

"So? I'm not following your line of reasoning."

Andy said casually, "Well, if this number *is* still good, there's a chance that Lydia might return a phone call from us whereas the police might scare her off."

A.J. opened her mouth but was forestalled by the arrival of the waitress. They ordered their meals—pistachio-crusted salmon for A.J. and ribeye steak for Andy—the waitress departed, and A.J. said, "Andrew Belleson, I'm warning you now. I'm *not* getting involved in another murder investigation."

"Really? What was the deal with me running out to the parking lot to scope out license plates while you pretended to be an autograph hound?"

"That was a fluke, our running into Jane Peters," A.J. said heatedly. "And you'll notice I turned that information straight over to Jake. I'm not going to play amateur sleuth again. It almost wrecked my relationship with him the first time."

"So it's serious with you and Robocop. I knew it." He was smiling, genuinely pleased for her, which vaguely nettled.

"It's not serious. Not yet. Actually, I have no idea what it is—but I don't want it ruined before I've had a chance to screw it up in the ordinary way."

"He should be so lucky." Andy thought that over. "And I mean that as a compliment."

"Uh . . . thanks."

"Anyway, if he cares about you, he won't want you to squelch your inner girl detective."

"I don't have an inner girl detective. I was just . . . in the wrong place at the wrong time before."

Andy tsk-tsked. Really, how the hell had A.J.—for ten years—missed the fact that he was gay? She simply could not imagine Jake tsk-tsking if his life depended on it.

"Don't do that. You know it bugs me. And for your information, sleuthing can be hazardous to your health. My health, in this case."

Andy sighed. "I'm disappointed in you, A.J. Your mother would take this case in a heartbeat."

He was teasing her—though not entirely. A.J. said, "Now might be the right time to break it to you that I'm not my mother. My mother—lucky for both of us—is cruising down the Nile even as we speak. And hopefully not triggering any international incidents. *And*, if I remember correctly, Nick wasn't thrilled about you being even peripherally involved in a murder investigation."

Andy's face tightened. An unpleasant thought sprouted in A.J.'s mind. Nick Grant was a big man and not particularly given to conversation. Was it possible he might have expressed his disapproval by hitting Andy? Knocking him down? She didn't know a lot about the gay lifestyle, but she had seen enough bad television to give her a sordid impression.

She couldn't help asking, "Is everything okay between you and Nick Grant?"

"Of course," Andy said quickly. Too quickly?

She wasn't sure she wanted to pry any further, and was saved from having to decide by the arrival of their meals.

Jake had not responded to A.J.'s message by the time she and Andy finished lunch and started back to Sacred Balance. She tried not to take it personally. Jake was in the middle of a homicide investigation; safe to say he was a little busy. Besides, for all she knew he was acting immediately on the information she'd given him.

"What's going on here?" Andy murmured as they pulled into the studio parking lot.

The hours between one and three were the least busy at Sacred Balance, but today the parking lot was packed. In addition to all the cars, there was a large truck half blocking the driveway entrance.

"What the . . . ?" A.J.'s voice trailed away, trying to see past the truck.

Suze stood at the entrance of the studio apparently trying to deny access to what appeared to be a film crew.

"Local news coverage?" Andy asked her.

A.J. took in the equipment and cameras scattered along the walkway curving up toward the studio. She shook her head. "There would be a van with the news station logo, wouldn't there? This is like a . . . a movie set."

Spotting a familiar tall, dark-haired woman arguing—loudly—with Suze, she reached for the door. "Let me out."

"Are you sure? If they're waiting for you—"

"They're not waiting for me. That's Barbie Siragusa arguing with Suze."

"Barbie Siragusa, as in *Barbie's Dream Life*? As in the mob boss's missus? *That* Barbie Sirgusa?"

"That's the one," A.J. said. "She wanted to film a segment of her reality TV show at Sacred Balance, and I told her no. Apparently she's not a very good listener."

"You told the wife of a famous mob boss *no*?" Andy said faintly.

A.J. tore her gaze away from the melee at the front of Sacred Balance. All those people and all that equipment in order to create . . . reality?

"I told her no," she said. "And I meant it. It's the last

thing Aunt Di would have wanted for the studio, so please don't tell me that it's a wasted opportunity for good PR. I don't think it would be good for the studio or the health and welfare of our clients."

"Uh, I wasn't thinking about the studio," Andy said. "Or your clients. I was thinking that telling a mob boss's wife 'no' might not be good for the health and welfare of *you*."

Nine

❦

"**Are** you sure you want me to abandon you like this?" Andy inquired as A.J. got out of the car.

That was almost too easy. A.J. opened her mouth but let it go. "I can handle it," she said.

Andy looked unconvinced.

"I've been managing just fine without you for over a year now."

He winced, and A.J. relented. "Thanks, but I can cope. Honestly. I'll see you back at the house this evening."

Slamming shut the sedan door, she started briskly up the walkway through the gauntlet of bodies and equipment.

Suze, blonde hair on end and looking like one of the Keebler Elves after a brawl, stood at bay, blocking the glass doors. A.J. could see movement in the building behind Suze, but no one was coming to the beleaguered instructor's aid.

Spotting A.J., she called out in relief, "A.J., I was just trying to explain—"

"What in the world is going on here?" A.J. demanded. She had to raise her voice—a lot—to be heard.

Barbie pushed through the crowd of people to meet her. Jabbing an acrylic talon at A.J.'s nose, she announced, "This is her!" She gestured to the cameraman in front of the horseshoe of people. "Get a close-up! A.J., we need to talk!"

"We *have* talked," A.J. told her, eyeing the cameraman warily. "I told you I did not want anyone filming inside Sacred Balance." And as the camera zoomed in on her, she said, "Please get that thing out of my face."

"This is about freedom of the press," Barbie said, and the camera swung her way. "You're standing in the way of free speech."

"And *you* are standing in the way of the front door," A.J. retorted. "Barbie, I'm trying to run a business here. What about my rights? What about the rights of all the other Sacred Balance clients?" Into the whirring eye of the camera, which had turned her way again, she said, "I asked you to stop filming."

"I warned you," Barbie said. "I gave you the chance to cooperate."

Apparently what you got when you crossed a mob boss's wife with reality TV was a close-up you could not refuse.

"This has gone too far already. Where's the director?" A.J. scanned the crowd of curious bystanders. "Or the producer. Who exactly is in charge here?"

"*I* call the shots," Barbie said. "Not the director. Not the producer. It's my show. It's my reality. And I gave you fair warning, A.J."

"You're right," A.J. said. "I should have paid more attention. Now I'm going to have to get a restraining order."

"You can't do that!" Barbie shrieked. "Don't you dare try it, you—!"

A.J. pushed past Barbie. Suze stepped back and A.J. slipped inside the glass door, locking it on Barbie's outraged protest. The glass door thudded beneath her angry fists.

"Oh. My. *God*. Is she for real?" Suze gasped, leaning weakly back against the closed door.

"I guess so. She's got the camera crew to prove it."

Inside the main lobby, the phones were ringing, unattended, and a few pleasantly horrified customers stood gazing out at the milling film crew.

Watching Barbie, who was now gesticulating like a SpaghettiOs commercial gone bad, Suze said, "Are you sure you should have done that? Bad things have a way of happening to people Barbie doesn't like."

"No," said A.J. "I'm not sure I should have done that. But I don't know what else to do. I can't have that film crew in here disrupting everyone's schedule." She headed straight for her office, Suze trotting behind.

"Well, okay, but we can't hold the customers hostage inside the building."

She resisted telling Suze to answer the phones and leave the rest to her. "We won't have to. I'm sure Barbie and her film crew will give up and go away in a few minutes."

In actuality, she was sure of no such thing, but she had bigger problems than Barbie. When it rained it poured. From down the hall, Lily was striding toward her, and for the first time A.J. understood the expression "a face like a thundercloud." She said to Suze, "Or you can just shove 'em out through the emergency exit."

"What in the world do you think you're doing?" Lily demanded.

A.J. unlocked her office. "Suze, could you get me Mr. Meagher," she told the younger instructor. She stepped inside her office and said to Lily, "If you have something to say to me, say it in here where we don't have an audience."

"As though an audience were a concern for you?"

Clearly A.J. had done something very wrong in a previous life; her karma had flatlined. First Barbie and now Lily.

Lily was in full spate as she followed A.J. inside. "You've turned this place into a circus, A.J. I will never understand what Di could have been thinking when she abandoned Sacred Balance to you."

A.J. told herself to count to ten. She closed the door to her office with great care. The electric fountain splashed musically in the silence. Reaching three and a quarter, she burst out, "That's not something either of us will ever know, Lily. But the bottom line is, we're stuck together. Deal with it!"

Lily's snapping-turtle eyes glinted dangerously. "*Deal with it?* Who do you think you're talking to?"

Months of struggling for understanding and patience—of biting her tongue—had come to an abrupt end. A.J. said, "I'm not any happier that Sacred Balance came with *you* attached than you are to find yourself in business with me. But this is what Aunt Di wanted. If you can't come to terms with it, I'll be more than happy to buy you out."

"Like hell!" Lily said. "If anyone is leaving, it's you."

"I'm not leaving."

"You're ruining this business. You're turning us into a laughing stock. Yoga for dogs, yoga for cats, yoga for babies, yoga for singles? My God, where will it end? Film crews, reality TV?"

"How is that last my fault?" A.J. objected. "I'm trying to keep that film crew out of Sacred Balance!"

"By antagonizing one of our most important clients."

Exasperated, A.J. said, "Do you want to be on reality TV or not? Because I don't understand—"

"This is my point." Lily was suddenly cool and patronizing. "You don't *understand*. You're out of your depth. It's obvious to everyone. Before you destroy Sacred Balance, and everything it stands for, why don't you let me buy *you* out?"

"Buy *me* out?" A.J. stared. "How in the world could you afford to buy me out?"

Lily smiled. "All that need concern you is that I'm now in position to do so. Name your price."

"I'm not going to sell Sacred Balance. Not to you, not to anyone. Aunt Di left the studio to me. We're co-managers, not co-owners, Lily."

"That was an oversight on Di's part."

"Aunt Di didn't *have* oversights. I'm not selling you the studio."

"Then at least let me manage it on my own, the way Di intended."

"She didn't intend that or she wouldn't have made us co-managers." A.J. lowered her voice and forced her knotted muscles to relax. "I understand that you're not any happier with this arrangement than I am, but until one of us is willing to concede, we're going to have to find a way to work together."

The intercom buzzed. Suze's voice said, "Mr. Meagher is on line one for you."

"If you'll excuse me," A.J. said to Lily.

Lily didn't budge. She said flatly, "We have to resolve this A.J. For the good of the studio. We can't have more incidents like this afternoon's."

"Well, we're not going to resolve it in the next two minutes," A.J. said. "I need to take this call."

It looked as though Lily might refuse to leave, but finally she turned and went, closing the door with the smallest suggestion of a bang behind her.

A.J. dropped down at her desk, her gaze seeking the enigmatically smiling photo of her aunt. She picked up the phone. "A.J. here."

"Ah, me darlin' wee A.J. So you've a minute to spare for your old Uncle Bradley, have you?" Mr. Meagher said in his musical Irish brogue. A.J. could see him in her mind's eye: a short and very tanned older man with a silver pompadour and bright, beady eyes. "And how is your wicked minx of a mam enjoying her holiday?"

"Oh, Mr. Meagher," A.J. said, and it all came pouring out—much to her own surprise.

Mr. Meagher listened in silence until A.J. paused at last for breath. Then he was brisk. "Now, as to your first dilemma, we've several options open to us. We can indeed go the way of placing a restraining order on Mrs. Siragusa. Are you sure that's what you wish to do?"

Having vented long and loudly, much of A.J.'s emotional heat had evaporated. She could hear the reserve in Mr. Meagher's voice, and she had respect for his legal—and other—instincts.

"I don't know," she admitted, raking a hand through her hair. "No way am I going to permit her to film inside the studio, and I don't think she's going to accept my decision graciously."

"She's an important client," Mr. Meagher pointed out.

"I suppose so," A.J. said. "She's a wealthy client, certainly. But I don't know that having the wife of a crime boss on our roster is necessarily a coup."

"Let me put it this way," Mr. Meagher said. "Having Mrs. Siragusa as an enemy is unlikely to prove good for business. Or anything else."

A.J. thought this over silently. *Bad things have a way of happening to people Barbie doesn't like*, Suze had said.

Of course, Barbie hadn't had anything to do with Nicole's death. At least . . . it wasn't likely, was it? The time element was off. Barbie would have had to race from the studio and make straight for Nicole's, murder her on the spot, and then escape—all without being spotted by an army of people. And Barbie was not exactly the inconspicuous type.

Mr. Meagher knew when to hold 'em and when to fold 'em. He cleared his throat and said, "Now, me darlin' . . . regarding the other matter. There's no question Ms. Martin is an unpleasant young woman. We've talked this over before, and the terms of your aunt's will are quite explicit. It was Diantha's wish for the two of you to work together. One of you may decide the situation is intolerable and leave, but neither of you can force the other out."

Till death do us part, A.J. thought grimly. She said, "What if it could be proven that the partnership is detrimental to the welfare of the business?"

"Is it indeed?"

She was silent. As dearly as she longed to blame Lily for everything that had ever gone wrong at Sacred Balance, the truth was little had gone wrong. Business was thriving, and the numbers bore it out regardless of Lily's feelings on the matter.

"I think Lily feels that it is," she said.

Mr. Meagher made a dismissive sound. "It's yourself that owns the studio. It would not be Ms. Martin's feelings on the matter that would be interesting to a court. If the studio fails, it's yourself who would lose out."

"I was afraid you'd say that." A.J. sighed. "Okay. I'm sorry for wasting your time, Mr. Meagher. I guess I'll wait and think things over before I do anything."

"It's never a waste of time speaking to a beautiful woman," the gallant—and clearly inexperienced—Mr. Meagher returned. "And speaking of beautiful creatures, give me best to that mad, bad vixen the next time you speak to her."

For one truly insane moment, A.J. thought Mr. Meagher was referring to Lily. Then she realized he must mean her mother. Which was a relief—though a mixed one.

"That I will," she said, teasing him. She had no sooner replaced the phone than Suze was in her office.

"Charlayne just phoned in."

For an instant A.J. couldn't even remember who Charlayne was. Oh, right. Their one remaining receptionist—and the daughter of one of her oldest friends, Nancy Lewis.

She said firmly, knowing it was a bluff even as the words left her mouth, "If she calls in sick one more time, she's out. I can't run a business like this."

"She quit."

"She *quit*?"

Suze nodded.

"Just like that? She's not giving notice or anything?"

Suze shook her head.

"Did she give a reason?"

"Sort of. She said it's too hard working and going to school, and that's why she caught the flu."

"So . . . let me get this straight," A.J. said. "She was out sick with the flu most of last week, and now that she's feeling better, she's quitting."

"Yep." Suze sounded unreasonably cheerful about the whole thing. She perched on the edge of A.J.'s desk and said, "Don't worry, we've got it all worked out. Denise and Simon will take my classes and I'll cover the phones till you find us a new receptionist."

A.J. stared at the pile of resumes on her desk and moaned. "That's *two* new receptionists I now have to find.

And if you'll notice, I'm not exactly having great results finding *one*."

Suze giggled, but she was serious as she asked, "Are you going to ban Barbie from the studio?"

Meeting those bright blue eyes, A.J. shook her head. "I don't think so. Mr. Meagher doesn't seem to think it's a good idea."

"You know what they're saying, right? In town?"

Reluctantly, A.J. admitted, "That Barbie might have had something to do with Nicole's death?"

Suze nodded. "They're saying it's a mob vendetta."

A.J. was shaking her head. "That's . . . preposterous. I mean, it's just remotely possible she could have managed it time wise—if everything went like clockwork—but she had no real motive. People don't kill other people because . . . well, why exactly is Barbie supposed to have wanted to kill Nicole?"

"Because she was having an affair with Barbie's teen-age son."

After a moment A.J. closed her mouth. "*Oh*," she said.

"Yeah," agreed Suze.

A.J. slipped off her shoes and stepped over Monster, who was lying in the doorway between the kitchen and the hall—the better to keep an eye on their uninvited guest. The dog thumped his tail in greeting and she rubbed his fur with her stockinged foot.

"Hey," she greeted Andy, and he looked up from the table where he sat peeling a pan of potatoes.

The house was redolent with the scent of garlic roast pork loin and cornbread. Andy was cooking comfort food.

"Hi. How did it go?" he asked, and for a moment it might almost have been a time warp. Wonderful food was cooking, Lula Mae was curled on the windowsill watching birds in the garden, and music was playing—one of Gus Eriksson's old jazz records: The Don Rendell / Ian Carr Quintet.

"Just an ordinary day on the eightfold path. First I threatened to call the cops on the local don's better half and then I was convinced in the nick of time not to start legal proceedings against my business partner."

"I think you need more meditation."

"I think I need a drink." She moved to the freezer to get out the Bombay Sapphire, and noticed the phone machine was blinking.

"Who called?" A.J. asked, and Andy made some noncommittal reply.

The first message was from Nick Grant, Andy's partner. Nick sounded self-conscious and a little grim. He didn't say what he was calling about—maybe he thought it was self-evident; he did say he would call back later. According to the phone machine, he had phoned at three thirty. Andy should have been back from lunch by then, but if he'd heard the message, he obviously hadn't picked it up.

"Nick called," A.J. informed him, which probably wasn't necessary since Andy was sitting only a foot or so away.

"Yes," he said politely.

And that seemed to be that.

The second call was from Jake, asking A.J. to call when she got in and maybe they could go to dinner.

She wasn't sure why he hadn't called on her cell phone. Was this message partly for Andy's benefit? Who knew how men reasoned these things.

She rang him back, and Jake—brief and business-like, which meant he was somewhere he couldn't talk—said he thought he could make time for dinner if she was available.

A.J., equally brief and businesslike, said she thought that could be arranged.

They made a plan to meet later.

Feeling unreasonably guilty, she replaced the receiver and said, "It looks like I'm going out to eat with Jake."

"Oh." Andy's expression was disappointed.

A.J. resisted the temptation to apologize to her ex-husband for wanting to have dinner with her boyfriend.

Andy said, "There's plenty of food. You could eat here. We could discuss the case."

"I . . . don't think so"

He nodded but continued to look dashed. "Were you going to call Nick?" A.J. probed.

"I'll call him after a while," Andy said. His voice and face revealed little, but A.J. wasn't betting much on Nick's chances of getting a buzz that night.

They chatted for a few minutes and then, after they had exhausted such neutral topics as how unreliable teens were in the workforce, and how much A.J. would like to rid herself of Lily Martin, Andy inquired, "Have you given any more thought to calling Lydia Thorne?"

"No, and I'm not going to."

"Why not?"

"Are you serious about this?"

Apparently he was. He even had the nerve to look slightly puzzled as he met her gaze.

"We've been through this," A.J. told him severely. "If you think it's such a great idea, *you* call her, although I think I ought to point out that bringing yourself to the attention of a psycho might not be the best idea you've ever had."

"A strange man calling is liable to sound more threatening," Andy said. "I think it would be better if you rang her."

"Why do I get the feeling you're not really listening to

me? Anyway, we don't even know if the number is still good. And even if it is good, what's the point? The police have probably called her by now."

"You can verify that one way or the other when you go to dinner," Andy said.

"I don't want to verify it. What part of *I don't want to interfere in Jake's homicide investigation* did you miss?" A.J. inquired.

"Come on," Andy said. "Of course you're curious. It's only natural."

Was it? Maybe it was. And Andy was right. She *was* curious. Not as curious as he was, though. A.J. studied her ex-husband's tired, preoccupied expression. There was something going on here that she didn't understand. Andy was too interested in this murder case. It was more than the normal interest anyone showed when violent crime touched so close to home. It was as though Andy were latching onto Nicole's death as a distraction from his own worries.

She excused herself and went to change from her work clothes into a pair of Prada jeans and a D&G yellow silk crepe camisole with lace trim. She gave her hair, now grown out and reshaped to a sophisticated bob, a flick of the brush and retouched her makeup. She added a pair of silk tassel earrings with Swarovski crystals as the final touch.

Andy whistled as she reappeared in the kitchen. "The simple life suits you."

"Ha."

He was smirking as he handed her a piece of golden cornbread warm from the oven.

"Mm. I can taste the cheddar."

"Sure you don't want to stay for dinner?"

She was saved from answering as the door bell rang. Monster trotted down the hall, uttering a friendly woof, his tail wagging.

"That will be Jake," A.J. said, brushing hastily at her chin for crumbs. She met Andy's knowing gaze and felt herself blush. It was annoying.

"Have fun tonight," he said slyly.

"I'm not sure how much fun we can fit into an hour and a half," she mumbled.

"A lot—if you don't waste time."

"Uh . . . right." It wasn't just her, right? Surely there was something a tad odd about her ex-husband ushering her off on a date with a new boyfriend? "See you later."

"Not if you handle things right," he called cheerfully.

"My God, he's worse than my mother!" A.J. told Monster who was sitting at the front door waiting with a doggy smile while Jake, exhibiting flattering impatience, rang the buzzer again.

A.J. slid the bolt, opened the door, and blinked at the sight of the tall, elegant figure framed there.

"No need to look like that, pumpkin," issued the familiar and dulcet tones. "All's right with your world now. Mummy's home!"

Ten

❧

"**Mother?**" A.J. said in disbelief.

"In the flesh," Elysia returned cheerfully—and, given the skimpiness of her zebra-striped shift—that wasn't entirely exaggeration.

Elysia Alexander—the former British sex kitten and TV personality formerly known as Easy Mason—was a small and shapely pocket Venus. Her artfully tinted raven hair was coiled fashionably on her delicately molded head. Her eyes, framed by lustrous fake lashes, were limped pools of Lakeland green. Her full, pouty mouth had once been described as equally perfect for kisses or wisecracks.

Obediently bussing a cool cheek scented of cigarettes and Opium, A.J. said, "But what are you doing here? You're supposed to be sailing down the Nile."

"Destiny . . . like the water of the Nile." Elysia closed her eyes, savoring her memories. "Blue waters dancing beneath an ancient sun, the warmth of the wind scented by the green mango trees . . . those bloody loudspeakers shrieking their interminable disco music . . ." The silky lashes lifted as Elysia brushed these delights aside. "How could I enjoy myself when it meant abandoning my only child to death and danger?"

"What are you talking about?"

"Pumpkin, it's not as though we were in some Third World country. We did have news coverage." Elysia gazed ever so innocently into A.J.'s eyes—much like the cat who swallowed the canary must have looked when the canary's owner showed up.

"Egyptian news covered the death of a minor U.S. TV star?"

"Why ever not?"

A.J. could think of dozens of reasons why ever not. She opened her mouth to voice her suspicions but fell silent as Jake's police SUV rolled silently into the yard. He parked between Elysia's Land Rover and Andy's rental car.

At the sound of the SUV door slamming, Elysia glanced over her shoulder and made a little moue of annoyance. "I see John Wayne is still hanging around."

"Mother," A.J. warned her. "Hi there!" she called cheerfully as Jake raised a hand in greeting. "I'm just grabbing my purse." And resisting the temptation to hit her mother over the head with it.

She moved fast, but if she'd hoped to head off a social collision, she was doomed to disappointment—delayed by a couple of crucial seconds in finding her bag.

Skidding down the hall, she found Jake on the porch steps, nodding a greeting to Elysia. "So. The mummy returns."

Elysia sniffed. Actually, it was more of a snort.

"You're back early, aren't you? Was it voluntary or did they expel all the diplomats?"

"You're so amusing, Inspector. Perhaps that's what holds

my daughter captive. I'd been thinking handcuffs." Elysia smiled a chilly pointed smile—which disappeared in a blaze of pleasure as Andy appeared behind A.J.

"I thought I heard voices. Why is everyone standing on the porch?" Andy inquired.

"*Andrew!* Dearest boy! *What* a delightful surprise." Elysia whirled to A.J. "Is there something you want to tell me, pet?"

A.J. tore her gaze from Jake's unrevealing expression, and blinked. "What? No!"

Dear God. Was she . . . surely Elysia wasn't imagining A.J. and Andy were reuniting? Elysia's beaming expression seemed to say so. A.J. watched in mild horror as her mother and ex-husband hugged in genuine—and mutual—delight.

"Oh, I've missed you!" Elysia exclaimed. *Mmwah!*

"Same here!" Andy said. *Mmwah!*

Jake met A.J.'s gaze. He raised his eyebrows. And suddenly it was just funny.

"I think we should leave them to it," he said, and A.J. nodded, scooting past her mother and ex.

Elysia tore her adoring gaze from Andy's equally adoring countenance. "Where are you going, pet?"

"To dinner," A.J. said. "We've already got plans."

"But . . . but I've only just got in." There it was, the wounded look that Elysia wielded with the expert and deadly precision of a fencing master.

"If I'd known you were coming . . ." A.J. tried to be firm, but it wasn't easy in the face of that pretty—if well-practiced—distress.

"I've traveled half the world and you abandon me my first night home?" It was a little broad for the small screen, but Elysia was playing it for all she was worth.

Andy came unexpectedly to their rescue. "This will give us a chance to catch up, Ellie. Come and tell me all about your adventures. A.J. needs a little time with her beau."

"Beau? *Beau Geste*," sniffed Elysia, but she let herself be drawn away. In afterthought, she threw, "We'll talk tomorrow, pumpkin—or perhaps I'll still be here when you return."

"I'm thinking all-night diner," A.J. told Jake as they strolled across the grass to his car.

He laughed—a little crisply. "She's really crazy about me. I can tell."

"Don't take it personally. When Andy and I divorced, she tried to adopt him—and make him her sole heir."

Jake snorted.

Inside the SUV they studied each other quizzically. "Hello again," A.J. said.

Jake smiled, a genuine smile, and he moved, wrapping her in his arms and kissing her. His mouth was warm and surprisingly sweet on hers, and A.J. was conscious of what a long week it had been without him—although, in fact, she had seen him the night before when he'd come to question her and Andy.

Somehow the official Jake was like a totally different person.

He let her go, smoothed a self-conscious hand over his hair, and turned the key in the ignition. After a brief debate, they decided on Bill's Diner, which was relatively close and one of their favorite places when Jake was on duty.

"How's the case going?" A.J. inquired as they drove down the road while the twilight shadows lengthened. Butterflies fluttered in suicidal swoops ahead of the SUV grill.

"It's going," Jake said noncommittally.

"Have you zeroed in on anyone?"

"All avenues of investigation remain open."

"Is that from the *How to Talk Like a Cop* manual?"

He met her eyes. "Page one."

She smiled but knew it was time to drop the subject. After that they chatted mostly about A.J.'s day, and she filled him in on her run-in with Barbie at the studio. Jake was suitably and satisfyingly astounded.

"Do you want me to have a word with her?"

"You mean, have your people talk to her people?" A.J. grinned. "I don't think so. I'm hoping the threat of taking legal action will be enough."

"You do understand who you're dealing with? It's a family not known for taking the threat of legal action real seriously."

"I got that. You know, half the people in Stillbrook believe Barbie whacked Nicole."

Jake's mouth curled derisively. "I heard a rumor to that effect."

"Is it true Nicole was having an affair with Barbie's teenaged son?"

"The kid's twenty. Young for Nicole, but she wasn't robbing the cradle." Jake glanced her way. "Where'd you hear that?"

"So it *is* true?"

He said cautiously, "It appears to be true. We downloaded a hundred and thirty-seven text messages from someone named Ball Boy."

"*Ball Boy?*" Then it clicked. "Oh, right. Oz Siragusa is supposed to be some kind of tennis pro."

For a time neither of them said anything. A.J. was thinking what an awful thing it would be to have strangers, police or not, pawing through your most private and intimate correspondence—reading through your e-mail and letters, listening to phone messages, reading your journal—not that Nicole seemed like the Dear Diary type.

She thought about how awful it would be for people to learn your nickname was Ball Boy.

"So how long is he staying?" Jake asked abruptly, and A.J. didn't bother to pretend she didn't know who he meant.

"Andy? Just a few days."

"And why is he staying with *you*?"

A.J. examined her instinctive flare of resentment. Jake had reason to ask, right? They were seeing each other, even if not exclusively, and gay or not, the fact that Andy was her ex-husband certainly put a different spin on things than if he'd simply been a longtime pal of the masculine persuasion.

She said, "I think something has gone wrong in his relationship."

Jake snorted.

"I mean, really wrong," A.J. said. "I've known Andy a long time. Since college, and I've never seen him like this. Like all the stuffing has been knocked out of him. I think . . . I think Nick might have hit him. When he showed up Saturday evening he was limping. And his face was bruised."

"I noticed that on Sunday," Jake said. "It didn't look to me like someone punched him, but that doesn't mean he wasn't shoved into a wall. Either way, this isn't something you want to get involved in. Domestic disputes are poison."

Yes. A.J. could vouch for that. Yet she heard herself say, "It's not that simple."

"It is, yeah. After what that guy did to you? It's that simple. Let him work his own problems out."

The parking lot at Bill's Diner was empty, which was a

surprise because when they walked inside, the first person A.J. spotted was J.W. Young. He was in one of the red leather booths with Bryn Tierney, and they were eating supper.

The eating supper was not the amazing thing—neither was the fact that J.W. and Bryn were dining out together. What was amazing was the absence of any reporters or news vans. A.J. had received several phone calls asking for *her* "story," and she knew J.W. would be the focus of near-relentless media attention for some time to come—certainly until Nicole's murder was solved.

Awkward! A.J. thought, glancing up at Jake. He had noticed J.W. and Bryn as well, and he asked the waitress for a booth on the other side of the room. A.J. suspected he wasn't being considerate of J.W.'s feelings so much as positioning himself the better to watch the other two without being observed himself.

Patsy Cline was singing "A Church, A Courtroom, Then Good-bye" as Jake and A.J. were seated beneath a long row of colorful vintage lunchboxes. A.J. ordered a Diet Coke, Jake ordered coffee, and the waitress departed.

Staring across the empty dining room, A.J. could see Bryn talking quickly, agitatedly, while J.W. listened gravely and nodded.

Jake was watching, too, and A.J. asked, "Was my phone call about Jane Peters helpful?"

His green eyes met hers. "Very. Thank you." A grim smile touched his mouth. "It turns out Jane Peters is J.W. Young's estranged wife."

"Wife? You mean ex-wife?"

Jake shook his head. "Wife. They never divorced."

"Nicole's boyfriend's *wife* was seen fleeing a few minutes before Nicole's body was discovered?"

"Yep."

"So . . ." A.J. worked it out. "That's why you were able to take time for dinner. You think you have your killer?"

Jake's hard mouth curved into brief smile. "I made time for dinner because I miss you."

The direct honesty of that warmed her cheeks. "Oh." A second later, she said, "But you do think Jane Peters is your killer?"

"Too soon to say. She's sure got some explaining to do." Jake added, "First we have to find her. We've run a couple of local spots asking for information on her whereabouts, asking her to come in. There hasn't been any word since you spotted her in town."

"She must not want to be found."

He shrugged.

The waitress—humming along with Patsy Cline's warm alto—dropped off their beverages, took their meal orders, and headed over to J.W. and Bryn's booth. Bryn hastily wiped her eyes. She had been crying—although it appeared to be more of a drizzle than a downpour.

"I guess you didn't call Lydia Thorne?" A.J. asked, tearing her attention away from the other table.

"We tried. The cell phone number Nicole had was out of date. There's no indication that she ever knew the Thorne name was an alias, and without Thorne's real name we don't have much chance of tracking her down. From what we can tell, she and Nicole stopped being pals several months ago."

"About the time the cyber attacks started. What exactly happened between them?"

"No one seems to know. Or at least no one is saying. From all appearances Thorne wasn't replaced as president of Manning's fan club until after she started writing nasty reviews. The hate mail dated from the point that Manning fired her."

"So . . . the nasty reviews weren't supposed to be personal?"

"I have no idea how this stuff works. Those reviews seemed pretty personal to me."

A.J. said, "I worked with a lot of people when I was doing marketing and PR—a lot of different egos—and I can tell you that very often people miscalculate how vulnerable we all are."

Jake stirred his coffee. "How so?"

"Everyone talks about the male ego and the professional ego and the adolescent ego and the artistic ego, but the truth is, *everyone* has an ego, and no one enjoys having it bashed."

"Sure," Jake said with the easy confidence of the possessor of a stainless steel ego. "But a person in Nicole Manning's profession must be used to criticism."

He didn't say—didn't have to—*especially with Nicole's lack of talent.*

"Yes and no. I'm sure Nicole had toughened up considerably when it came to anonymous reviews or professional reviews, but a venomous review from someone she considered a friend and a fan? That would hurt."

A lot. A.J. could guarantee that having watched Elysia's reactions to the critics through the years. Happily, her mother's methods of coping had improved from the days when she had drowned her sorrows in Gilbey's and Noilly Pratt.

A.J. added, "I'm betting from the tone of those reviews that Lydia Thorne has as much ego as anyone—and that somehow Nicole managed to wound it."

"That makes sense, I guess," Jake said. "Hell hath no fury and all that. Jane Peters's ego must have taken a hit when her husband took up with Nicole Manning."

They both glanced over at the other booth. Bryn was chuckling—a watery sort of chuckle—but whatever the crisis had been, it seemed to be over. J.W. was listening and nodding while he studied the bill. Observing them, A.J. decided that they probably *were* innocent of any involvement in Nicole's death because surely guilty people wouldn't be so dumb as to be seen together following the death of a spouse.

They made a nice couple, though. Not stunningly good looking, but attractive in a non-Hollywood way. And they were obviously comfortable with each other, obviously liked each other.

She said quietly to Jake, "I guess Jane was still in love with J.W.?" How terribly painful that would be. It was impossible not to remember the shock of those first days after Andy had told her he was leaving her, that he had fallen in love with someone else. At least in Andy's case it had been more than a simple falling in love with another woman—maybe it should have made it worse, but somehow it was easier for A.J. to accept knowing that Andy had been fighting his own nature, his own sexuality.

Jake cautioned, "We don't know for sure that the Peters woman killed Manning. It's a pretty big coincidence that she was running away from the house after Nicole was dead, but . . ."

A.J. followed his train of thought and said, "How long had Nicole been dead when I found her?"

"About an hour."

Why would Jane Peters have hung around for an hour after killing Nicole? That was what Jake was wondering, A.J. knew.

Jake said slowly, "You know, I really shouldn't be discussing this with you."

"Believe it or not, I can be discreet. And it's not like I'm involved this time. I mean, unless you suspect me of knocking Nicole off."

"No." And he didn't even crack a smile! "It's just . . . this isn't the kind of job you can talk about to your girlfriends."

Girlfriends. In the plural. Well, good to know where she stood.

Malicious humor flickered within A.J. "Even when your girlfriend is the local incarnation of Miss Marple?"

"Ha." Jake looked anything but amused. "Yes, I saw the paper this morning."

"Now don't worry," A.J. assured him. "I'm not going to take over your case. This time."

Jake met her eyes. After a long moment, his mouth quirked into a reluctant grin. "I hope not. It's going to put a real crimp in our relationship if I have to throw you in the hoosegow for interfering in police business."

"So you threatened once before."

"Yeah. Well . . . I blame the last time on your mother."

"Me too." A.J. was smiling, her good humor inexplicably restored as Jake laughed, too.

They looked up as J.W. and Bryn paused beside their table on the way out of the diner. Up close and personal, they both looked tired. Bryn's eyes were red-rimmed from crying. There were little lines of tension around J.W.'s eyes and mouth.

"Is there any news?" he asked Jake.

"I'm sorry. Nothing since we spoke this afternoon." A.J. liked Jake's combination of sincerity and professionalism. There was a distance there, but there was also compassion.

J.W. slanted a look at A.J.

She offered her hand. "A.J. Alexander. We met at the April reopening of Sacred Balance. I'm so sorry about Nicole."

"Thank you." He shook her hand but then stiffened. "You're the one who said she saw Jane running away."

Bryn caught her breath.

"You're wrong about Jane," J.W. said. "I don't care how it looks or what anyone saw."

"Hey," Jake said, and it sounded like a warning.

J.W. ignored him, frowning down at A.J., and she felt compelled to say, "I didn't really *see* anything. I mean, I saw Jane running away . . . but that's all I saw."

"I don't believe Jane was there." J.W. didn't raise his voice, but there was no doubt of his intensity. "And if she was, she had a damn good reason—and it didn't have anything to do with what happened to Nikki. Jane is a genuinely good person."

Unmoved, Jake said, "Good people do bad things. Everybody makes mistakes, and sometimes those mistakes are fatal ones."

"Not Jane," J.W. said.

Bryn watched him without comment, her expression unreadable. Meeting A.J.'s gaze, she looked faintly apologetic, but A.J. was not offended. J.W. was not aggressive, just absolute in his belief in Jane's innocence. It was sort of nice, really.

J.W. said to Jake, "I've been doing what you asked: racking my brain trying to think of anyone who might have wanted to hurt Nikki. Did you know she received threats from some kind of koala preservation league?"

"But I thought Nicole was active in koala preservation?" A.J. said. Nicole had her faults, but she had been generous with the causes she believed in.

"She was," Bryn put in. "But Nicole wanted to start her own mini preserve here in New Jersey, and not all conservationists agreed with her on that. In fact . . . none of them did."

J.W. said, "Nikki had the best intentions, but she had a tendency to view all animals as . . . potential pets. That didn't go over well with wildlife preservationists."

"Let me get this straight," Jake said. "You're saying wildlife preservationists threatened your wife?"

"Nicole and J.W. weren't married," Bryn said.

"Right," J.W. said, although whether he was answering Bryn or Jake, A.J. wasn't sure.

"You have letters from these wildlife activists?"

J.W. turned to Bryn. Bryn shook her head. "We didn't take them seriously. Nicole didn't take them seriously." She said earnestly, "But the fact that someone used that koala ice sculpture to kill Nicole . . . well, that can't be a coincidence."

A.J. could see from Jake's expression that he was unconvinced on that point. Personally, she thought it was probable the killer had grabbed whatever was handy to clobber Nicole. It seemed unlikely these crazed conservationists would know what the planned table décor was for Nicole's party.

"Maybe. Maybe not," Jake said. To Bryn, he added, "Do you think you can locate names or contact information for these koala kooks?"

"I can try."

He nodded approval. "Do what you can. We'll look into this, of course—let you know what we find. In the meantime"—and this was directed toward J.W.—"if you do hear from Ms. Peters, let us know as soon as possible."

"Will do." J.W. nodded a curt good night to Jake—and then to A.J. He followed Bryn out of the diner into the May night.

A.J. watched Jake watching J.W. and Bryn.

"What do you think?" she asked.

His expression was sardonic. "Very touching," he said. "You don't often hear exes speaking so loyally about each other." He added, "Present company excepted."

A.J. did not want to say good night to Jake. His mouth moved on hers with warm expertise, but as pleasurable as it was to be in his arms again, she couldn't quite manage to forget that although the grassy front yard of the farmhouse was empty of Elysia's Land Rover, the light in the front room indicated Andy was home—possibly even waiting up for her.

She swallowed hard—it was sort of a gulp—as Jake's mouth trailed down her throat, burning softly through the thin silk of the camisole covering her breasts. Nice. Very nice. It had been a long time since A.J. had acknowledged these feelings—well, maybe not the feelings themselves, but the unsettling power of those feelings. Jake's touch was setting her nerves on fire, setting uneasy desire crackling through her. He couldn't have had worse timing if he'd planned it.

"How long is Belleson staying again?" he murmured against her skin.

A.J. shook her head. It was hard to find words. Heck, it was hard to find coherent thoughts.

Jake stroked her hair, her face, ran his hands over her bare shoulders, down her arms, but he was not gathering her close. He sighed, drew back, and said, "I guess that's just as well. I have to get back to work."

And though A.J. was disappointed, she was also a little relieved. She wasn't ready to move her relationship with Jake forward, was she? Not to mention the fact that she just couldn't relax knowing Andy was a few yards away. He might even be peering out the window at this very moment.

"Good night," she said hastily, shoving open the door of the SUV.

"I'll call you," he said—and there was a funny note in his voice.

The phone was ringing as A.J. let herself into the house.

She patted Monster and swiftly crossed the hall—pausing as she spotted Andy sitting motionless in the front room.

"Hi there! When did Mother leave?"

"About half an hour ago. Let it go to message, A.J.," Andy ordered as she moved to the phone.

"What?" She was already picking up the receiver.

"Hi, A.J." The voice that answered her greeting was male, deep, and attractive—unfamiliar to her. "This is Nick Grant." Into her silence Nick added, "Andy's partner."

Like she could possibly have forgotten the name of the man Andy had left her for?

"Hi, Nick," she responded coolly.

Andy had moved to the doorway. He shook his head fiercely in answer to her glare.

Okaaaaay . . .

Nick said very casually, "I've been out of town for a few days and . . . anyway, I wondered if by any chance . . . Andy was staying with you?"

A.J. looked at Andy. He stared back at her, willing her to say nothing. No. Willing her to lie for him.

Which took a fair bit of gall given their history and the fact that she was unlikely to be sympathetic to the idea of Andy lying to anyone ever again. But as she glared at him she couldn't help noticing how drawn he was—the faded bruise on his cheekbone stood out starkly—and she heard herself say, surprised at how calm and collected she sounded, "No, he's not. Is he supposed to be?"

"Not that I know of," Nick said. There was an undernote

in his voice that A.J. couldn't quite pinpoint. Disappointment? Frustration? Worry? She could imagine how hard this must be for him, having to call his lover's ex-wife and basically admit that he didn't know where Andy was. Presumably Andy had a good reason for this subterfuge. Because if he *didn't*, this wasn't just selfish, it was downright cruel.

"I'm sorry, Nick," she said. And she meant it.

There was a beat, and then Nick said quietly, "Me too. If you hear from him, will you ask him to give me a call? Please?"

"Yes," A.J. said, scowling at Andy. "I will."

The phone was replaced softly on Nick's end. Not so softly on A.J.'s. She turned to face Andy.

"Well, that was interesting. Maybe you better tell me what's going on."

She thought he wasn't going to answer, but at last Andy scrubbed a hand across his face. His gaze met hers. "I've left Nick."

Eleven

"Oh, I think I got that part," A.J. said, beginning to give in to her temper. "Did you bother to tell Nick you were leaving him? Because he sounds a little confused."

"I left him a letter."

"A *letter*?"

For a moment A.J. was so angry she wasn't sure she could speak without screaming. This was the relationship for which Andy had shattered their own decade-long marriage. And now, after less than a year, he was walking away from that, too, this time leaving his bewildered spouse with nothing more than a letter to explain his hurtful, cowardly, selfish actions.

"Who *are* you?" she demanded.

He said with difficulty, "You don't know . . . the full story."

"Well, what's the full story?" Her suspicions returned. "That bruise on your face. Nick hit you, didn't he?"

There was no mistaking the genuineness of Andy's reaction as he gaped at her. "*Nick?* You think Nick *hit* me?"

"Didn't he?"

"Hell no!"

"Then *what* is the big mystery? You show up without warning, you're limping, your face is bruised, you won't talk to Nick. What is going on?"

"He's never laid a hand on me. He's . . . he wouldn't ever . . ." Words seemed to fail Andy.

"Then what? You want to play the field? What?"

"*A.J.*" He stopped. Took a deep breath. "I have MS."

She stared. "What?"

"I've been diagnosed with multiple sclerosis."

A.J. knew she should say something but nothing occurred to her.

Andy said with surprising steadiness, "I found out for sure a few days ago. I've been having problems with my balance and coordination, stiffness in my joints. Tremors in my hands. My vision goes in and out. I'm tired and feeling weak all the time. I kept thinking it was different things. Stress or fatigue or . . . Anyway, about a week ago I fell down. Just . . . fell. That's when I got this." He touched his cheekbone. "And I knew something was really wrong."

A.J. felt winded. She groped for words, found them at last. "And you haven't told Nick?"

Andy shook his head.

"Why on earth not?"

"Because we were already having problems. Arguing over his schedule and the fact that his job comes before everything else."

"Oh my God, Andy. And so . . . what? You don't want to burden him? It's not a burden when you love the person."

"Of course it is! It's just that when you love someone

you're willing to take on the burden. But Nick and I . . . we don't have that kind of relationship."

"I thought you were both *so* in love." She couldn't help the trace of acid there, although she did try.

"We do love each other. But Nick didn't bargain for this."

"How do you know? You haven't given him a chance—"

Andy interrupted sharply, "I know, all right? Before this ever happened we talked about our schedules and the future and what we both want and . . ." He struggled briefly with his emotions, then said more calmly, "The kind of MS I have is the kind that progresses fast. I'm . . . probably going to be disabled. I mean, like in a wheelchair."

What a way to realize you still loved someone. A.J. took a deep breath. "Are you . . . going to die?"

Andy shook his head. "MS doesn't usually mean a shorter life span. But I'm going to be more and more dependent, and I can't—I don't want to do that to Nick. Even if he wanted that. Which he wouldn't."

All at once A.J. understood Andy's desire to lose himself in amateur sleuthing. No wonder he didn't want to deal with his own real-life problems. She said, "But you're not giving Nick the choice."

He said a little bitterly, "Nick didn't have time for me when I was well."

She absorbed that silently. Nick Grant didn't strike her as the nurturing kind, that was for sure.

"I still think you should tell him."

She saw the tension leave Andy's face as he realized he had won the most immediate battle. "I will," he promised. "I just need a little more time to come to terms with it myself."

There really wasn't much she could say to that.

* * *

"**'Everything** happens for a purpose.' As the Bard said."

A.J. quit trying to calculate whether the difference in fat content between a skinny iced cinnamon dolce latte and a chai frappuccino would compensate for a slice of zucchini nut bread. She stared at her mother.

"I think that's the Bible, isn't it?"

"Is it?" Elysia blinked at her. Granted, Bible study had not played a large part in the Alexander family's curriculum.

They were sitting in the small crowded patio outside Starbucks where they had met for an early breakfast.

Elysia brushed away the minor difference between God and the Bard with a lazy wave of her bronze tipped fingers. "My point, pumpkin, is that Andy has come back into your life—"

"No he hasn't."

"—at a time when you both—"

"No we don't."

"—need each other most."

"No." A.J. scowled at Elysia. "No. No. *No.*"

Unperturbed, Elysia sipped her black coffee and gazed soulfully up at the blossoming tree in the center of the patio. "I know you far too well, Anna, to believe you would turn your back on your husband in his hour of need."

Anna. So—incredibly—she was quite serious. This would take delicate handling. Which meant that hysterical laughter was probably out of the question. A.J. drew a deep breath, but all the deep, cleansing breaths in the world weren't going to help. A wet vac wouldn't help.

"Mother, Andy and I are divorced, remember? Remember the part about Andy leaving me for another man?"

Elysia's face tightened, conveying vast world-weariness. Or perhaps she was merely doing her facial exercises. "Don't be so unforgiving, pet. There is a reason Andrew has turned to you in his darkest hour."

An alarming thought occurred to A.J. "Did Andy tell you he wanted to get back together with me?"

"Not in so many words," Elysia hedged.

"How many words did he use, and what were they?"

"Men don't discuss these things like women do." Elysia cast A.J. a measuring look as though seeing whether she was buying it.

A.J. was not buying it. In fact, this was the last thing she was in the market for. She gritted her jaw against a lot of things she would regret saying, and finally managed, "I understand that you mean well, Mother."

Elysia made a sound of near horror.

Before she could open her mouth to protest, A.J. had changed the subject. "You still haven't explained why you cut short your cruise."

The gray green eyes narrowed. "But of course I have. I heard—"

"Yes, so you said. But I don't see why you felt you had to end your vacation just because there was a murder in Stillbrook. What is it you're not telling me?"

Elysia reached for her pack of cigarettes, ignoring A.J.'s look of censure. She said, "There are many things I don't tell you, pumpkin, as I'd imagine there are many things you don't share with me. But why I should have to explain my perfectly ordinary desire to return to my own home and hearth—and Tempur-Pedic mattress—"

"All right already," A.J. said. "But you looked like you were having such a wonderful time."

"I was. Mostly."

"Who was the good-looking young guy who seemed to be with you in all those photographs?"

Elysia froze. It was just for a split second. "Hmmm?" she murmured. "Oh. That would be Dicky." Her eyes met A.J.'s. "Dakarai Massri. He works for the SCA."

She did it beautifully, but A.J. was certain she hadn't imagined that odd break.

"I have no clue what the SCA is."

"The Supreme Council of Antiquities."

"So he's an archeologist or . . . ?"

"Something like that," Elysia said vaguely.

"Very nice," A.J. admitted. "If you like them newly hatched. You know, I think Mr. Meagher missed you. A lot."

"Bradley Meagher! That old fox." Elysia's honey-brown cheeks flushed prettily. "Why, we've been mates forever."

"I don't think he thinks of you as just one of the lads." A.J. glanced at her watch. "Damn. I've got to get over to the studio. I'm interviewing receptionists this morning." She rose and tossed her plastic cup in the trash.

"Come and have supper this evening," Elysia invited. "You and Andrew. It'll be like old times."

How could it possibly be like old times?

Watching her, Elysia coaxed, "Humor your dear old mum. Besides, don't you want to see the lovely prezzie I brought you?"

"You don't have to bribe me to visit, Mother."

"Lawks. Times *have* changed," Elysia cooed. "See you both at six."

"Do you drug test?" Dana Pickles asked, glancing at her cell phone for the third time in two minutes.

"Uh . . ." We do now, A.J. thought.

Dana was the fourth and last candidate of the morning. Candidate number one had started the interview by asking to use the restroom and then spending the brief remainder of her interview time asking about the holiday work schedule, sick pay, and overtime. Candidate number two had turned out to be a cub reporter from the local paper hoping to score an interview with A.J. Candidate number three had been a no-show.

Ms. Pickles was the most promising of the lot—and that was not saying much.

"So!" A.J. automatically double-checked the list of questions on her notepad. "Why do you want to work for Sacred Balance?"

Dana shrugged. "We were all talking. Me and my peeps. Oz said that this one sounded like an easy gig."

"Oz?"

"Oz Siragusa." Dana raised her immaculately groomed eyebrows at A.J.'s ignorance. "The tennis star?"

"Barbie Siragusa's son?"

"That's right." Dana yawned. "After I got fi—left Tea! Tea! Hee!, I was trying to think of someplace else that might not be too big a PIA to work."

"And you thought of us," A.J. murmured. "We're honored."

"Actually, Oz thought of you." Dana—an unexpected stickler for accuracy—added, "Barbie takes classes here."

A.J. remembered the hundred and thirty-seven text messages from Ball Boy downloaded from Nicole's phone. Beyond the fact that Oz Siragusa was young, handsome, and spoiled rotten by his adoring mother, A.J. knew very little about him, although he had briefly—very briefly—taken a yoga course for athletic training.

"Lots of people take lessons here. Nicole took lessons here." A.J. wasn't sure why she tossed that out. Maybe the sleuth reflex *was* genetic.

Dana glanced down at her cell phone again. "I guess." She couldn't have sounded less interested.

"So is it true? Were Oz and Nicole seeing each other?"

"Sure," Dana said indifferently. "They *were* seeing each other. Till Nicole blew Oz off."

Apparently the idea that Nicole might have a previous commitment—like to her live-in boyfriend—had not occurred to Dana and her peeps. "Why would she do that?" A.J. asked.

Dana shrugged, texting a lightning-fast message on her cell phone before looking up again. "Something about being too old for him. It's total bewshit."

Bewshit?

"How old is Oz?" A.J. couldn't recall, but she wasn't sure he was over eighteen.

"Twenty."

Twenty in boy years. Which in real life translated to . . . what? Sixteen? "Nicole was in her thirties. There was something like fifteen years between them."

"Yeah, she was old," Dana said with the brutal frankness of a girl who had never seen a line in her face that didn't come from a pillow crease.

"Was Nicole . . . ?" This was so hard to imagine. "Did Nicole hang out with all of you?"

Maybe it was even harder to imagine than she thought because Dana giggled, actually raising her eyes from her cell phone for an instant.

"How did Oz take getting dumped?"

Dana rolled her eyes. "*Dude.*"

Which A.J. translated as *not so much!*

"And Barbie knew about all this?"

Dana looked puzzled. "Sure. Barbie's cool."

Not that cool, A.J. thought. Nobody's mom was that cool.

"Anyway," Dana said. "It wasn't Oz getting dumped that pissed Barbie off. If you get what I mean."

Oh yes, A.J. got what Dana meant. She inquired with faint trepidation, "Did the breakup happen on an episode of Barbie's reality show?"

Dana went into peals of laughter at the idea. "No way!"
So much for reality TV.

Apparently it really wasn't merely a rumor. Nicole had
been having an affair with Barbie's twenty-year-old son.
Granted, the age of consent in New Jersey was sixteen, so
while the relationship was liable to offend mothers, live-in
boyfriends, and television viewers across the country, as
scandals went, it wasn't exactly the stuff of front page *National Enquirer*.

"So?" Dana asked.

"So what?" A.J. asked.

"Do you drug test?"

"Yes."

Dana made a face and put her cell phone away.

A.J. asked, "What did Barbie say?"

"About what?"

"About Nicole dating her son?"

"Oh," Dana replied, unperturbed. "She said she'd kill her."

Twelve

A.J. gasped. Andy braked gently as a rabbit darted out from the side of the road—changed its mind in the nick of time—and disappeared back into the tangle of underbrush.

"He found a reason to live after all," Andy declared.

A.J. snickered at the reference to *The Book of Bunny Suicides*. They were on their way to Starlight Farm for supper with Elysia. Always a pretty drive, it was especially lovely in the pink-veined dusk, dogwood flowers glimmering palely beside the road, lights from old farmhouses and new mansions winking through the trees.

"I don't think there ever was an important phone call from a Hollywood producer," she said, picking up the thread of their discussion once more. "I think Nicole was panicking over the idea of her cell falling into the wrong hands. Those multifunctional phones are like tiny laptops. Voice mails, e-mails—it would have all been there, including one hundred and thirty-seven text messages from the besotted scion of a mob family."

"*Besotted scion!*" Andy threw her an amused look. "This is why you used to be so good at marketing. That special turn of phrase." He continued, "It makes sense, though. It also explains why this important caller wouldn't just dial in on the landline."

"Yes, except . . . how secret could this affair with Oz Siragusa have been? Oz's pals seem to all know about it, and they aren't exactly the closemouthed type."

"Maybe they found out after the fact."

"Maybe. I didn't think to ask. Even so . . . Bryn must have known. She was Nicole's PA. It would be hard to conceal an affair from her; at least part of her responsibilities would be scheduling Nicole's daily activities."

"A big part of that job description is knowing how to keep your mouth shut."

"True. But Bryn and J.W. seem awfully chummy."

"Oh ho?" Andy glanced away from the road again, eyes lighting with interest. He had insisted on driving that evening, and he did seem more energetic than he had when he had first arrived on Saturday.

"Maybe not *that* chummy," A.J. qualified. "But friendly, certainly."

"If J.W. Young knew about Nicole's affair, that would give him a motive for murder."

"Not necessarily. Not everyone turns into Othello when they're betrayed." She hadn't been thinking at all about their own situation, but Andy's sudden silence indicated her words hit home. A.J. said hastily, "Besides, J.W. was flying in from Mexico at the time—"

Her cell phone rang and she reached down to her purse.

"Jake," she identified, and pressed to answer. "Hi!"

"Hey," Jake said. "What are your plans for this Sunday?"

"Nothing that I know of."

"I've got the day off. I was thinking maybe we could do something. Go somewhere."

"Sure!"

"Where?"

"Sorry?"

"Where would you like to go?"

"Oh. I don't know." Usually A.J. and Jake just went to eat or see a movie. Sometimes both. This sounded more complicated—and more entertaining.

"Well, you think about it," Jake said.

They chatted a little more—and that was different, too. Jake usually didn't make time for small talk on the phone.

"How is the case coming?" A.J. asked. "Have you found Jane Peters yet?"

Sounding uncharacteristically weary, Jake said, "No. She's apparently dropped off the face of the earth."

"Well, she's probably hiding."

"Then she's doing it like a pro." His voiced faded away, then he came back on and said, "Got to go. Talk to you later."

And with that he clicked off.

A.J. tucked her phone back in her purse and tried to get her smile under control. Her gaze slid sideways and caught Andy's.

"Don't say it," she warned.

Andy chuckled.

The emerald green door to Starlight Farm swung wide. Elysia stood framed in the arch of roses around the entranceway. Tanned and rested from her recent holiday, she looked radiant in a gorgeous red silk caftan, her dark hair coiled elegantly on her head. She looked like an older version of herself in the 1972 racy historical epic *A Night with Nefertiti*. In fact, A.J. would have suspected her mother of setting up one of her "entrances," except that Elysia was staring as though she had never seen them before.

"Well, well!" she said brightly, after a funny pause. "Pumpkin. Andrew. What a lovely surprise."

"It shouldn't be." A.J. said. "You invited us to dinner."

"*I* . . . ?" Elysia blinked and then seemed to re-collect herself. "But of course! Of course, I did. Come in, pet. Andrew, darling boy, how are you feeling?"

"I'm fine, Ellie," Andy said quickly, clearly uncomfortable with the suggestion that he might not be hale and hearty to his buffed fingertips.

"*Such* a brave lad," Elysia said, patting his cheek. She was moving them—shooing them, in fact, straight through to the living room. "Sit, lovies. What would you like to drink? Lemon squash? Fruit juice? Soft drinks? Coffee or tea?"

"Iced tea," Andy requested.

"Same," said A.J. She could have used a real drink, but Elysia, now a successful nine years sober, did not keep alcohol on the premises.

"Right-o!" Elysia said brightly. "Tea for two coming up. Make yourselves comfy. As the Bard said, '*Mi casa es su casa.*'"

"No way did the Bard ever say that," A.J. muttered to Andy as Elysia bustled away down the hallway lined with watercolors of eighteenth century London.

"I think she forgot we were coming to dinner," Andy remarked. He was studying the piano-top collection of gold-framed photographs of A.J. and himself. The gallery started with their college romance and ended with the final summer Elysia had visited them in Manhattan. Theirs had been an extremely photogenic union, which just proved the old adage about appearances being deceptive.

"She seems . . . rattled," A.J. agreed, turning away. She still found the photographs painful—although less so these days. "I hope she's not going to a lot of trouble. We could just order in pizza."

"Pizza sounds fine to me," Andy said indifferently. His appetite had been off since his arrival. A.J. wasn't sure if that was depression or his illness—or both.

She started down the hall, but Elysia appeared at the other end with two glasses of ice tea. She hastened toward A.J.

"What's this? Sit, sit! You've had a long day bending and stretching and whatever-it-is-ing you do at the gym."

"Studio." A.J. retreated back to the living room, falling back before her mother's onslaught.

Elysia delivered their drinks. "*Relax*, darlings. I'm going to whip a little something up—"

"We can just order in," Andy started.

At the same time A.J. began, "Mother, why are we sitting in here when you're . . . ?"

But Elysia had vanished down the hallway once more.

"Okay, this is getting weird," A.J. told Andy.

His eyes laughed at her over the rim of his glass.

"Have you ever known her to serve anything that wasn't on a tray? Drinks, hors d'oeuvres, popcorn? I mean, even for my mother, she's behaving oddly."

"Actually, I've always thought the tray thing was the odd bit. This seems—"

A.J. was shaking her head. "She's up to something."

That appealed to Andy's weird sense of humor. He wriggled his eyebrows. "You're right. She's as jumpy as someone in a bedroom farce."

"Ha. Very funny." A.J. took a sip, then set her glass down. "I'll be right back."

"Are you sure you should . . . ?"

A.J. missed the rest of that as she started down the hallway. At the same instant Elysia poked her head out the kitchen doorway and jumped. She had so obviously been checking whether the coast was clear that A.J. stopped dead.

"What's going on?"

Elysia smiled a wide insincere smile. She really was *not* a very good actress.

"Sorry?" She was walking toward A.J. and A.J. realized that she was once more being steered away from the kitchen.

A horrible suspicion entered her mind. Could her mother be drinking again?

No. Please, God, no. There had been no hint of alcohol on Elysia's breath, and while she was definitely acting a little peculiar, she seemed steady enough.

All the same, A.J. couldn't help advancing suspiciously on her mother. "What are you doing in there?"

Elysia held her ground. "It's called cooking, pumpkin. Sometimes it's a wee bit more involved than pouring a bottle of milk over a bowl of cereal."

Refusing to be sidetracked, A.J. said, "I know you. You're up to something."

"Nonsense! And I very much res—" Elysia broke off as A.J. brushed past her. "Anna Jolie! I did *not* raise my daughter to behave like something calved in a stable. . . ."

A.J. stopped short. A young woman stood at bay beside the kitchen table. Her face was white beneath freckles, her short red hair stood on end as though she had been running her hands through it. Her blue eyes were wide with fear.

"Y-you were at the restaurant…"

"Oh my God," A.J. breathed. She turned to Elysia. "You've *got* to be kidding me!"

"Wait! Please!" the woman pleaded.

A.J. ignored her. "Do you know who this is?" she demanded of Elysia. "This is Jane Peters. The police are looking everywhere for her."

Elysia's chin tilted. "Clearly not."

A.J.'s jaw dropped. "Mother, you're harboring a *fugitive*. They can throw you in jail for that. They *will* throw you in jail for that!"

Elysia announced defiantly, "Jane is innocent."

There went any hope that her mother was unwittingly sheltering a criminal. A.J. snapped, "Says who? Jane?"

"Yes. And I believe her. Why, I've known Janie for years," Elysia asserted. "Ever since we worked together on *The Spy Who Came to Babysit*. She was the most adorable tyke. Why, I've practically watched her grow up."

Both of her—because that would have been during the years Elysia spent drinking herself cross-eyed. A.J. was ashamed of that mean-spirited thought, but it was difficult when she remembered how oblivious to her own daughter Elysia had been during A.J.'s formative years.

"I didn't kill anyone," Jane burst out desperately. "I know you saw me leaving Nicole Manning's house, but she was dead when I got there."

"What were you doing there at all?"

Jane looked at Elysia, who nodded encouragingly. "I went to see J.W. I didn't realize he was out of town."

"You didn't call first to see whether he would be home? Isn't New Jersey a little out of your way?"

It was pretty much out of everyone's way, so that was a safe bet.

Jane bit her lip. "I just . . . took a chance."

"So did whoever killed Nicole."

Jane glared at her. "I didn't kill her! I had no reason to kill her."

"According to the tabloids, she stole your husband," A.J. said. Reading her mother's gaze, she added, "You can't avoid reading those covers in the checkout lines."

"What's going on in here?" Andy asked, appearing in the kitchen doorway.

Jane took the opportunity of that distraction to run for the door.

"Don't let her go!" A.J. cried, and Andy stepped in front of Jane. She crashed into him, and Andy grunted and went down, flimsy as kindling. Jane tripped over him and landed on her knees on the polished wood floor. She began to crawl up the hallway.

"Stop it this instant!" Elysia shrieked. "Stop it, all of you!"

"Are you all right?" A.J. demanded, pausing long enough to see that Andy hadn't been seriously hurt by his fall. Grimacing, he was using the door frame to pull himself up.

"*Get her*," he said, sounding—for Andy—quite vicious.

A.J. sprang after Jane, who had scrambled to her feet and was making for the front door.

Catching her up before she could get the front door open, A.J. fastened a hand on Jane's arm. Although Jane had changed her outfit, she was still wearing those ridiculous red platform shoes, and she nearly toppled over again.

"Leave me alone!"

"You're not going anywhere."

"You have no right!"

"Enough!" Nefertiti herself couldn't have sounded more commanding as Elysia wriggled between them, wrapping a surprisingly steely hand around each young woman's arm.

The fight went abruptly out of Jane, and she began to cry.

Elysia patted her soothingly. Meeting her accusatory gaze, A.J. said, "Don't give me that look."

"What look shall I give you then? Brawling like a common street urchin!" Elysia delivered the lines like the grand dame in a drawing room drama. All she was missing was a lorgnette and the sal volatile.

"Mother—"

But she was talking to herself. Elysia was already urging Jane Peters back to the kitchen. "Now let's sit down and talk this out like civilized people."

"There's nothing to talk out," A.J. said.

Neither Elysia nor Jane Peters responded, and A.J. looked heavenward. She followed her mother and her unorthodox house guest. Jane Peters's heavy shoes clomp, clomp, clomped down the hardwood floor.

In the kitchen Andy was applying a towel filled with ice to his elbow. He grimaced, meeting A.J.'s eyes. "Sorry," he said.

"*I'm* sorry," she returned, going to join him at the sink.

And she was sorry. Jane Peters could have been armed for all she knew; she hadn't thought twice about it. And Andy . . . she had always looked at Andy as her protector; it was shocking to realize he might now be in the position of needing protection himself.

"Are you okay?" she asked.

"Oh hell yeah," he said. There was a long scrape down his forearm, but it didn't look serious.

"You should *both* be sorry!" Elysia scolded.

"Don't even start, Mother," A.J. said sternly, and at her tone, Elysia fell silent. A.J. looked from her mother to Jane Peters. "Look, I have no idea what you two think you're doing—what your harebrained plan might be—but we *have* to call the police. If we don't, we all become accessories after the fact."

Elysia said with great certainty, "Not if Janie is proven innocent."

"Well good luck with that. As far as I can see all you

have is her word and all she has is an awfully shaky story."
A.J. added to Jane, "No offense."

"I know how it looks," Jane responded, wiping her wet
cheeks. "But I didn't kill Nicole. I do love J.W., and I was
devastated when he left me. That's true. But I didn't go
there to kill Nikki."

In Jane's position A.J. wouldn't have stressed the loving
J.W. and being devastated part, but it did have the ring of
truth. "Then why did you go there? To try and persuade
J.W. to come back to you?"

Once A.J. had known the truth about Andy, she'd have
died before she begged him to come back to her. Even so,
she could understand—and pity—the feelings of despera-
tion and bewilderment.

But Jane was shaking her head. "No. I didn't go there to
beg J.W. to come home. I went there to try to get him to
sign our divorce papers. I've been trying to get him to sign
them for the past six months."

A.J. met Andy's gaze.

"It's goofy enough to be true," he commented.

"And that's why I didn't dare call ahead," Jane continued. "Every other time I've tried to arrange with J.W. to
sign these damn papers, he dodges me. I thought if I caught
him by surprise, he wouldn't have a choice. He'd have to
sign. I had no idea he was out of the country again. I knew
Nicole was celebrating her birthday, and I assumed he
would be there."

"It's perfectly obvious that that horrid Sargasso woman,
the gangster's moll, twepped poor Nicole," Elysia said
briskly. "It's up to us—"

"No, it most certainly is *not*." A.J. met the gazes of the
other three and hardened her heart.

"How can you say that? This poor child is obviously
innocent."

"It's not that obvious to me," A.J. said. "Sorry," she told Jane. "But I'm just not convinced. And even if I was convinced, this would be something for the police to handle."

"Oh, the police!" Elysia exclaimed in disgust. "That inspector of yours couldn't find his arse with both hands. *We*—you and I—were the ones who solved the murder of my poor dear sister."

"She's got a point," Andy said.

"Don't *you* start!"

Andy shrugged.

Elysia said slyly, "Besides, as you've pointed out, if you hand Jane over to the Gestapo—"

"The *Gestapo*?"

"I'm quite likely to be nicked as her accomplice."

"Jake wouldn't." Despite her confident tone, A.J. was sure of no such thing. Jake did take his job very seriously.

"It's certainly not a chance I'm willing to take," Elysia said. "However, if you're going to grass me out . . ."

A.J. looked skyward for assistance, but no sign from above was forthcoming.

"What is your plan?" she asked tersely. "You seem to think you have one."

"It's very simple. We solve Nicole's murder."

Silence.

At last A.J. inquired, "Just out of curiosity, how do you imagine we would do that?"

"The same way we did it before. We ask questions of everyone involved. People will talk to us in a way they never would to the police."

"*That* I don't doubt."

Elysia smiled reminiscently. "I remember once on *221B Baker Street* we had a similar situation with Lew Collins. Adorable man. He played a soldier of fortune who returned from the war and was accused of murdering the husband of his former fiancée."

"I *loved* that episode," Andy enthused. Meeting A.J.'s stare, he sobered. "Well, I did."

"Of course you did," Elysia said. "Everyone did." She eyed A.J. "Nearly everyone. It's a great source of pain to me that A.J. has never shown the least bit of interest in my work."

In fact, A.J. had seen every episode of *221B Baker Street* several times, but in her opinion it wasn't a good idea to encourage her mother's incipient megalomania. She said, "Am I the only one here who sees that this could be dangerous as well as dumb?"

Elysia shook her head—apparently in sorrow at A.J.'s lack of sleuthing spirit. "We're not going to place ourselves in harm's way, pumpkin. We're simply going to ask a few questions and glean enough information to place Jane's guilt in doubt in the minds of the filth."

"The minds of the *what*?"

"The filth. The plods. The coppers."

"Charming."

"I'm sure your inspector has been called many worse things than that, petal."

A.J. opened her mouth but let it go. The other three gazed expectantly at her.

"Please," Jane said, wiping at her tears. "I know you don't have any reason to trust me. You don't know me at all. But I didn't do this thing. I'm innocent. And I need your help."

Andy said reasonably, "You could give it a day or two. See what happens."

It could happen! The Sacred Balance slogan popped into A.J.'s mind. She wondered suddenly what her unconventional aunt would have done if presented with this kind of situation.

Slowly, reluctantly, she said, "All right. I guess we can wait a day or two. Maybe the situation will resolve itself."

"Bravo!" Elysia exclaimed, beaming. "I'm proud of you, pumpkin."

A.J. smiled weakly.

"It's kind of like . . . we're The Three Investigators," Andy said. "You're Pete Crenshaw and I'm Bob Andrews and—"

"Oh my God," A.J. said looking at Elysia. "*Jupiter Jones?*"

"I have no idea who this Jupiter Jones bloke is, pumpkin," Elysia said. "But it's a lovely stage name. And, in any case, what could *possibly* go wrong?"

Thirteen

"A.J. can I speak to you?"

A.J. looked up from her laptop where she had been reading about MS on the National Multiple Sclerosis Society website. Lily stood in the doorway, and although she had framed her command as a request, it was clearly expected that A.J. would drop what she was doing.

"Of course," she said politely, clicking out of the computer window.

Lily thrust a sheet of paper beneath A.J.'s nose. A.J. noted absently that Lily's hand was shaking. "I understand this was your idea."

A.J. reached for the paper, reading over it. It was a copy of the letter she had drafted and distributed the day before to the clients of Sacred Balance officially restricting the use of cell phones within the studio.

"That's right." She raised her eyes to Lily's glowering countenance.

"Are you trying to put us out of business?"

"I'm going to assume that's rhetorical."

"You can't treat clients like this!"

A.J. said carefully, "I don't feel that requesting clients leave their cell phones in their cubbies during class is particularly harsh treatment."

Lily gave her a short, disbelieving laugh. "The most amazing thing to me is that you apparently made some kind of a living working with the public before Di gave you a chance here." She made it sound like A.J. had been slinging burgers at Carl's Jr. before her aunt rescued her from a life of food stamps and public transportation.

"No, the most amazing thing," A.J. retorted, "is that you're under the delusion that *you* have a winning way with people."

"*I* know how to get results," Lily said. "And I get them without antagonizing the important people."

"The difference between you and me, Lily, is I believe *everyone* is important—from Suze to Mrs. Siragusa."

"You know what I mean."

"I think I do, yes!"

Lily snatched the Xeroxed letter away from A.J. "It's only fair to tell you that I'm looking into finding legal representation. The studio is mine by rights, and I don't intend to let you destroy it with your well-meaning incompetence."

"Oh. My. God." A.J. shoved back her chair and rose. Lily took a step back at whatever she read in A.J.'s face. "Is there an echo in here? You've been threatening to sue me for control of the studio since the day I arrived. Well, go right ahead, Lily. It's not going to be as easy as you think—speaking as someone who has tried to find a way to get rid of *you*."

The color drained from Lily's face and she stared at A.J. "You're trying to cut me out of my share of the studio?" She seemed genuinely stricken. So much so that A.J. unexpectedly found herself trying to soften her words.

"I'm not trying to cheat you. We can't work together, Lily. That's obvious by now. I'm looking for a way—"

"I can't believe you would try to rob me of my inheritance!"

"Isn't that what you're trying to do to me?" It wasn't the right answer, of course. A.J. wasn't trying to rob Lily of anything. She had come to the end of her tether as far as working with the other woman, but she fully intended that their separation be a fair and equitable one.

Lily drew herself very straight. She said with unexpected dignity, "I'm trying to do what's best for Sacred Balance. I'm not trying to cheat you or rob you. And I haven't tried to go behind your back."

"I'm not trying to rob you!" But A.J. was speaking to the door as it slammed shut in Lily's wake.

A.J. was surprised at how much she enjoyed working with the youngest students at Sacred Balance. She liked kids but had never experienced any burning desire for children of her own. Ironically, Andy had been the one who had been most interested in beginning a family.

But as A.J. observed her pint-sized practitioners hissing enthusiastically as they assumed cobra pose, she found herself laughing, the tension of the morning's unpleasant encounter with Lily evaporating like a popped bubble.

Lily, of course, disapproved of A.J. teaching any courses—even suggesting that the Doga courses were pushing A.J.'s limits—despite the fact that A.J. had completed her accreditation with flying colors. And A.J. had to admit, gazing over the class of little yogis—some of whom were now attempting to slither snakelike across the slick floor and bite each other—that the class might on the surface seem to lack a certain seriousness or structure. But the truth was that yoga had many benefits for children beyond the obvious physical ones of increased strength, flexibility, and coordination. Yoga helped children improve their concentration and focus, even helped reduce their stress.

In fact, until A.J. had begun teaching Yoga for Kids and Itsy Bitsy Yoga, she'd had no idea of how stress-filled some of these tots' lives were. It probably made sense, given their parents' stress levels. Now more aware, A.J. had developed a relaxed and fluid teaching style, no longer insisting on perfect alignment—even occasionally letting the kids make up their own poses. She used songs to help teach breathing, and a number of props, including books and toys, to gently instruct her students in yoga's philosophy. The response from parents had been terrific so far—and the response from the young students even better.

She wouldn't have dared admit it to Lily, but she sometimes felt the kids were teaching her as much about yoga as she was teaching them. Either way, A.J. was convinced she was bringing something needed, something valuable to Sacred Balance. She felt sure she was doing what her aunt would have wanted, that she was taking Sacred Balance in a direction Diantha would have approved, despite Lily's equal conviction that she was on the wrong path and endangering everything already achieved. Still, A.J. couldn't shake the feeling that her inability to work with Lily was a failure. True, the failure wasn't hers alone, but that didn't lessen the fact that it *was* failure.

She wondered if there was any possible way to start over with Lily. It seemed unlikely given Lily's personality. In fact, the only real question seemed to be what form Lily's inevitable retaliation would take.

*   *   *

Several fashion magazines and a hardcover book featuring a smug-looking koala sat next to a yellow bowl of violets on the polished table in Nicole Manning's elegant living room. The scent of lemons mingled with the fragrance of freshly mown grass drifting through the open window.

"It's lovely of you to see us on such short notice," Elysia was saying, using her fork to break off a small bite of almond cheesecake. She directed a pointed look A.J.'s way, and A.J.—caught with her mouth full—murmured assent. Her mother had somehow wrangled this impromptu meeting with J.W., and A.J. had reluctantly abandoned the stack of resumes on her desk and in her e-mail to provide "backup."

"No," J.W. Young replied, gazing at his own cheesecake without appetite. "This place is like a mausoleum without Nikki. I'm grateful for some company."

"J.W., don't forget you've got a conference call with Margaret Sciorra of Lazarus Films at three thirty," Bryn said, sticking her head around the doorway.

J.W. waved thanks, and Bryn ducked back out again. J.W. picked up his coffee cup.

Again, A.J. was struck by his ordinary attractiveness. He was tall and lean, with a neatly trimmed beard and intelligent eyes. There was nothing particularly Hollywood about J.W. In fact, his jeans and plaid flannel shirt seemed a little out of place in this room with its silk brocade upholstery and marble fireplace. The living room was very much a woman's room—a woman with an expensive interior decorator—but then the house was very much Nicole's house.

"Is Bryn staying on then?" Elysia asked, and A.J. studiously avoided looking her way. Subtlety had never been Elysia's strong point.

But J.W. answered easily enough. "For now. God knows, I'm grateful for her help in winding everything up."

"She seemed devoted to Nicole," A.J. said.

"Yeah." He sipped his coffee, swallowed. "She is. Was. But she has her own life, and I've asked her to put it on hold long enough."

At Elysia and A.J.'s inquiring looks, he said, "Bryn's supposed to be getting married next month. She's engaged to a great guy. He's a Navy SEAL just home from Iraq. Anyway, from what I understand they're planning this giant wedding. Last week was supposed to be her last, but Bryn's been kind enough to stay on and help me sort through . . . everything."

He fell silent, staring out the window at the rolling green meadow.

There was a strange, awkward break. To A.J.'s surprise, her mother gracefully filled it.

"You mustn't feel guilty," Elysia said warmly. "I know you're telling yourself that if you'd been here—"

J.W. drew in a harsh breath. He looked at Elysia and then looked away. "Yeah. You got that right. It's still so hard to believe."

A.J. stared as her mother continued in that sincere, frank way, "Jane is such a sweet girl. I worked with her a few years ago in London, you know."

"Jane didn't have anything to do with it." J.W. gave A.J. a hard look.

"No, of course not," Elysia agreed. "No one who met Jane could possibly think any such thing. A delightful girl." And she, too, couldn't resist directing A.J. a look.

A.J. asserted, "I'm not trying to cause trouble for Jane. I wasn't the only one who saw her leaving here that day."

However A.J. was the only one who had been able to identify the fleeing woman as Jane Peters, and they all knew it.

J.W. sighed. "I know. It's just . . ."

Elysia reached across and patted his hand. "We understand. How did Jane and Nicole get along?"

"They didn't." J.W. grimaced. "Nikki was jealous as hell, and Jane . . . well, no way was Jane ever going to forgive me or forget the way I treated her. I don't think she blamed Nikki, though. It's just . . . they wouldn't have had anything in common other than me."

"Ah," Elysia said wisely. "And when did you and Jane get divorced?"

J.W.'s gaze fell. "Well, to be honest, we're not divorced. Not officially. It's just a technicality, of course."

"Of course," A.J. said shortly, wondering how Nicole had felt about that little technicality. She knew how *she'd* feel.

There was another one of those pensive pauses.

J.W. drew a deep breath and said with an attempt at briskness, "So what is it that I can do for you ladies?"

A.J. had almost forgotten their cover story. "Oh! Well, I wanted to talk to you about the possibility of you doing some kind of a piece on Sacred Balance."

His brows drew together. "I really don't do commercial—"

"I was thinking more of a documentary. As you know my aunt was a legend in the yoga world, and I was hoping that there might be a way to combine a biography of her life—and work—with a film about the studio."

"So this would be for promotional purposes?"

"Yes. Er . . . sort of." What was the right answer? A.J. had no idea. Elysia moved to the rescue.

"I'm afraid I put the idea in her mind," she apologized charmingly. "I'm such a great admirer of your work. That PBS documentary on those Illinois death row pardons was brilliant." She shivered. "Utterly chilling."

J.W.'s tanned cheek creased in a smile. "Thanks."

"And you were filming in Mexico . . . recently?"

"I've been working on a documentary about the 2006 teacher's strike in Oaxaca." He paused inquiringly. Both A.J. and Elysia looked blank.

"It's an amazing story—and a precursor of things yet to come in Mexico."

"One can only imagine." Elysia—apparently channeling Barbara Walters—inquired, "Now would you consider reality TV a form of documentary?"

"God no."

Elysia looked at A.J. "You see, pet. You're perfectly right to stick to your guns." J.W. looked a question, and Elysia explained, "A.J. recently butted heads with one of her celebrity clients. A rather awful woman by the name of Barbie Sargasso."

"Siragusa," murmured A.J.

Elysia nodded distractedly. They both stared hard at their host while trying to look casual.

"That bimbo." J.W. was dismissive, nothing more, and surely if he was aware of the rumors surrounding Barbie's son and Nicole he would sound more than politely interested. Was it possible he didn't know about the illicit relationship? Just how buried in his work had he *been*?

A.J. said, "Barbie wanted to film a segment of her reality show at Sacred Balance. When I refused she blamed Nicole for my decision."

"Really?" J.W. seemed genuinely puzzled. "I know there was some suggestion she might have had it in for Nikki because she knew the character of Bambi Marciano was loosely based on her, but I didn't get the feeling the cops took that very seriously."

He really didn't seem to know.

A.J. and Elysia exchanged looks.

Elysia said, "I suppose it was difficult for Nicole—so far

away from her Hollywood friends. What were her plans now that her television show was ended? Was she considering new projects?"

J.W. put his coffee cup down hard in its china saucer. "Yeah. In fact, we were planning on starting our own production company."

"Really? How exciting. What was the first project to be?"

He pinched the bridge of his nose hard, then managed a strained smile. "We were still turning over the possibilities."

"*Such* a tragedy," Elysia remarked sadly. "I suppose you've gone over and over it in your mind. You must have your own theory on who might have done such a monstrous thing."

"None," J.W. said curtly. "It's not something I care to speculate on."

That was clear enough. Even Elysia couldn't seem to figure a way to storm that barricade. They chatted briefly about the pretend documentary A.J. wanted made and then Bryn summoned J.W. to his conference call.

"*Verrrry* interesting," Elysia remarked as the white colonial mansion grew smaller and smaller in the Land Rover's rearview mirror.

"But not particularly helpful."

"Oh, I don't know about that."

A.J. eyed her mother skeptically. Elysia was smiling enigmatically to herself, apparently going for the All-knowing Master Detective thing, but A.J. wasn't buying it. J.W. Young never had been high on their list of suspects—nor had he volunteered any information that offered any particular insight into anyone else's possible motives. He believed implicitly in Jane Peters's innocence, but that wasn't proof.

Elysia dropped A.J. off at the studio and headed into town for a late lunch with Mr. Meagher.

A.J. settled down to work in her office. She had been looking into purchasing a software program along the lines of Yoga Sage, something that might prove useful for generating operational and strategic reports. Naturally Lily had objected to the idea, claiming that A.J. wanted to implement software to manage the studio long-distance.

"Dr. Lewis on line five," Suze said over the intercom.

"Thanks, Suze." A.J. picked up the phone and greeted one of her oldest friends in Stillbrook. "Hey, Nancy!"

"I cannot apologize enough to you," Nancy said without preliminary. "If I could practice retroactive birth control, I would, but your mother would just find me out and turn me over to the police."

A.J. laughed. "It's okay. I know Charlayne was bored working at the studio."

"In fairness to my daughter, she *is* carrying a heavy class load this semester. I know that doesn't excuse the way she's left you in the lurch."

"It's alright," A.J. said again. But a thought occurred to her as she glanced down at the notes she had made earlier that day when she had been sifting through the confusing pages upon pages of medical information on MS. "*Although*, if you really want to make it up to me, you could meet me for lunch. I'd like to consult you—informally—about a friend."

"A friend?" Nancy said doubtfully. "Well, how about tomorrow? I'm free then."

They made plans to meet and said good-bye. A.J. got back to work, but a few minutes later Suze interrupted again.

"Your four o'clock is here."

"My four o'clock?"

"Your four o'clock interview," Suze clarified. "Emma Rice."

"Crap," A.J. muttered, shuffling quickly the papers stacked on her desk. If there was a resume from Emma Rice, she didn't seem to have it.

Well, maybe that was a blessing in disguise. Sooner or later she had to hire someone, and maybe no resume would give Ms. Rice a better shot.

"Send her in," she told Suze, and a few moments later there was a brisk rap on her office door.

"Come in," A.J. called, rising.

The door opened to a short, slender, elderly black woman. A.J.'s heart sank. Emma Rice's hair was gray and cropped close; her shoes were sensible. It was difficult to determine exactly how old she might be—but it a safe guess she was anywhere between sixty-five and a well-preserved eighty.

"Ms. Rice," A.J. said, offering her hand. "Won't you sit down?"

She was already consigning Ms. Rice to the also-rans pile. It wasn't anything personal, but Sacred Balance had a certain image, and the geriatric Ms. Rice in her sensible shoes and pince-nez eyeglasses just wasn't going to cut it.

"How do you do?" Ms. Rice asked, taking A.J.'s hand in what felt like a stevedore's grip. "Or maybe I shouldn't ask." And she laughed heartily and sat down in the chair next to A.J.'s desk.

"I'm sorry?" said A.J.

"Honey, you're a little shorthanded, in case you hadn't noticed."

"I . . ." A.J. began sifting through papers again. "I don't seem to have your application."

"Is that so?" Ms. Rice sounded unsurprised and slightly amused. "What would you like to know? I taught high school English for thirty years, I'm a widow with two grown children, and I am sound in hoof and wind."

A.J. controlled her expression with difficulty. *Sound in hoof and wind?* And yet . . . and yet there was something about the cool, collected way that Emma Rice sat there watching A.J. with those alert, intelligent eyes. . . .

She thought of the questions she typically asked during an interview: What are your long-range goals and objectives? What historical figure do you admire and why? How do you work under pressure? Where do you see yourself in ten years time?

She settled for, "Why do you want to work here?"

"I like to keep busy," Ms. Rice said. "I like to work with young people. I like to be needed." She studied A.J. over the top of her specs. "And I've never worked for a detective before."

"I'm not a detective, Ms. Rice," A.J. said.

Ms. Rice raised her eyebrows. "Honey," she said, "call me Emma."

Fourteen

"She's kind of like a cross between Shaft and Mary Poppins," A.J. told Andy later that evening.

"Sounds promising. Does she have references?"

"Impeccable professional references. Although I don't know how relevant they are. Personal references . . . she's supposed to be a great pal of Stella's."

Stella Borin was A.J.'s nearest neighbor. She had been Aunt Di's tenant and friend for many years, and had inherited Little Peavy Farm after Diantha's death. In addition to farming, Stella was a psychic. According to local gossip, she was supposed to be a very good one, although it was hard to imagine a psychic being in high demand in a small, rural community like Stillbrook.

Andy looked up. "Stella . . . as in Stella your mother's arch enemy?"

A.J. nodded. She could see from where she sat at the kitchen table that the phone machine light was blinking again.

"There's a recommendation." Andy was combining

bacon, bell pepper, cucumber, cherry tomatoes, green onion, and the leftover cornbread in a large bowl.

"You know, my mother is not an infallible judge of character."

"I can't say I've noticed that."

A.J. snorted. "I wonder what the problem *is* between Mother and Stella."

"Have you ever bothered to ask either of them?"

"Yep. They both change the subject. Quickly." She picked up Lula Mae, who suffered her attentions for a much-tried few seconds before Monster rose from the rug to come and investigate, whereupon she took a swipe at his black nose. "Hey!" A.J. held the cat away.

"What's he doing to her?" Andy frowned at the mournful-looking Lab.

"I hate to tell you, daddy, but your little girl is a thug." She let Lula Mae go and the cat bounded lightly across the table and curled up in the broad windowsill where she proceeded to hurl insults at Monster.

"Hm." Andy picked up another bowl and stirred ranch salad dressing into mayonnaise and sour cream. "You have to admit, Stella Borin is a nut."

"She's a little eccentric," A.J. admitted. "And so, I have a feeling, is Emma Rice."

"Did you hire her?"

"I did."

Andy looked up and laughed.

"Hey. It's not like I have a lot of options. You should see the candidates I've interviewed this week. It's just a receptionist position."

"Your receptionist is the first impression anyone gets of your business."

"Thanks a bunch. Speaking of answering phones, who called?"

His attention apparently on selecting exactly the right spoon for mixing, Andy answered, "Nick."

"Are you ever going to tell him what's going on?"

She thought he wasn't going to answer, but Andy muttered finally, "Of course."

"I'm not trying to push you. I just don't think you're being fair to him."

Andy's smile was bitter as he mixed the ingredients in the bowl.

"What are we having for dinner?" she asked.

"Cornbread salad."

A.J. studied him unobtrusively as he moved around the kitchen. He had always been so quick and graceful, naturally athletic although he had never been much for sports or organized activities. Now he moved with a careful deliberation, compensating for a slight but definite stiffness.

"Plans for this evening?" he asked abruptly, jerking her out of her thoughts.

"No," she replied. "No, unfortunately my boyfriend is scouring the countryside for a murder suspect who just happens to be hiding out at my mother's house."

"Er . . ."

"Exactly. Meanwhile my ex-husband is hiding out from *his* boyfriend at my house. I think it's safe to assume my social life won't be back to normal anytime soon."

That shut Andy up.

He was still quiet and preoccupied over dinner. The food was delicious, and A.J. tried to do it justice if only to make up for the fact that Andy was eating so little. Although he responded sympathetically to A.J.'s account of her day, it was clear he was on automatic pilot. Even relating her visit to J.W. Young's with Elysia barely pricked his interest— although he did make an effort.

"What about this PA of Nicole's? She certainly had access. Maybe she had motive, too."

A.J. responded, "According to J.W. she's getting married next month to a Navy SEAL."

"So she says. What do you want to bet she comes up with excuse after excuse for why the wedding can't take place?"

"If you're right, it won't take long to prove it. Last week was supposed to be her last. She's staying on for a few days to help J.W. sort through . . . everything. But I can't imagine that would take more than another week or so."

Andy nodded, but apparently he'd already lost interest. A.J. wished she knew what to do to help him—besides simply being there.

The chimes on the patio tinkled softly in the night breeze. Crickets chirped in peaceful symphony with the frogs in the garden.

A.J. was lying on her bed, decompressing from the day with her evening workout.

It really wasn't what most people considered a "workout." In fact, an actual workout would not have been conducive to winding down and going to sleep. Instead, A.J. did a few gentle stretches and practiced her deep breathing while concentrating on releasing the tensions of the day.

Outside the window she saw the stars twinkling cheerfully. In her old life she would have spent the evening talking business with Andy, watching a little TV, and then going to bed to read for a few minutes. It occurred to her now how little time for simply *thinking* she had allowed back then. Maybe that had been a defense mechanism; had she thought too much she might have realized that she was not actually happy.

Was she happy now? A.J. blinked at the stars blinking back at her, and she concluded that she was. Granted, she never knew what the day would bring . . . but maybe that spontaneity was part of what gave her joy now.

She expelled a long, heartfelt sigh. Tucking her knees into her chest in Happy Baby pose, she inhaled and gripped the outside of her feet, spreading her knees and drawing them to her underarms.

With ankles directly over her knees and shins perpendicular to the mattress, she flexed her feet. At the same time she pulled gently down creating resistance as she drew her knees toward the sheets.

A.J. pressed her buttocks into the mattress, lengthening her spine and relaxing her neck and the base of her skull. She held the pose, breathing deeply and evenly for nearly a minute.

Happy Baby was good for the lower back and hips. A.J. followed it with Goddess pose, which was great for the groin. Still lying on her back, but now with knees bent, still relaxed and breathing evenly, she pressed the soles of her feet together and let her knees fall open forming a diamond shape. Her arms rested relaxed on the cool sheets. She breathed slowly and deeply, pressing her back into the mattress, focusing on her sense of relaxation and peace.

Nancy Lewis was working her way through a glass of cabernet and a basket of rolls when A.J. slipped into the booth across from her.

"Sorry I'm late." A.J. double-checked her wristwatch.

"You're not late," Nancy reassured her. A.J.'s old high school pal was slim and blonde and very pretty. She looked more like an aerobic instructor than a doctor. "I had to get out of the office before *I* had a heart attack."

"That bad?"

"Sometimes I think your aunt was right. It seems like ninety percent of the health issues my patients face are related directly or indirectly to diet." She reached for her wineglass. "Diet and exercise."

A.J. now had firsthand experience on that score. "It seems so simple and yet . . ."

"Believe me, I know." Nancy reached for another pat of butter. "And just for the record, I don't usually eat like this." Not since she had reached adulthood, anyway. Nancy had been a pudgy teen back in the days when she and A.J. had been adolescent outcasts in the high school social hierarchy.

Finishing buttering her roll, Nancy said casually, "You know, when people ask for a consultation on behalf of a friend they usually mean themselves."

A.J. smiled wryly. "Not this time." She held up her three middle fingers. "Girl Scout's honor."

"We got kicked out of the Girl Scouts, remember? I blame it on our failure to sell enough Thin Mints although I think the official reason had something to do with being caught smoking in a national forest."

"I blocked that out as too traumatic to remember. Anyway, it's not for myself. Andy, my ex, has recently been diagnosed with MS."

"Oh, I'm so sorry," Nancy said.

"It's a shock," A.J. admitted. "I want to help however I can. I've been reading up, but there's so much information, and a lot of it is confusing."

She paused as the waitress arrived to take her drink order. A.J. ordered a glass of merlot.

"The joke in med school is that medicine is not an exact science," Nancy said when the waitress had departed. "What has Andy told you?"

A.J. told Nancy everything she knew and Nancy listened attentively. When A.J. had finished, she said, "I have to be honest, this is way outside of my area of expertise . . . which is, um, general medicine. From what Andy's told you and the symptoms you've described, it sounds like he's suffering from primary-progressive multiple sclerosis."

"I don't know what that means."

"It's relatively rare." Nancy gnawed her lip. "The main thing is that it doesn't go into remission. No course of treatment has been proven to modify its course. The patient experiences a steady increase of disability—sometimes slowly, sometimes not."

Abruptly A.J. had no appetite. She pushed her bread plate away. "God."

"It usually develops in older adults. It's quite difficult to diagnose. I'm assuming Andy's had a full battery of tests?"

"He seems to think so." A.J. said with difficulty, "His neurologist told him he'll probably be in a wheelchair within a few years."

Nancy sighed. "You know, every case is different. And like any illness, a positive attitude with MS makes all the difference in the world. Not just to the prognosis but to the quality of life." She hesitated. "Are you and Andy thinking about getting back together?"

"No."

Nancy sat back in the leather bench. "I'm glad to hear it because I *think* Jake Oberlin has a little bit of a thing for you."

"What gave it away? The fact that he threatens to throw me in jail on a regular basis?"

Nancy laughed. "Noo. It has more to do with the way he looks at you when he thinks no one is watching him."

A.J. felt her face warm. "I'd like to think you're right. I sort of have a little bit of thing for him."

"I sort of guessed," Nancy teased.

The waitress arrived with A.J.'s wine and jotted down their meal selections. A.J. and Nancy chatted about life in general until their food came.

"Heavenly! Remind me again about food being the root of all evil?" A.J. inquired, breathing in the delicious fragrance of the garlic, basil, and white wine wafting from her plate of linguini and white clam sauce.

However, she didn't hear Nancy's response because at that moment she caught a glimpse of Barbie Siragusa entering the restaurant dining room followed by a tall, black-haired, hawk-faced young man in a polo shirt and white jeans. Even if he hadn't born a remarkable resemblance to his mother, A.J. would have recognized Oz Siragusa.

A number of the other diners were also watching the reality TV maven, but Barbie ignored the stares, and A.J. had to give her credit. Barbie had nerves of steel, no doubt about it.

Following the hostess through the maze of tables, Barbie and her son walked past A.J. and Nancy's table. Barbie's dark eyes met A.J.'s. She stared right through her.

A.J. glanced at Nancy, and Nancy arched her eyebrows, not missing that deliberate diss. They watched curiously as Barbie and Oz, neither of them appearing to be in very good humor, took their seats and picked up their menus.

Nancy sipped her wine and said, "Anyway, what were we saying? Oh. Andy's going to need a lot of support—emotional and practical. Is he still with his . . . um . . . partner?"

"I don't know what's going on there," A.J. admitted. Judging by the ferocious eyebrows, Barbie and her son were now scowling at their menus—and still not speaking.

"In sickness and in health, right?"

"Till death do us part, too, but that didn't happen the first time around."

Nancy said a little sourly, "Sometimes I'm amazed anyone stays together. Charlayne's father bailed when he found out I was pregnant."

"I remember. And yet for some couples kids are the glue that holds them together."

Eyes on Barbie, Nancy said in the tone of one thinking aloud, "I guess it partly depends on whose kid it is."

Meeting A.J.'s startled look, she grimaced. "I shouldn't have said that."

"So Barbie *is* pregnant?"

"Damn. A.J., I *cannot*—"

"She's taking prenatal Pilates courses at Sacred Balance."

"Oh." Nancy relaxed. "I was afraid I was being indiscreet."

Nancy had *always* been indiscreet, but no one was kinder or more conscientious.

A.J. said slowly, "But if Barbie is pregnant, who's the father? It can't be the Big Bopper. He's safely tucked away in a maximum security facility in Colorado."

"Now I *am* being indiscreet, but since Barbie isn't being particularly coy about it . . ." Nancy leaned forward across the table and said very softly, "According to Barbie, the father of her unborn child is J.W. Young."

Fifteen

❧

"It's a simple process of elimination. Let's see what we have." Elysia nibbled on the end of her purple pen. "Suspect number one." She looked around the circle of faces. A.J. and Andy were at Starlight Farm having what Elysia blithely referred to as a "council of war." "Anyone?"

"J.W. Young," Andy said obligingly.

A.J. shook her head, and speared a forkful of lettuce from her salmon salad.

"Hmmm." Elysia squinted down the length of her pen as though considering perspective. "Husbands do make wonderful suspects, I agree. I remember once on *221B Baker Street—*"

"So do wives," A.J. interjected, eyeing Jane.

Jane flushed.

"Motive?" prodded Elysia.

"He inherits Nicole's money and house," Andy said.

"Do we know that for a fact?" A.J. questioned. "Because

they weren't married, so he's not necessarily Nicole's heir.
She could have left everything to the baby koalas."

"Very good, pumpkin!"

"Please don't call me pumpkin."

Andy said, "Nicole was having an affair with Oz Siragusa."

"But did J.W. know about it?" A.J. questioned. "I don't
think he did. He didn't bat an eye when mother and I started
discussing Barbie."

"Nicole wasn't having an affair with Barbie."

"*Actually*," started A.J., but she was interrupted by
Jane.

"J.W. didn't kill anyone. He wasn't even in the country
when it happened."

"Do we know *that* for a fact?" Andy asked. "Because
that's one of the oldest—"

"J.W. is not a murderer!"

Elysia scratched notes on her lavender legal pad, sipped
from her glass of iced mineral water, scratched more notes,
and looked up. "We must review all the evidence, Janie. We
have to be utterly cold, ruthless professionals about this.
Did you ever see Yul Brynner in that film where he's search-
ing for his son?"

A.J. and Andy looked at each other. Jane merely looked
puzzled.

"J.W. Young." Elysia seemed to savor the name. "Husbands and wives are always prime suspects. With very
good reason. J.W. may or may not have inherited Nicole's
money—which he may or may not need. He may or may
not have an alibi. Lovely." She made a lavish check mark
on her lined pad. "Suspect number two?"

"Oz Siragusa," Jane said. "He was having an affair with
Nicole and she dumped him. That gives him a stronger motive than J.W."

"How do we know she dumped him?" Andy objected.

"His friends seem to think she did," A.J. said.

"Find out for sure from Inspector Oberlin," Elysia ordered.

A.J. opened her mouth and then closed it.

"The other thing about J.W.," Andy reflected aloud, "is it's his house. He had the best chance of sneaking in and out unnoticed. He'd know all the side and back entrances, and everyone's patterns."

"You really are determined to pin this thing on him." A.J. speared another piece of salmon.

Andy shrugged. "If you watch those true crime shows, it's always the husband or the wife."

"No one gets under your skin like a spouse, that's true," A.J. said.

"Unless it's an ex-spouse."

"Does Oz Siragusa have an alibi?" Elysia interrupted, inquiring of the room at large.

The other three shrugged or looked at each other.

Elysia pointed her pen at A.J. "Another one to verify with the inspector."

"Detective, Mother."

"Same difference, pu—pet."

"Puppet?" Andy inquired, grinning.

"If you weren't ailing, I'd kick you," A.J. informed him.

"Suspect number three," Elysia announced. "Any takers?"

"Lydia Thorne, the barking mad reviewer," Andy said. "She was obsessed with Nicole, sent her threatening e-mails, wrote nasty reviews, and in general behaved very badly."

"We don't even know if she was in the state at the time, let alone Nicole's neighborhood," A.J. said.

"That's because you refuse to call her and ask."

Elysia looked up, eyes gleaming with interest.

"Let me guess," A.J. said. "Another one for my list?"

Elysia's smile resembled the Cheshire Cat.

"Suspect number four."

"Barbie Siragusa," A.J. said.

"*Exaaactly*." Elysia purred. "Her enmity to Nicole was of long-standing—as we used to say on *221B Baker Street*."

A.J. groaned and Elysia stretched across and rapped her knuckles with her pen. "Ouch!"

Elysia said, "Barbie's son was having an affair with Nicole, and to add insult to injury, Nicole treated the boy badly."

"And J.W. was having an affair with Barbie," A.J. put in. "Which gives her another motive. She wanted Nicole's man."

"*What?*" Jane's voice cracked. The others stared.

"According to Barbie, she was having an affair with J.W."

"No," Jane said. "It's not true."

"Suspect number five," A.J. said quietly. "Jane."

"Yeowch," murmured Andy.

"Thanks a lot!" Jane said unsteadily. Tears filled her eyes. She wiped at them with the edge of her hand.

"Anna," Elysia cautioned.

It did seem a little bit of a stretch. Could anyone look less like a murderer? That annoyingly fresh-faced pixie quality of Jane's: it was like suspecting Pippi Longstocking of taking a hatchet to a playmate.

"Do you still have the divorce papers?" A.J. asked suddenly.

"What divorce papers?" That was Elysia looking from Jane to A.J.

"You were there when Jane explained why she went to

J.W.'s house, Mother. The papers she says she brought J.W. to sign the afternoon Nicole was killed. She's been on the run since it happened, so she should still have them."

Jane gave her a strange look, and then without speaking, rose and left the room. She was back a few moments later with a fat cream-colored envelope which she handed to A.J.

The flap was tucked in, not sealed. A.J. opened it and drew out the papers, examining the envelope's contents. Sure enough the documents enclosed included a marital separation agreement.

Jane said shortly, "I went there to ask J.W. to sign the papers. That's the truth. If I thought about Nicole at all, I thought it would be a—a kind of birthday present for her."

"But you didn't announce yourself when you arrived?"

"I know how it sounds, but I couldn't find anyone. The hall was full of people—caterers and florists—but none of the household staff as far as I could make out. There was some problem with the drain in one of the downstairs bathrooms. And some of the wrong booze had been delivered.

"I just thought I would see if J.W. was in his study." Her blue eyes met A.J.'s and she made a face. "Okay. *Yes*. I admit I was a little curious. You can't imagine how different that house was from the place J.W. and I lived. *Rented*. I poked my head in a couple of rooms just to . . . see how the other half lived."

"And?"

"It was sort of depressing, really. It didn't look like a home, it looked like a magazine layout. I couldn't imagine living there."

"That's not what I meant," A.J. said.

Jane bit her lip. "Oh. Well, I could tell immediately which room was Nicole's office. Her face was plastered all over the walls." She shook her head. "The music was blasting, so I knew she was there, and I stepped inside just to say a quick hello and happy birthday. I wanted to get the papers signed and get out of there." She closed her eyes.

"But she was already dead," Elysia stated. She didn't notice the irritated look A.J. directed her way.

Jane opened her eyes and nodded. "Yes. It must have just happened. She was lying behind the sofa . . . twitching. But I could see it was too late. She wasn't breathing. Her head was . . . it was awful. There were bits of bloodied ice everywhere. I saw what was left of the koala sculpture smashed on the floor." She swallowed hard. "And I knew I had to get out of there fast. I could see exactly how it was going to look, and I knew my only chance was to run—and pray that no one recognized me."

Into the silence that followed her words, Elysia said briskly, "It makes perfect sense to me."

Nobly, A.J. refrained from comment. As the other two women gazing expectantly at her, she said, "I don't *dis*believe you, Jane. But you must know how this will sound to the police. It's weak. Yes, it could have happened exactly like you describe, but I can also see how someone might argue that you deliberately sneaked into the house when everyone was busy, grabbed the first available weapon—"

"Why wouldn't she bring her own weapon if she was planning to murder Nicole?" Elysia demanded. "You can't have it both ways. She either planned it or she didn't."

"Fair enough. And I happen to agree with you," A.J. said. "I'm just pointing out how it's going to look to Jake."

Elysia's expression spoke volumes on her concern over Jake's opinions.

A.J. said, "It's not like we're making any progress coming up with an alternate prime suspect. Yes, plenty of people disliked Nicole, but moving from not liking someone to actually killing them is a big jump."

"I think we've all agreed Barbie Siragusa looks very good for it," Elysia retorted.

"I agree she's our best suspect so far. She still can't even bring herself to be polite about Nicole, and she did sort of threaten her. But no one reported seeing her at the house—and the timing is just a little too close."

"But not impossible," Andy said.

"No, not impossible. But everything would have to have gone like clockwork, and how does that happen when she couldn't have planned the murder?"

"Who says she couldn't have planned it?"

"Well . . ." A.J. considered. "I guess she could have faked the scene in the studio."

"She is an actress."

"That's debatable." Elysia spoke at the same time Jane said, "Ha!"

A.J. admitted, "She's got the best motive of anyone. Two best motives. Her teenage son was seduced by Nicole, and she's pregnant with Nicole's lover's baby."

"Which, now that I think of it, does give J.W. another motive," Elysia commented.

"*What!*" Jane stared from Elysia to A.J. "Are you saying you think Barbie is pregnant with *J.W.'s* baby?"

"Barbie's saying so," A.J. said. "I mean, I don't know if she's made a public announcement yet, but she's apparently told a few people."

"Has she told J.W.? He'll be fascinated to hear that one!"

"What do you mean, lovie?" Elysia inquired, narrow-eyed.

Jane laughed, although it was a shaky laugh at best. "I don't know if that woman is delusional or what, but J.W. is *not* the father of her child. J.W. is sterile."

Sixteen

In an unexpected and utterly unprecedented move, Lily called in sick the following morning for the second day in a row.

"On a Friday?" A.J. cried when Suze delivered the message Lily had left on the answering machine. "That's like publicly announcing she's taking a day off."

"Some people do get sick on Fridays. Especially if they were already sick on Thursday."

"Not Lily. She never gets sick. Her body wouldn't dare permit a germ access. She's doing this to me on purpose." Catching Suze's expression, A.J. said glumly, "I sound paranoid, don't I?"

"Yep." Suze grinned. "But I think you're right."

It was probably the worst morning A.J. had had since taking over the studio. Lily carried a full roster of classes five days a week. She was the number one teacher at the studio, and the gap her unplanned absence made in the schedule was not pretty.

Emma Rice was the heroine of the day, coming in at a minute's notice—and three days earlier than she was supposed to officially begin work—to help cover the front desk. A.J. taught her own Itsy Bitsy Yoga and Yoga for Kids classes, then took the Beginners class. Her muscles were already feeling the strain even before she realized that after lunch she would have to cover Simons's Seniors and later Suze's Teens and Tweens to free the two more-experienced instructors to cover Lily's advanced sessions.

It was more teaching than A.J. had done since she started, and when she finally escaped back to her own office, her muscles were aching—along with her ego. She was reminded in no uncertain terms of the vital role Lily played within the studio. There was no pretending she was ready—or even wanted—to take on Lily's role as head teacher.

Although no one came right out and said anything, it seemed to her that—with the exception of Suze—the other instructors were looking at her with silent accusation.

"I feel like I'm getting the silent treatment. They can't be blaming me. Can they?" she asked when Suze brought her the mail.

Suze looked a little uncomfortable. "Um, the opinion seems to be that you should have consulted Lily before you drafted that letter to all the clients about not using their cell phones in the studio. I guess it looks a little high-handed."

A.J. stopped rubbing her back and straightened in her chair. "Compared to the stuff Lily does?"

Suze shrugged. "The thing is, Lily has been here forever, so everyone is sort of used to her little ways."

Her little ways? That was like referring to a piranha attack as a case of the munchies.

"Plus . . ." If possible, Suze looked even more awkward. "We all always knew—thought, anyway—that Lily was going to be taking over the studio. So it looks sort of bad that you're trying to maneuver her out of her share."

It took A.J. a moment to recover from the shock of realizing Lily had made their conflict public. And Lord only knew what version of the truth she was handing out.

"I'm not!" she lowered her voice hastily. She repeated, "I'm *not*. I'm just trying to eliminate having to work with her. She's threatened to do the same thing."

"But you actually consulted a lawyer."

"Well, yes." A.J.'s bewilderment grew. "The partnership would have to be dissolved legally." She remembered Lily's accusations. "Suze, you know me. You all know me. I'm not trying to cheat her. I'm trying to find a fair and equitable way out for both of us."

"But she doesn't want out."

"She wants *me* out."

Suze looked sympathetic but noncommittal. It gave A.J. plenty to think about as she worked through the rest of the morning—and not all her thoughts were pleasant.

She was eating a Ding Dong at her desk when Jake poked his head in the door.

"Uh-oh," he commented. "The hard stuff, huh?"

It was utterly irrational the way her heart leapt at the sight of him—not that his rugged handsomeness wasn't the stuff guilty dreams were made of. Long and lean, he lounged in her doorway, that crooked smile creasing his tanned cheek.

Silently A.J. offered him a piece of Ding Dong, absurdly pleased when he took a small bite. Immediately and hastily he wiped at his mouth.

"What are you doing here?" she asked.

Jake lifted a broad shoulder. "I have a couple of free hours. Do you have time for lunch or did you plan on drowning your sorrows in chocolate frosting and cream filling?"

"Wow. To what do I owe this honor?"

There was a hint of color in Jake's lean face. "It's not like we never have lunch."

"True. But not usually when you're immersed in a case." And all the more remarkable because Jake didn't have many cases like this one. Stillbrook and its environs were usually pretty peaceful.

He spread his hands. It was . . . disarming. So was the way his eyes smiled into hers.

A.J. crumpled the silver cake wrapping, tossing it in the trash. "I would *love* you to take me to lunch," she said and stood up.

They lunched at Patty's Pantry near the village green. It was a cute little café decorated in cottage style with flowered chintz cushions and swaths of Swiss dotted curtains like a doll house. There were bowls of silk roses on the tables and the dishes were Blue Willow. The food was simple but good: pot pies, quiches, stews, casseroles—and homemade ice cream and fresh baked pie for dessert.

A.J. tried to eat salad for lunch whenever she could, but it was hard to resist Patty's chicken pot pie. Even reflecting sheepishly on the linguini of the day before couldn't stop her from opting for carbs when the waitress arrived to take their orders.

"So when is the ex moving out again?" Jake asked after their meals were served.

"It's . . . complicated."

"Yeah?" His eyes were very green as they met hers. "Uncomplicate it for me."

"Andy's . . . not well." She proceeded to explain how unwell Andy was, and Jake listened without expression.

When she had talked herself to a standstill, he asked, "What does this mean for you and me? Are you planning to get back together with him?"

A.J. shook her head. "No."

His face was without expression. "Are you sure about that?"

"Did we just wander into a Bette Davis movie? Yes, I'm sure. I care about Andy, I want to help the best way I can, but I'm not in love with him. He's not in love with me."

Jake relaxed a fraction. "Okay."

Her heart rose at his well-concealed but definite relief. Now this *was* encouraging.

"So what are his plans?" Jake inquired. "Because, I'm sorry for the guy, but he's kind of putting a cramp in our relationship." His gaze held A.J.'s, and the directness there brought a faint warmth to her face.

"I don't know," she admitted. "He's not confiding in me, but I know he feels overwhelmed. He's not sure he'll even be able to keep working, and I know he's eating his heart out over Nick Grant."

"Where is Grant in all this?"

A.J. shook her head. "Andy hasn't told him yet. He doesn't believe Nick will be willing to deal with . . . well, whatever the future entails."

"I hate to say it," Jake said, "but he's probably right. That's pretty much the gay lifestyle."

A.J. was surprised at her instinctive irritation at Jake's offhand comment. "I don't know anything about the gay lifestyle," she admitted. "Unless you count watching a couple of episodes of *Torchwood*, and I don't think Captain Jack is Mr. Gay Average. I guess I was assuming the gay lifestyle wasn't that different from anyone else's lifestyle."

"What about his family? Can't they help?"

A.J. sighed. "Like me, Andy's an only child. His parents disowned him when we divorced." At the time it had been a small but significant comfort to A.J. Now she regretted their attitude. "Andy was always closer to my family." To

Elysia, at least; Aunt Di had not been any fonder of Andy than he had been of her.

Jake studied her for a long moment. His mouth curved wryly. "You're a good person, A.J."

"Can you forgive me?"

He laughed.

They were nearly through dessert when A.J. found an opening to ask about the investigation into Nicole's murder. Jake didn't exactly avoid talking about—well, come to think of it, maybe he did avoid talking about it.

"I've spoken to J.W. Young about doing a documentary on the studio."

Jake looked up from his pecan pie à la mode. "Any particular reason you picked Young to do this film?"

"Mother recommended him. She's a fan of his work."

"Oh, brother," said Jake. "Tell me she's not poking that pointy nose into this thing."

"Hey. Lay off my mother's pointy nose."

"I'll be happy to—provided she stops sticking it in my business."

If he only knew. A.J. decided to overlook that last comment. "J.W. is absolutely adamant that his ex-wife is not involved, isn't he?"

"Jane Peters is not his ex. They never divorced."

"Right, right. So . . . that means J.W. *doesn't* inherit under the terms of Nicole's will?"

Jake gave her a long look.

She did her best to look innocent. "Just asking. It's public record, isn't it?"

"I guess so. Manning left everything to a couple of wild-life organizations."

She would.

"And J.W. would know that, of course."

"Of course."

"For what's it worth," A.J. said, "I don't think he has—or at least *had*—a clue that Nicole was fooling around."

Jake studied her impassively. "Go on."

"When we were discussing filming this documentary, the subject of Barbie Siragusa came up a couple of times, and he never flinched, and I think if he knew Nicole had been unfaithful with Barbie's son . . . I mean, there was *nothing* there. Mother agreed."

"Oh, well now I'm convinced."

"Okay, maybe we're not trained law enforcement professionals—"

"*Maybe?*"

A.J. forged on. "But in our own way we're each also in the business of reading people, and we agreed that J.W. Young had no idea what Nicole was up to."

If she had hoped that by volunteering this information, he would be wooed into sharing his own thoughts, she was doomed to disappointment. Jake continued to eat his pie with the careful attention of a man who knew he wouldn't be getting another meal break any time soon.

"And," she pressed, "by the same token I don't think J.W. is the father of Barbie's baby."

Ah. At last she had his attention.

"Say that again."

"Barbie's taking prenatal Pilates courses. The rumor—a rumor *she* started—is that J.W. is the father. Except . . ." she stopped realizing she had almost made the disastrous blunder of revealing Jane's information that J.W. was sterile.

"Except?" Jake asked, watching her closely.

"Except . . . I don't think it's true." She regained a little confidence. "And for the same reason. J.W. didn't react an iota to Barbie's name, and surely he would if they were having an affair?"

Jake rubbed his jaw meditatively.

A.J. asked curiously, "Besides being at the scene of the crime—which includes a lot of people, including me—is there some particular evidence against Jane Peters? Why are you so sure she's your killer? Does she have a violent past or anything like that?"

"Why do we want to bring her in? You mean besides fleeing the scene—and her continuing efforts to evade a police dragnet? Let's see. She's still married to Manning's live-in lover. She showed up without an appointment at Manning's home on the afternoon of Manning's death. After her husband left her for Manning, she made public threats against her."

"Oh."

Jake's smile was sardonic.

A.J. thought it might be a good time to change the subject from Jane Peters. "Have you eliminated Barbie as a suspect yet?"

"We haven't eliminated anyone as a suspect yet," Jake said shortly. "We've got motives galore here. In addition to means and opportunity." His cell phone rang. He glanced at it, glanced back at A.J. "Sorry. I've got to get back."

A.J. nodded. She sighed wistfully. "Hey, as the Bard would say, 'a policeman's lot is not a happy one.'"

Already on his feet, Jake threw her a reluctant grin.

"How come the Master Detective is giving us the evening off?" A.J. inquired as she and Andy ate dinner that evening.

She had been talking to him about some of the online articles she had read regarding yoga and MS. Everything she found indicated yoga appeared to be as beneficial as any traditional aerobic exercise program in helping MS patients combat loss of flexibility, balance, and coordination, and cope with stress and fatigue. Fatigue, in particular, seemed to be one of the most disabling aspects of the disease. A.J. could already see the change in Andy, who had always had boundless energy, and she knew he was frightened by it. It *was* frightening.

Although extensive study remained to be done, there was every indication that yoga appeared to enhance both physical health and quality of life in MS patients. No one had yet determined the impact of yoga on the disease itself, but a number of doctors and yoga practitioners—as well as patients—theorized that yoga might even slow the progression of the disease. Stress seemed to acerbate MS, and yoga was excellent for addressing stress.

In between covering classes, A.J. had read numerous accounts of people with MS practicing yoga and reporting benefits. It was certainly something to think about, but Andy—although he listened politely—seemed unimpressed.

Maybe he was still hoping for a silver bullet, and she couldn't blame him if he was. Coming to terms with chronic illness wasn't something that happened easily or quickly.

"Maybe she needed an early night," he suggested *"Mother?"*

"She's not a kid anymore, A.J." Andy smothered a yawn.

"I know she's not a kid," A.J. said a little irritably. It was not a grown up response, but she didn't like thinking about her mother aging. Aunt Di last year . . . Andy's illness . . . the people closest to her were all too mortal, and it was a scary realization. "It's too quiet on that side of the valley," she continued darkly. "What's she up to?"

They were interrupted as Lula Mae and Monster got into it. Or, more exactly, Monster yelped and scrambled for the doggie door while Lula Mae smugly investigated his abandoned dinner bowl.

"Lula Mae," yelled A.J. *"Bad kitty."*

Andy snickered. "And she acts like she doesn't even care."

"She *doesn't* care." A.J. balefully eyed Lula Mae, who was now twitching her whiskers in finicky disgust at Monster's dinner. "She doesn't even like dog food, but she swaggers in here with her broken beer bottle and threatens poor Monster. I think he's on the verge of a breakdown."

Andy was chuckling as A.J. rose and cleared their plates. It had been another very good dinner. Andy wasn't eating much, he was mostly cooking for A.J., and she was appreciative, but she was also starting to wonder how much longer they were going to continue to play house. As fond as she was of Andy—and as concerned as she was—her lunch conversation with Jake had made her eager to have her privacy again. The fact that she was spending Friday night with her ex-husband . . .

"What did you want to do this evening?" She dumped the dirty dishes in the sink and ran water over them.

Andy shrugged and then his gaze sharpened. "We could try calling Lydia Thorne."

A.J. turned off the water and rejoined him at the table, propping her chin on her hand. "What a super idea! Who wouldn't love to spend a quiet evening chatting with a psycho stalker? Then again, we could always just play Scrabble."

"Well, I wasn't thinking purely of our pleasure. Our names were mentioned in an article about Nicole's problems with her fan club."

A.J. sat up. "You're not serious."

"I wish I wasn't."

"I can't believe anyone would bother to drag that up. It was *years* ago."

"They don't have anything else to talk about," Andy said. "There haven't been any major breakthroughs in the case so far."

A.J. groaned and ran her hands through her hair. "Did the papers really mention our agency?" She raised her head to stare at him.

Andy nodded wearily. "Don't worry. I realize it's not your problem. You're out of it now. I bought your share of the business."

A.J. said quickly, "Of course, it's my problem too. And, anyway . . . I'm as curious about this as you are."

"You are? Seriously?"

"Process of elimination, right?" she said staunchly. "Maybe we can cross her off the list once and for all."

This seemed to cheer Andy up. He went off to find the phone number, presenting it to A.J. a few minutes later. "You want to call from here? I'll get on the other phone and listen in."

Now presented with the deed, A.J. felt slightly uneasy. "You know, she's probably not going to answer. . . ."

"Sooner or later, she has to."

He seemed so touchingly sure. A.J. said reluctantly, "Should I leave a message if she doesn't pick up? Andy, I have no idea what to say to this woman."

"It'll come to you," he assured her, moving down the hall to the other phone.

A.J. gazed after him in disbelief. She shook her head and then quickly dialed the number before she had time to chicken out.

The phone rang once, twice—and to A.J.'s utter shock someone picked up. A deep voice, which could have been—but was not necessarily—feminine, said sleepily, "Hello?"

"Lydia?"

There was a pause and the voice said warily, "Who's asking?"

"This is . . ." A.J. blanked for a second and then pulled a name out of thin air. "This is Alice Hart. I'm the . . . the current president of Nicole Manning's fan club. I was wondering if I could talk to you for a few moments."

"Why?" The voice was harsh, but A.J. was now certain "Lydia" was a woman.

"Well, after the terrible tragedy of Nicole's death—" A.J. broke off as Lydia burst into raucous laughter.

"I'm sorry?"

"I'm not! That conniving bitch deserved exactly what she got." Lydia finished starkly, "I don't have anything to say to you or anyone else."

The phone slammed down.

The dial tone buzzed in A.J.'s ears for a few heartbeats before she held the receiver away as though she could stare down the line.

"Holy Hell," Andy called from the other room. "So much for letting bygones be bygones."

"One thing for sure: whatever happened between Lydia and Nicole, Lydia hasn't forgiven her."

Andy appeared in the doorway. "Too bad you couldn't keep her on the line."

"Yes, what a darned shame! We were really hitting it off." A.J. replaced the receiver. "I have to tell Jake about this call. At the very least, Lydia Thorne's attitude is . . . suspicious. He'll want to question her further."

Andy looked thoughtful. "He's not going to be happy if he finds out you've been meddling in his case."

"That's what I keep telling all of you!"

His blue eyes met hers solemnly. "The thing is, if you tell Jake about Lydia, there's going to be an argument, and if during that argument you neglect to tell him about Jane . . ."

A.J.'s eyes widened. "I . . . see what you mean." Only too well. In fact, she had already trespassed into this ethical no man's land during their lunch that afternoon.

"I'd wait till you can make a clean breast of it," Andy advised into her stricken silence. "It's not like we really have anything at this point. Sure, Lydia Thorne's attitude is suspicious, but Jake already knows that she hated Nicole."

"Very Machiavellian," A.J. said shortly, and it wasn't a compliment.

Seventeen

Barbie Siragusa lived in a monster mansion by the Delaware River. Fans of *Barbie's Dream Life* were aware that the property included a custom movie theater, popcorn machine, an indoor swimming pool, and an even more spectacular outdoor pool enhanced by waterfalls, caves, and a Jacuzzi. There were tennis courts behind the 35,000-square-foot house and a large wine cellar with a sit-down tasting area where regular viewers had enjoyed a memorable episode in which pals of Oz Siragusa had filled nearly forty-five minutes of prime time with embarrassing personal revelations as they drank themselves stupid (not that anyone could really tell the difference). There was also a full-sized professional gymnasium and a personal trainer on staff although Barbie preferred to work out at Sacred Balance. Barbie always enjoyed an audience.

A.J. was grateful to see that no television cameras were in evidence when she and Elysia arrived on Saturday afternoon.

Barbie greeted them from a lounge chair positioned beside the azure blue waters of the seventy-foot lagoon-style pool. Flawlessly made up, she wore a shirred emerald green Roberto Cavalli swimsuit with a spectacular diamond-shaped jeweled ornament across her midrif. If she truly was pregnant, she hadn't yet begun to show. She certainly didn't *act* pregnant. Granted, the jury was still out on the effects of light to moderate drinking in the first weeks of pregnancy, but the martini Barbie was guzzling was obviously not her first.

"Can I offer you some foreplay?" she offered lazily, then laughed at A.J. and Elysia's expressions. "Cocktails, ladies. Don't get your hopes up. Vanilla infused vodka, Golden Pear liqueur, and sour lime." She held up her glass. It winked like distilled sunshine in the light.

"Very pretty," Elysia remarked. She didn't look a lot older than Barbie in her gauzy tangerine Shay Todd romper. Not that the idea of one's mother in a "romper" wasn't scary. "D'you know, I've never yet come across two identical recipes for foreplay."

Barbie guffawed, nearly spilling her drink. "You make it too easy!"

"Do I, ducks?" Elysia murmured, meeting A.J.'s eyes fleetingly.

Barbie laughed again. "She's so cute," she informed A.J. "Like one of *The Golden Girls* . . . only with that limey accent."

Elysia arched one eyebrow, and A.J. had to bite her lip.

"Help yourself, by the way." Barbie gestured lazily to the pitcher on the bar at the end of the patio. Her gaze never left them, though, her hard, unexpectedly alert eyes watching over the rim of her glass. "So, to what do I owe this honor?"

"I've been reconsidering my decision about allowing

you to film at Sacred Balance," A.J. said. This was the story
she and Elysia had cooked up to gain entrance to the castle,
but surprisingly they hadn't needed it. Barbie had agreed to
see them without any convincing.

Now she sat up straight—or at least as straight as the
lounge chair permitted. "Is that so?"

"Yes." A.J. couldn't help watching as Elysia wandered
over to the bar set up and began to fill a tall glass with ice
using a pair of silver tongs. She had far too many distress-
ing memories of her mother in similar circumstances . . .
parties, graduations, A.J.'s wedding . . . She said automatically, "I'm not making any promises, but I thought I should
give you the chance to explain your side of it."

Elysia poured a glass of tonic water, added a squirt of
lime and returned to the tableau by the pool. She smiled
cheerfully at A.J.

Folding gracefully on the foot of one of the lounges, she
said, "All publicity is good publicity, that's what I told A.J."

"That's right," Barbie exclaimed. "That is exactly right.
I'm trying to do you a favor, that's what you don't seem to
get. Just because a lot of Hamptons rejects don't want to see
their fat asses on TV!"

Elysia made a little sound like a hiccup, but when A.J.
and Barbie stared at her, she was unruffledly sipping her
tonic water. A.J. said carefully, "Well, I have to admit that
now that Nicole is gone—"

"I knew it!" Barbie was up and pacing beside the pool in
one lithe movement. "I knew the whole time that hag Nicole was behind your refusal."

"What do you think it was Nicole had against you?"

At the same instant, Elysia inquired, "I suppose she re-
sented your attitude toward her relationship with that handsome young rascal, Izzie."

Mother and daughter locked gazes. "Ozzie," A.J. said, and Elysia bowed her head, graciously conceding a point.

Barbie had frozen in her tracks. "There was nothing between Oz and Nicole. *Nothing*."

"So we heard," Elysia agreed. "Why do you suppose Nicole broke it off like that?"

"He's just a kid!" Barbie cried. "What would he want with a tramp like her?"

Elysia's expression rearranged itself into sympathetic lines. "'The heart has its reasons which reason knows nothing of.'" She sipped her tonic water and added, "Shakespeare."

"Does Pascal know the Bard is stealing his material?" A.J. murmured.

Barbie was stalking up and down the side of the pool. "It's because of Oz's dad. The police want to pin this on him because of Sam. The sins of the father. That's what they think."

"One never hears about the sins of the mother," Elysia remarked. "I wonder why. After all, I think mothers have *far* greater influence on their children. At least when I . . ."

"Do you think Nicole was using Oz to get at you?" A.J. interrupted.

Barbie came back to the chaise lounge and dropped down on the flowered cushions. "Nicole was a vampire. She fed off other people, off their energy and talent and love. She never gave a thought for anyone but Nicole."

"You don't think she was ever serious about Oz?"

"Oz is a terrific kid, don't get me wrong," Barbie said. "But he *is* a kid. His main interest in life is tennis. And cars. And partying with his posse. It wasn't serious for him. And it sure as hell wasn't serious for her. He was never anything more to her than a fling."

One hundred and thirty-seven text messages in the course of a few hours seemed to indicate a certain level of seriousness on Oz Siragusa's part—or maybe just adrenaline—but A.J. didn't think it would be useful to point this out.

"And, after all," Elysia drawled, "Nicole did have that deliciously earnest J.W. waiting for her at home."

Barbie snorted. "Waiting at home for her? That's a laugh. I don't think it's a coincidence Mr. IDA is always off working in foreign countries. Think about it."

"Mr. IDA?"

Elysia explained, "International Documentary Association."

"Oh." A.J. *had* been thinking about Nicole's relationship with J.W. Safe to say, if there had been an affair with Oz Siragusa—and it seemed pretty certain that there had been—there were significant problems in Nicole's relationship with J.W. Young.

And wasn't that underlined by the fact that J.W. had apparently resisted divorcing Jane Peters?

She waited for Barbie to bring up the fact that she was supposed to be carrying J.W.'s baby, but Barbie didn't say a word.

"They weren't married," A.J. said. "Nicole and J.W. Either one of them could have walked out at any time."

Barbie opened her mouth, but the French doors leading onto the flagstone courtyard swung wide. Oz Siragusa stepped out.

"Speak of the handsome young devil," Elysia murmured. Barbie threw her an unfriendly look.

"What are you doing, baby?" Barbie called.

"What does it look like I'm doing?" Prince Charming returned. "I'm going for a swim."

"I'm entertaining some people right now."

"So entertain!" He tossed his plum-colored towel to one of the lounge chairs and dove into the pool, clean as a knife.

Barbie met A.J. and Elysia's twin gazes and shrugged. "Kids these days."

"They're so precious at that age," Elysia agreed.

They did not glean anything much more useful than that from Barbie, and when Oz eventually pulled himself out of the pool and stalked, dripping, back into the house, the royal audience was ended—Mrs. Big Bopper seemingly recalled to her maternal duties.

"I'll call and let you know one way or the other," A.J. promised vaguely in answer to Barbie's demand for permission to bring her film crew back on Monday morning.

"Don't disappoint me," Barbie said. She was smiling, but the effect was similar to a shark viewing something scrumptious flailing in the water.

Neither A.J. nor Elysia spoke till they were in the Volvo heading back to Starlight Farm.

"What do you think?" A.J. asked as the summer scenery slid by.

Elysia said slowly, thoughtfully, "Not sure."

A.J. threw her mother a quick look, glad—if a little taken aback—that they seemed to be on the same wavelength.

"Ditto. I was sort of betting on Barbie. Don't you think it's odd she didn't say anything about carrying J.W.'s baby?"

"She hasn't formally announced her pregnancy, has she? Probably saving it for prime time. It's not as though the two of you were close."

"No, but she seems to be the one who started the rumor

of her pregnancy, so why wouldn't she take the opportunity to spread it to us?"

Elysia shook her head.

"Unless she's given up on trying to pull her story off? If Jane is right, it wouldn't be hard for J.W. to puncture that balloon."

Elysia said, "She doesn't strike me as the type to think very far ahead of her mouth."

"The thing is, if she's not pregnant with J.W.'s child—and I don't think she could be—that probably means there was no affair, which eliminates one motive for her wanting Nicole out of the way."

"Barbie hated Nicole. Still hates her. She doesn't strike me as the type to plot and plan, but she might strike out in a fury."

"I don't think anyone could have plotted or planned to whack Nicole with an ice sculpture," A.J. pointed out.

"No. But by the same token, it couldn't have been an accident. No one accidentally picks up an ice sculpture and coshes someone over the head."

"Not premeditated, but deliberate."

"I think so."

"When she left the studio, Barbie was in a fury. If Nicole had been standing in the middle of the road, I think Barbie would have mowed her down. But to drive twenty-something minutes and still be angry enough to kill when she arrived at Nicole's? And at that point she would have to be intending Nicole harm because she'd have to sneak past all the servants and caterers."

"Hmmm. Possibly." Elysia seemed to look inward. Considering how she might pull off such a crime? "There's the chance that she simply walked in unnoticed, argued with Nicole, and bopped her over the head."

"Can you really picture Barbie walking in unnoticed anywhere?"

"There is that."

"It's possible that *someone* might have walked in unnoticed. There were so many people wandering around that afternoon it would be easy—well, possible anyway—to overlook one more. I mean, that's Jane's story right?"

"Certainly if that someone happened to be dressed like a delivery person or one of the caterers . . ."

"That brings us back to premeditation."

Elysia was silent.

"Are you so completely convinced of Jane's innocence?" A.J. probed delicately.

"I am. Yes."

"Why?"

Elysia flicked her a look. "I have an instinct for these things, pumpkin."

"Mother . . ."

"No, no. I know what you're going to say, but it's true. I've known Jane since she was a kid. I only worked with her twice, but we just . . . connected. You know how that happens with some people?"

A.J. nodded tightly. She did know. It was a little hard hearing how her mother had instantly connected with Jane Peters when she hadn't tried to connect with her own daughter, but . . . what the hell.

"We became friends. I believe her."

"Okay," A.J. said. "I respect that. I do. But I knew Andy all through college. He was my best friend and my business partner. We were married for ten years—and I had no idea he was gay. No clue." Well, she had had many clues, but she hadn't recognized them for clues at the time. "And I would have said that I knew Aunt Diantha very well—I think Lily would have said she knew Aunt Di very well—but neither of us expected her to leave the studio to us in joint partnership. Even people we think we know can surprise us. And not all of those surprises are happy ones."

Elysia said simply, "Sometimes you have to trust your instinct, pet."

A.J. expelled a long breath. "Mother, I have to tell Jake about Jane."

She could feel Elysia's silent stare. She kept her own eyes on the road.

"I don't know if Jane is guilty or not. What I do know is how Jake will feel when he discovers that I've taken part in harboring a fugitive. We're breaking the law—*I'm* breaking the law—and Jake is not going to be okay with that."

"Don't tell him."

A.J. threw her mother a bleak look. Elysia raised a bony shoulder. "Suit yourself. You always do."

It took A.J. a second to catch her breath at the unexpectedness of that attack. She kept her voice steady with an effort. "That isn't fair. I've gone along with this thing, but it's getting too complicated—and we're not making headway."

"Nonsense. We're making marvelous progress. We just need a little more time."

"We don't have more time. Time is running out. And the longer I deceive Jake, the worse it's going to be. For all of us."

Elysia's jaw tightened, but she said nothing.

"I can give you until this evening. That gives you time to persuade Jane to give herself up, which is going to look much better than if she tries to run again. If you went to Mr. Meagher—"

"Thank you, Anna. I'll figure out what's best from here."

They drove in silence the remaining few miles to the farm. A.J. pulled in the front drive, and Elysia got out, self-possessed as always. Her cat-green gaze flicked to A.J.'s.

"Mother—"

"I'll see you tonight—at the head of the posse, I suppose."

"Mother!"

Elysia slammed the Volvo door and stalked away, heels crunching on the white gravel walk.

Eighteen

Andy was leaving Sacred Balance when A.J. arrived at the studio after dropping Elysia off at Starlight Farm.

Dressed in gray sweats and wearing a T-shirt with a towel draped around his neck, he was climbing into his rental car as A.J. pulled up next to him. She rolled her window down.

"Hi! What are you doing here?"

He looked sheepish. "Taking a beginning yoga course. I thought about what you were saying last night. And you're right. The better the shape I'm in, the better I'll be able to handle . . . whatever is coming."

"How did it go?"

He laughed. "I've stretched parts of my body that I don't believe God intended to bend."

"But you feel all right?"

"Tired. But I'm always tired, so that's okay." He climbed into the sedan and said, "I'll see you tonight?"

A.J. nodded. She waited till he'd backed out and driven

away, then got out of her car and went briskly up the walkway past the gardeners who were planting pink and lavender annuals in front of the stone wall bearing the bronze
plaque with the scripted words *Sacred Balance*. Students
bearing gym bags and dressed in yoga togs passed her
going to and from the parking lot and building.

Even on a gorgeous Saturday afternoon, the lobby was
reasonably crowded, and A.J. felt a surge of satisfaction.
She spotted Bryn Tierney by the front desk speaking to
Emma Rice. From their expressions, it looked fairly serious. Emma looked up and noticed A.J.

"Honey, here's Ms. Alexander. Why don't you tell her
what you've told me?"

Bryn turned. She wore a crisp yellow-checked sundress
and her hair was faultlessly French braided. She looked, as
always, neat and cool and competent.

"A.J., I've come to clear Nicole's things out of her
locker."

Taken off guard, A.J. said, "I didn't realize . . . not everyone keeps a locker here."

"Nicole did," Bryn said confidently.

A.J. thought it over. "Okay. Well, let's have a look." She
went behind the counter and unlocked the key box, finding
the correct key to the locker assigned to Nicole.

"You won't need that. Nicole used her own padlock."
Bryn held up a key.

A.J. happened to catch the expression on Emma Rice's
face. She had a feeling it mirrored her own. "Right," she
said coolly. "Lead on."

Bryn turned and marched upstairs, A.J. following. Nicole's PA went straight to the showers and pointed out the
bank of lockers.

"Second from the left on the top." She handed the key
over to A.J.

A.J. opened the locker and Bryn began to lift out Nicole's belongings, putting them into a brightly designed yoga bag: Nicole's yoga mat, a baby blue sweatshirt, an iPod . . .

"I think," A.J. said slowly, "we'd better bring this all down to my office so I can inventory it."

Bryn stared at her. "Why?"

A.J. shook her head. "We've never really had a situation like this before. If something turns up missing later, I don't want there to be any confusion of whether it was lost at the studio or not."

Bryn seemed to think it over, and then she shrugged, handing the bag over to A.J.

"How are you holding up?" she asked Bryn as they headed down the staircase again.

"I'm okay. I mean, I miss Nikki, naturally. It's J.W. I'm worried about. He's really having a hard time with this."

"I guess that's not surprising."

"No."

"Any idea of when the funeral will be held?"

"Tomorrow evening. The police have finally released Nikki's body."

That was a conversation killer if there ever was one. Unspeaking, they carried the items into A.J.'s office and A.J. emptied out the yoga bag and made notes on a legal pad as they went through everything again. It didn't take long.

"Poor Nikki," Bryn said absently, folding the pastel sweatshirt. "She could be . . . well, you know. But she . . . meant well. She really did have a kind heart."

"I know," A.J. said. "Last year she donated a designer dress to one of our financially disadvantaged students for the prom, and she always contributed generously whenever the kids had a charity drive—I mean, I'm pretty sure Nicole wasn't actually eating all those candy bars or reading all those magazines."

Bryn laughed. "No. She was good about that stuff, and great about making time for her fans. She did a lot of appearances—benefits and that kind of thing. Especially anything to do with animals. She felt very strongly about animal rights."

"How long were you her PA?"

"Four months." Bryn smiled. "She tended to go through personal assistants pretty quickly."

"J.W. said congratulations were in order."

Bryn looked puzzled.

"You're leaving to get married?"

"Oh!" Bryn blushed. "Yes. Well, with Nikki gone . . . I'd be leaving in any case now."

A.J. nodded. "I guess it will be hard for J.W. without you."

"He's a sweetie. I wish . . ."

A.J. looked inquiring.

"Nothing," Bryn said hastily. They both looked down as a velvet jewelry box, rolled up in the yoga mat, fell to the floor.

Bryn knelt, picked the case up, and opened it. It was a tennis bracelet; over thirty stones glittered like stars against a blue velvet sky.

"Oh my God," whispered Bryn.

"Those don't look like cubic zirconium."

"No, I think they're real."

A.J. stooped to pick up the small card that had fallen to the floor with the box.

Always, O

Bryn couldn't seem to tear her gaze away from the card. A.J. asked softly, "Did J.W. know about the affair?"

"*No.*"

"You sound pretty sure about that. Everybody else seems to know."

Bryn looked up, but she didn't appear to see A.J. "J.W. is obsessed with his work."

"How did Nicole feel about that?"

Bryn said sourly, "She had an affair. That's all this is about." She nodded dismissingly at the bracelet. "Nikki felt neglected. It wasn't serious."

"Maybe not on Nicole's part, but it looks like Oz Siragusa had invested something in it."

Bryn reached for the card, but A.J. shook her head. "You know I have to hand this over to the police."

Bryn bit off an exclamation. "All this is going to do is hurt J.W."

"I have zero wish to hurt J.W. Or anyone. But someone killed Nicole."

"And you think this gives J.W. a motive?" Bryn's eyes were hard.

"Actually," A.J. said, "I was thinking more about Oz Siragusa's motive. He seemed pretty besotted with Nicole, and she dumped him. Not everyone takes being dumped graciously."

Oz Siragusa had not exactly looked prostrate with grief the two times A.J. had seen him. Of course people dealt with bereavement differently.

"Is J.W. pretty broken up over Nicole?"

"Of course," Bryn said without any great conviction. She continued to stare at the tennis bracelet as though she wanted to snatch it away. "He's burying himself in his work; that's how he deals with it."

"I guess that's how a lot of us deal with tragedy."

Bryn said nothing, continuing to look angry and troubled.

An idea occurred to A.J. "Did you ever meet Lydia Thorne?"

If possible, Bryn's frown deepened. "Lydia Thorne? The

woman who used to run Nicole's fan club?" Her expression changed, grew speculative. "Is that what you're thinking? Yes . . . I could see that. I'm surprised the police haven't looked a little closer there. I was working for Nicole when Lydia turned on her. Like a mad dog."

"What do you think happened?"

Bryn said promptly, "I think Lydia expected Nicole to help her get started in Hollywood."

"You mean she wanted to act?"

"She wanted to be a screenwriter. She wrote a script for Nicole."

"Was it any good?"

"I don't think so. It was called *Interstice* or something."

"Catchy."

"Yes. Anyway, Nicole wasn't interested in the script, and she wasn't interested in referring Lydia to her agent or anyone else in Hollywood. And . . . unfortunately she wasn't very tactful about it."

"And so Lydia began writing all those awful reviews?"

Bryn nodded. "That was only part of it. She started cyber-stalking Nicole. She would send all these horrible anonymous e-mails, but they were usually from the same IP address—and they all had the same . . . *voice*. And anywhere that Nicole's name was mentioned on the web or one of her films reviewed, Lydia would post some nasty comment. She was obsessed. Her entire life revolved around Nicole."

"Did she ever make any specific threats against Nicole?"

"You mean like threaten to kill her? No."

"Did the police ask you about her?"

"Not really." Bryn looked vague. "It's hard to know what to tell the police. A few facts and they begin twisting everything."

A.J. finished noting the last of Nicole's belongings and let Bryn take everything but the bracelet and note. Those she put with the list of Nicole's locker's contents in her desk drawer.

She was tempted to call Jake then and there, but if she called him, she would have to tell him about Jane Peters, and her relations were strained enough with Elysia. She had promised to hold off until the evening, and she would keep that promise. It would be better to make the phone call from Starlight Farm. Better all around if it looked like everyone was cooperating. And a couple of hours were unlikely to make any real difference to the investigation.

Her reluctance to be on her mother's bad side surprised A.J. given how often she deplored Elysia's unrealistic approach to the world.

She locked her desk, locked her office, and left for Deer Hollow.

A.J. let herself quietly in the house. If Andy was sleeping, she didn't want to wake him. Monster greeted her with a full body wag, his air that of a shipwreck victim sighting the rescue planes.

"Has Lula Mae been picking on you again?" she sympathized, kneeling down to fuss over him. She could hear Andy on the phone, and even from down the hall she picked up the tension in his tone. To give him a moment, she stayed in the hallway, gently tugging Monster's ears. The dog panted up at her.

"I'm not blaming you," Andy was saying. "It's no one's fault. We just made a mistake. It happens. We might as well be civilized about it."

A rather lengthy silence while the other person on the phone gave Andy an earful.

"I just don't see the point," Andy said. "I don't want to haggle over stuff. If there's something in particular you want—"

Another silence.

Andy said, "I'm not angry. Nick, I've already agreed it isn't anybody's fault. Okay? We *both* made a mistake. I'm . . . glad that we've admitted it and can deal with it. I just don't want to drag it out."

"What's he doing?" A.J. whispered, and then recoiled as Monster licked her face. "You need breath mints," she informed him. Not offended, Monster tried to lick her again. "And a girlfriend," A.J. added.

"Look," Andy said shortly—and A.J. heard the uncharacteristic anger in his voice. "I've said I'm sorry. I meant it, but I can't do more than apologize. I know you're angry. Apparently there's no point trying to work out the details until you've had time to cool off."

Another considerable silence.

"Now you're being ridiculous," Andy said. "I'll give you a call next week."

A.J. heard the phone slam down on the receiver. She rose and went into the kitchen where Andy was lowering himself into a chair by the table. He jumped and then seemed to force himself to relax.

"I didn't hear you come in."

"I just got home. What was that about?"

"Loose ends."

"*Loose ends?* I guess I should be grateful. At least you had the courage to deal with our loose ends in person."

Andy raised his head and his expression shut her up. She'd never seen so much pain on the face of someone who wasn't actively dying. It seemed to her that the struggle to contain all that pain and grief was worse than if he'd let it out in one long primal howl.

She dropped into the chair across from him. "*Andy.*"

"Don't," he said tersely. "I can't take sympathy right now."

"Are you sure you're doing the right thing?" she asked.

"Yes."

"In sickness and in health," A.J. reminded him.

Andy's face twisted. "It wasn't working for us before this happened. I don't see my getting sick helping anything. Anyway, it's done. It's over. I don't want to talk about it. My mind is made up."

"Oh, well great. Did *he* get to have his say?"

"Yes."

A.J. scrutinized his drawn face. "Did you tell him what was really going on?"

"Since when do you care about Nick's feelings?"

"I don't," A.J. said. "I care about you. And you can tell me till you're blue in the face that you're okay with this and you've made your decision and blah, blah, blah. Anyone can see you're totally miserable."

"I'll get over it."

"Will you? Will Nick?"

He turned a stony profile to her.

"Did you tell him the truth or did you tell him some stupid lie like you don't love him anymore?"

Andy was silent. He said at last, "Can we not talk about this now?"

A.J. sighed and, leaning across, kissed his cheek.

Although for different reasons, neither of them felt much like eating the dinner Andy had prepared. When they had finished picking at their meal, they got in A.J.'s Volvo and headed across the valley to Elysia's farm.

The evening was mild; a pair of bats flew over the golden meadow as the red ball of the sun sank beneath the trees. A.J. put The Killers' *Day & Age* in the CD player and neither of them spoke.

Are we human or are we dancer? Well that was the question, wasn't it?

They rounded a curve in the road and Starlight Farm lay before them. The front yard was crowded with police vehicles, red and blue lights glittering in the dusk.

"Uh-oh," Andy said.

Nineteen

❦

A.J. braked hard. "Oh *no*."

Andy said faintly, "You don't think Jane . . . ?"

Ran amuck and murdered her mother? A.J. swallowed hard. "No, of course not." But if Jane had not murdered her mother, A.J. was going to. She took her foot off the brake, advancing slowly into the yard. A state trooper ran toward their car and flagged them to a stop.

A.J. pressed the button and the window rolled down.

"Sorry, you'll have to go back." Despite the late hour, the trooper was still wearing mirror sunglasses. A.J. could see her tense face reflected in twins.

"My mother lives here. Is she all right?"

"Your mother?" He looked back over his shoulder, and then said, "Maybe you should pull over to the side there beside the hedge. Remain in your vehicle, please."

"Is she all right?"

"No one's been injured." He gestured impatiently, and

A.J. pulled carefully over to the side and parked behind the emergency vehicles.

She turned the engine off and peered through the gloom at the house.

"The police must have discovered Jane was staying here."

Andy said nothing.

"She must be all right, don't you think? Mother, I mean."

He started automatically, "I'm sure she's—" He broke off. "Oh hell."

Two uniformed officers escorted Jane—arms handcuffed behind her—out of the house. They marched her over to a marked police car.

A moment later Jake appeared on the front doorstep.

A.J., hands frozen on the wheel, said faintly, "Do you think he's arrested Mother?"

Andy said grimly, "Him? Probably."

A.J. swallowed hard. She felt a little lightheaded. They waited. Jane was put into the police car, the officers got in, and the car drove slowly away. The trooper who had directed them over to the side went to speak to Jake. As they talked, Jake stared at A.J.'s car.

After a brief discussion Jake turned and went back in the house.

The trooper crossed the lawn to A.J.'s car.

"You can go," he said.

"Is my mother being arrested?"

"I don't know anything about it."

"But—"

The trooper made another of those brusque move-it-along motions.

"Move it," Andy said out of the side of his mouth. "Robocop is liable to arrest you, too."

Hands shaking, A.J. put the car in reverse, inching painstakingly past the wedge of official vehicles, before finally reaching the safety of the open road.

"Should I call Mr. Meagher?" she asked as they drove swiftly back to Deer Hollow. "He won't really arrest her, will he?"

Andy just shook his head.

Back at Deer Hollow, A.J. paced up and down the living room while Monster, head on his paws, watched her. Andy sat on the sofa absently stroking Lula Mae.

"Why doesn't she call?" A.J. demanded as the clock slowly ticked down the hours.

Andy shook his head again—it was starting to get on her nerves.

"What can they be *doing*? They can't be interrogating her, can they?"

"They're probably getting out the rubber hoses and bright lights as we speak."

She glared at him. "Very funny."

"Sorry. She'll be okay, A.J. You know, Ellie. She'd probably get a kick out of being arrested. And if she needed Mr. Meagher, she'd have no hesitation yelling for him."

The phone rang, shattering the silence that followed Andy's words.

A.J. jumped to answer it.

"Mother?"

There was a pause and then a voice—muffled and indistinct—said, "Keep your nose out of Nicole Manning's murder if you don't want to end up like her."

The phone clicked down.

A.J. looked to hit redial, but the phone in the hall was an old model, refurbished from the fifties, and did not have such fancy doodads.

Returning to the front parlor, she said, "Somebody just threatened me. Us. Me."

"That narrows it down."

"I'm serious. Someone just called and said to butt out of investigating Nicole's murder if I didn't want to end up like her."

Andy stared at her with dawning consternation. "You *are* serious. Did you recognize the voice?"

She shook her head. "It was pretty low tech. Someone disguising his voice and talking through a handkerchief."

"He?"

"I don't know." A.J. lowered her voice and spoke in menacing tones, trying to emulate the caller. "It. Could. Have. Been. A. Woman."

"Don't do that, okay? It's scary." Andy tilted his head. "Maybe it's a prank?"

"Nothing gets me laughing like a death threat. It's that stupid article about me being the local Miss Marple—I bet it caught the attention of some nut."

Andy looked worried. "If it's not a prank, we must be getting close."

"Close to what? Close to who? How could we be getting close without knowing it?"

"Well, then maybe it *is* a prank."

Wide-eyed, they gazed at each other.

Andy was sleeping on the sofa when the phone rang the next time. He groggily lifted his head, and A.J. said, "I've got it," and went into the hall.

She lifted the receiver and Elysia hissed, "Trust no one!"

"Mother?"

"The police have taken Jane."

"I know. We were there this evening, but it wasn't me. I

didn't tell Jake. I was going to call from your house so that it would make it clear we were all cooperating."

Elysia who had been making a soft shushing sound as A.J. spoke, turned up the volume like a hissing tea kettle on the verge of explosion, cutting off with a sharp, "SHUSH!"

A.J. shushed.

Elysia said, "I know it wasn't you, pet. The Grand Inquisitor wouldn't be so angry with you if you were the fink."

"*Fink?*"

"The coppers received an anonymous tip about Jane. *We are being watched.*"

"What? By whom?"

Elysia spluttered, "How should I know by whom? But they may be listening to us *at this very moment.*"

This jolted A.J. into silence. Then sense reasserted itself. "How could they be listening to us? And what makes you think it's a *they*? I doubt if it's a conspiracy—"

Elysia was hissing again. A.J. shut up, and Elysia whispered, "We can't take that chance."

"Mother . . ."

"Meet me tomorrow at eight—no, I need a decent night's rest. Make that ten o'clock—at the place your father took you for your ninth birthday."

"But—"

Elysia hung up.

A.J. stared at the phone in disbelief before replacing the receiver and returning to the room where Andy was sleepily scrubbing his face.

"Who was that?"

"Mother. I think she's finally snapped. She thinks we're being observed by an unknown nemesis. She says the police were tipped off about Jane by an anonymous caller."

Andy lifted his head. "I thought that was you."

"You thought *I* told the police that my mother was hiding a fugitive?"

"I did. Sorry." He said slowly, "Someone *is* watching us."

A.J. nodded. "We're starting to make someone nervous."

After Andy turned in, A.J. sat in the parlor listening to the crickets outside the open window and the chimes moving softly in the night breeze.

It was nearly midnight when she heard the sound of an engine approaching. Monster thumped his tail heavily on the floor. Lula Mae stretched luxuriously and showed her claws.

A.J. rose from the sofa and went to the window.

Jake's SUV gleamed in the moonlight. The car door opened and he got out, a long-limbed shadow crossing the grass and coming slowly up the porch.

A.J. opened the door before he rang the bell.

He stared at her for a long moment.

"Will you come in?" she asked.

He shook his head. "I can't stay."

"Jake, I know what you're going to say . . ."

"No," he said levelly. "I don't think you do." And something in his tone held her silent.

"I like you, A.J. A lot. Hell, I even like your mother. Sort of. But . . . I don't like this. I don't like the games you play."

"It's not a game," she tried to interject. "I know how it looks, but I was going to—I was trying to—I had already told Mother—" She stopped, horribly aware that she was making it worse with every word out of her mouth.

Jake spoke over her, and although he didn't raise his voice, every word hit her as hard as a pelted stone.

"I asked you to stay out of it. You're not dumb, so you must know that you put me in an impossible position when you cross the line between my personal and professional life. Worse than that, you lied to me."

"I didn't lie."

"Come off it. You lied by omission. We sat right there at lunch talking about Nicole and your mother and Jane Peters, and you never said a word. Not a hint that you knew where Peters was. Didn't it occur to you that you had a responsibility to come forward? I'm not just talking about your responsibility as a law-abiding citizen, I'm talking about your responsibility—call it your *loyalty*—to me. You're the girlfriend of a cop. It didn't occur to you that some of these stupid, reckless decisions would reflect on me?"

And even though she knew Jake was right to be angry, A.J. was starting to get mad, too. "I wasn't thinking about your image, no. And I *was* going to tell you, Jake. Tonight—"

"My *image*? I'm not talking about my goddamned image. I'm talking about the fact that you've potentially compromised a police investigation. I'm talking about the fact that I could lose my job over this. And because of you, because of my feelings for you, I'm continuing to make bad decisions. I should have arrested your mother tonight along with Jane Peters. I should have arrested you and your damned ex-husband. But I didn't. Once again, I didn't do my job because of my feelings for you."

She could feel the blood draining out of her face as the full ramifications of what she had done finally sank in— along with the realization of the extent of Jake's feelings for her.

And although she tried to be rational, she couldn't help pleading. "She's my mother, Jake. It's not so easy to choose between loyalties like that."

"I know." He just sounded weary now. "So let's call it a

draw. You should have confided in me, but I should have arrested you. So we're quits."

"Quits."

He nodded, drew in a long breath, and expelled a longer one. "Yeah. We could go back and forth on this, but the upshot is . . . I don't think it's going to work between us."

She opened her mouth and then closed it.

"Good night," Jake said.

She watched until his figure merged with the darkness.

Twenty

A.J.'s cell phone was ringing.

She stopped pacing in front of the empty parking lot of the Wild West City in Byram and snatched it up.

"Where are you?" she demanded.

Elysia's voice crackled back indignantly, "Where are *you*? I've been waiting here since nine bloody forty-five!"

"Waiting *where*?"

"At Fairy Tale Forest in Oakridge."

"What on earth are you doing there? You said to meet you at Wild West City."

"I said we would meet where your father took you for your ninth birthday."

"Which is Wild West City."

"But I-I distinctly remember—" There was a funny pause.

Oh.

Elysia's moment of doubt was understandable. Her memory of those years was sometimes a little cloudy, but not this time. In this particular case A.J. and her father had pulled a fast one, jettisoning the mater-approved fairy tale theme park in favor of the western amusement park. Funny how A.J. had forgotten all about that switcheroo until this moment.

She felt almost guilty remembering the illicit delight of that stolen day . . . the excitement of hay rides and make-believe gun fights . . . the pleasure of having her workaholic father all to herself, the relief of not having to worry about whether her mother would get through the day sober. If she closed her eyes she could once more smell the sawdust and popcorn and leather and horses. . . .

A.J. snapped out of it. "It's moot, anyway, Mother. They're *both* closed this time of year."

She could practically here the wheels turning. "Were you followed?"

"Was I—?" A.J. turned to stare at the wild green hills behind the carefully reconstructed frontier town. It felt eerie out here all on her own in this little ghost town. The faded signs creaked in the wind. "No. Why would I be followed?"

"Because I made sure to shake any tail."

A.J. closed her eyes, summoning inner strength. Alas, after the past few days she seemed to be running alarmingly low on inner strength. And the fumes were making her giddy. "Why would someone follow *either* of us?"

"Pumpkin, use your loaf. To *stop* us. I remember on an episode of—"

A.J. couldn't take it. "Mother, if someone is following us, spying on us, planning to stop us from further snooping, then we've already done the worst possible thing. We've split up and we've both headed out to isolated areas where we could be picked off with no one around to help us."

Elysia inhaled sharply and began coughing.

"Mother? *Mother.*" A.J. walked up and down the parking lot, listening tensely.

After a delay filled by muffled hacking and coughing, Elysia's voice came on the line. "Never fear, pet," she said hoarsely. "Just swallowed the wrong way."

"Oh for—!" A.J. leaned weakly against the side of a wooden building. With an effort she got control. "Look, there's no point skulking around because whoever is watching us already knows we've shared any information. The best thing is to get back to Stillbrook."

"We'll rendezvous at—"

"No." A.J. repeated, "No. We won't. I have to get to work, and you have to leave this alone. If you want to help Jane, then help her find legal representation, but we need to *stop.*"

"What's happened?" Elysia asked sharply. "Has someone got to you?"

Talk about leading with your chin.

"You mean threatened me? Yes, as a matter of fact. But that's not . . . that doesn't matter. Jake—actually, that doesn't matter either. But we have to stop this now. *I* have to stop this now."

"Has that rozzer been at you? Has he been bullying you?"

"No. No more than I deserve. Listen. I can't tell you what to do, but I can't go on playing cops and robbers. We're not accomplishing anything. In fact . . . we're placing ourselves in danger." A.J.'s eyes raked the verdant hillside as she strode to her car. She got inside and locked the door. "I'll call you later, all right?"

"But we're so close!" Elysia protested.

"Call me when you get back to town so I know you arrived safely."

"So you *do* think we're getting close."

"No, I don't. But someone else apparently does. I'll talk to you later." A.J. disconnected and started the engine.

What a way to start the morning. But her attempts to reach her mother at home and head her off had met with no success.

As A.J. drove, she listened to the local radio station: it was the usual mix of weather and traffic and the Boss—and then a special news bulletin. Wonderingly, she heard J.W. Young state to reporters that he believed in the innocence of his estranged wife, Jane Peters, and that he intended to stand by her.

"I'm going on record that I believe implicitly in the innocence of my wife, Jane Peters. Jane has remained a dear friend. She was a friend to Nicole. Anyone who knows Jane, knows the allegations against her are false and will be disproved."

The newscaster came back on talking about startling revelations in the Nicole Manning murder case, and then it was back to weather, traffic, and the Boss.

A.J. arrived at Sacred Balance without incident—or any sign of pursuit—and gratefully immersed herself in the day's work. She rarely worked Sundays, but work was what she needed right then. She needed to keep very busy because if she didn't, she would start to think about Jake, and she wasn't able to handle those thoughts yet.

Elysia called shortly after A.J. had settled down at her desk to say that she had arrived safely and that Mr. Meagher was arranging bail for Jane.

"How's Jane holding up?"

"It's not pretty. That child does not belong in a cell with the dregs of humanity."

It was hard to believe that the tidy little local jail house confined the dregs of humanity within its four brick walls. Not that A.J. wasn't sympathetic to Jane's plight. Being arrested would be . . . awful. She was abjectly grateful Jake had not arrested her—or her mother.

"Does Mr. Meagher think there will be a problem getting bail for her?"

"He said the fact that she fled the crime scene and continued to flee could be a problem. Have you had a chance to reconsider—?"

"Yes," A.J. said, cutting her off. "And no."

"But I don't understand. We're making such marvelous progress. Someone is getting nervous, pumpkin, and that's always a good sign."

"*I'm* getting nervous. And that is not good. It's the last thing I need right now."

"It's not like you to be so poor-spirited, Anna."

"I'm not poor-spirited. I'm being sensible. For once."

"Very well. If your decision is final." Tartly, Elysia added, "At least Andrew is committed to the cause."

"That's another thing. Leave Andy out of this. He's not in any shape to play detective. Stress is very bad for him."

Elysia said huffily, "Andrew doesn't find sleuthing stressful. There's a difference between stress and stimulation. The dear boy enjoys the thrill of the hunt as any right-minded person would."

A.J. bit back the words she would have—probably—regretted. Besides, Elysia was right about one thing. Andy did enjoy sleuthing. He was practically as big a nut as her mother.

"Are we still attending Nicole's funeral this evening?" Elysia inquired. "To pay our respects?"

"To pay our respects, yes. I'm attending the funeral. If you're attending it for any other reason than that, I don't want to know."

Elysia made a dismissive sound and rang off.

Confirming her mother's opinion, Andy seemed remarkably chipper when he stopped by A.J.'s office midmorning before his next beginning yoga session.

"Have you heard from Ellie? I got the weirdest call this morning."

"From who?"

She was immediately concerned that the anonymous caller might have phoned in with more threats, but Andy said easily, "From Elysia."

"Oh. Right." A.J. said, "I have heard from her. The sleuthing is on hold until further notice."

"Why?"

"*Why?*" A.J. explained why in no uncertain terms.

Andy listened with raised his eyebrows and made no further comment. When she finally paused for breath, he excused himself and escaped to his workout. Feeling a little better for unburdening her soul, A.J. returned to her paperwork.

After that, the day was beautifully ordinary and delightfully dull.

When the afternoon classes had concluded for the day, A.J. held a quick staff meeting and broached her idea of bringing a doctor on board as the first step to implementing several yoga therapy courses.

"Yoga Cikitsa?" Lily stared at A.J. with an odd expression.

"What are we talking about here?" Denise asked, looking from one to the other.

"Yoga as a therapeutic-based practice," Simon explained. "Medical or healing yoga. The program is grounded in classical yoga. We'd have to either get certified or hire another instructor."

A.J. said, "I've been reading up quite a bit, and yoga

therapy has been found to be useful in treating musculosk-
eletal problems, autoimmune disorders, MS, fibromyalgia,
Chronic Fatigue, arthritis pain, hypertension, diabetes,
asthma—"

"It would probably be very popular with my seniors,"
Simon put in.

Lily said slowly, "And it's had encouraging results with
PTSD and other stress-related disorders as well as ADD,
ADHD."

"You want to hire a doctor as well as a new instructor?"
Denise asked.

"I'm considering the idea."

"I would love to train and get certified in Yoga Cikitsa,"
Suze offered.

Lily made a dismissing sound. "The last thing we need
is an inexperienced yoga instructor working with ill and
disabled students. That's a lawsuit waiting to happen."

Suze flushed painfully. A.J. pressed her lips together and
kept her irritation to herself. Most Cikitsa programs required applicants to have three or more years teaching experience. Lily was right, but as usual she had phrased her
objections in a belittling and hurtful way guaranteed to
wither Suze's youthful enthusiasm.

But if Suze was chastened, the other three instructors
were guardedly enthusiastic, and A.J. felt that she had regained some of the ground she had lost in her recent clash
of wills with her co-manager.

When the meeting ended, she went down to her office
and to her surprise was joined by Lily a few minutes later.

"That wasn't a bad idea," she said grudgingly. "Actually,
neither idea was bad. Starting Cikitsa sessions and bringing
a doctor on staff. This doctor . . . did you have anyone in
mind?"

"Not really." Other than a couple of visits to a local chiropractor, A.J. hadn't even seen a doctor on her own behalf since arriving in Stillbrook.

She couldn't help it. Lily being pleasant made her more uneasy than Lily openly hostile. Warily, she asked, "Do you?"

"No. But I could ask around."

"That would be . . ." A.J. discarded several possibilities, settling on, "helpful."

Lily nodded, accepting her due.

A.J. waited. Lily seemed to have something on her mind. And after drumming her fingers absently—and irritatingly— on the edge of A.J.'s desk, she said, "Have you had a chance to look over the new slogans for the studio that we discussed?"

A.J. hadn't really thought that battle was over, had she?

She said, trying to keep her tone neutral, "Lily, I'm not convinced that we're at a point where Sacred Balance's image needs a facelift."

And Lily, also clearly striving to keep her tone nonconfrontational, said, "We've already been over this, A.J. And we agreed that it's time for a change."

"We've discussed it, but we didn't agree on anything. I said I would *think* about it."

"Do you really not see how unreasonable you're being?"

"I really don't!" And once again, despite her very best of intentions, A.J. was agitated. "Why is this so important to you? Why is it such a matter of urgency?"

"Why are you fighting me every step of the way?"

"I'm not. I just . . ." Her gaze fell on Aunt Diantha's photograph, and registering the serenity in her aunt's expression, A.J. made a conscious effort to let go of her defensiveness, her resistance.

Maybe if she could be more open, more vulnerable with Lily, they might make some progress. "Maybe it's because

I feel close to Aunt Di here. It's comforting for me to feel like I'm carrying on her legacy." She expelled a slow breath. "I guess emotionally I'm not ready to make a bunch of changes. Not that I won't ever be—just that it's too soon for me."

Lily said in the patient tone of one speaking to a child, "It's not just your decision, A.J. I'm co-manager here, and I think it's time for change. I think this is the strategic moment for such a change."

Okay. So much for openness and vulnerability.

"Then we're in a deadlock."

Lily smiled. "Maybe not. Why don't we ask the rest of the staff how they feel about a change? We could vote on it. You keep saying you want us to be a real team."

As A.J. stared at Lily she became uncomfortably, painfully aware that she did not want to put this motion before the rest of the staff—she wanted to have her own way on this. It was important to her. She did not want to compromise about something that meant so much.

And as this unpleasant realization took root, it occurred to her that perhaps this was why Aunt Diantha had thought it would be good for A.J. and Lily to work together.

"We could do that," she managed.

"Good!" Lily was still smiling. "I'll put something together for our next staff meeting."

Twenty-one

One week and a day following her murder, Nicole was buried in Blairstown, New Jersey.

The little chapel was crowded with mourners and media—and sightseers. Sure that she would run into Jake, A.J. had hoped to lure Andy into keeping her company, but he excused himself from the festivities on the grounds of fatigue—and, worryingly, he did seem exhausted again despite the care he was taking.

But his spirits were good, and she had left him reading a thriller on the sofa under the watchful eye of "Old Yeller."

Instead, Elysia volunteered to drive, and A.J., after delivering the now routine warning about no more sleuthing, gratefully accepted the offer. She was especially grateful when, entering the chapel, she came face-to-face with Jake. Jake, looking handsome and severe in a charcoal blazer, his dark hair disciplined into something like smoothness, nodded politely and looked right through her before moving on.

Elysia muttered a word not often heard in church, and they squeezed into a pew at the back of the chapel. A.J. couldn't help reflecting, as she observed her fellow mourners, that the odds were very high that someone in this crush of people had probably killed Nicole.

It seemed odd, now that she thought about it. Odd that someone as . . . frivolous as Nicole should have inspired murder. Yes, she had been superficial and self-centered, but those seemed like fairly minor sins.

The service was brief and then the mourners filed out in the sunshine to the graveside.

"No one should die in the spring," Elysia said as they walked through the old graveyard toward the grave site. A.J. threw her a curious look. She understood what her mother meant, though. It was a lovely, soft evening, and the dying light filtering through the trees and limning headstones and crosses in old gold made everything somehow more vibrant—poignant.

For the first time A.J. felt the haunting power of the words: *In the midst of life we are in death.*

The graveside ceremony was even briefer, and then the crowd slowly dispersed.

Nicole's parents were having a small group of people back to the house. A.J. had not been invited to this gathering, and she ignored her mother's hints that she should speak to J.W. and try to get them invited.

"You don't give up, do you?" she asked as they made their way back to the parking lot, trailing behind the rest of the crowd. "What part of *no sleuthing* do you not understand?"

"The part where we fail to catch the villain."

"Or he catches us."

"We cannot live our lives in fear." Elysia sounded like she was trying out for the part of Winston Churchill via Cate Blanchett.

"We also can't live our lives like characters in a TV show."

Elysia bridled. "It was a very good TV show, you know. The critics rather liked it. We had a nice long run."

A.J. laughed—against her will, because the last thing she wanted to do was encourage her mother in this lunacy.

She stopped laughing as she spotted Jake walking a few yards ahead. He moved well, at ease and confident, his alert gaze trained on J.W. Young and Bryn Tierney who were strolling ahead of him. Tracking them, A.J. thought cynically.

"Police at the funeral," Elysia remarked, apparently also noticing Jake. And after a beat, "He is a good-looking brute."

A.J. said nothing.

"Is it over between you then?"

A.J. glanced at her mother. Elysia's face gave nothing away.

"I think so."

"I'm sorry, pumpkin."

A.J. managed a twisted smile. "No, you're not."

"I'm sorry for anything that hurts you, love."

And A.J. couldn't find anything to say in answer to that.

As usual Elysia drove like the hounds of hell were in pursuit; A.J. wouldn't have been surprised to see flames shooting out the exhaust pipe of the Land Rover as they fled back to Stillbrook. Scenery flew by in picture-postcard flashes of old rock walls stained pastel shades from lichen, glittering snatches of the Delaware, an ivy-covered brick mill, the pink and silver shadows of the clouds unfurling in the blue dusk above the canopy of trees.

"Funerals do make me hungry," Elysia remarked off-handedly, downshifting past a truck hauling cattle.

"I wouldn't know. I think we left my stomach back on the interstate."

"Shall we stop and grab a bite?"

"Who are we meeting?" A.J. was resigned.

"Well, Bradley did mention . . ."

"How did I know?"

But A.J. didn't put up a fuss as they headed into Still-brook. Seeing Jake had depressed her, and the thought of going home and spending the evening with an equally heartbroken Andy was more than she could face just then.

They went straight to Mr. Meagher's office and waited for him while his pet cockatoo—if such an irascible creature could be called a "pet"—threw alternately salacious and insulting comments their way. When Mr. Meagher had wrapped up the day's business, the three of them drove to a nearby Italian restaurant.

It wasn't till they were seated and glancing over the menu that A.J. remembered Jake had brought her there on their first official date. Ironically that night had ended badly, too, and for the same reason: Jake's discovery that A.J. and Elysia were playing amateur sleuth.

"Jane Peters has been denied bail," Mr. Meagher informed them after the business of ordering drinks was concluded and they waited for their entrees. "She's been determined a serious flight risk."

"Now what would give them that idea?" A.J. wondered aloud, and her mother leveled a long look her way.

"There's some good news, though," Mr. Meagher said. "The forensics people finished with the clothes Jane was wearing the day of the murder and found nothing suspect. Never so much as a drop of Nicole's blood touched Jane's clothes."

"But that's excellent!" Elysia said.

"Aye," Mr. Meagher said, noticeably not jumping for joy.

"What is it?" Elysia asked.

"The Siragusa lad has an alibi. Airtight and cast iron."

"Bloody hell. You're joking."

From her mother's reaction A.J. gathered that Elysia had recently zeroed in on Oz Siragusa as prime suspect. The funny thing was her own instinctive conviction that her mother was on the wrong trail—funny because she had convinced herself she was not giving Nicole's murder any thought.

Regretfully, Mr. Meagher shook his head.

"He was at a bon voyage party for another tennis player from noon till four thirty when the news of Nicole's death came over the television. There are at least twenty people willing to swear to it. It seems the young man made a rare spectacle of himself calling and texting Nicole that day."

Elysia swore again, and Mr. Meagher blinked. "Is it possible they were bought off?"

Mr. Meagher shook his head. "Most unlikely."

"Then my next question is, *could* they be?"

As the other two gazed at her in consternation, Elysia gave an evil chuckle. "*Joking*, my darlings. A wee jest."

"What happened to Barbie? I thought she was your prime suspect?" A.J. asked, hurriedly steering the discussion from what felt like perilous waters.

"It won't wash. The timing is off."

"What do you mean? I thought we were agreed that the timing would be tight, but just manageable."

Elysia was shaking her head. "I tried it."

"You . . . tried it? What does that mean?" A.J. looked at
Mr. Meagher for clarification. He looked massively uncomfortable. What was that about?

"This morning. I made a couple of trial runs." Elysia
selected a bread stick and crunched into it with her small,
white teeth.

"Wait a minute," A.J. said. "Are you telling me you did
the drive from the studio to Nicole's mansion? At eighty
miles an hour?"

"Ninety-five on the second run. I still couldn't make it in
under half an hour."

"When did you . . ." A.J. had to stop to swallow. "When
exactly did you perform this suicide run?"

"At three and four thirty this morning. There's no traffic
at three and four thirty in the morning, which merely con-
firms my theory that Barbie couldn't possibly have got to
Nicole's in time. There would certainly have been traffic
last Saturday afternoon."

"Mother are you *crazy*? What if you'd hit a deer going
those speeds? Or a cow. You'd have been killed."

Elysia had the gall to look offended. "Really, Anna, I
was doing my own driving stunts when you were still in
your pram."

"That was thirty years ago. In a controlled environment.
And don't tell me you didn't have professional drivers
for all the really difficult stuff because I know damn well
you did."

Elysia waved these tiresome points away. "The important bit is that Barbie is—unfortunately—cleared. If Nicole
was dead for an hour by the time you arrived, and judging
by both the forensics evidence and the significance of the
phone being taken off the hook, she *was*, then Barbie
couldn't have done it."

"That leaves Jane."

"And J.W." Elysia's eyes glinted dangerously.

"J.W. has an alibi."

"Jane does *not* have a motive."

Mr. Meagher was shaking his head disapprovingly at the idea of motives.

A.J. said suddenly, "What about Bryn Tierney? Has anyone looked into her movements that day?"

Elysia brightened. "Oh, very good! Who better placed to move unseen through the house? But what's her motive?"

A.J. shrugged. "Maybe she has feelings for J.W.? She stayed on after Nicole's death and she certainly seems very loyal to him."

"Devoted," agreed Elysia.

"Granted, we've seen them together a few times and I've never seen anything that couldn't be explained away by friendship."

"She would have to be smart enough to hide the depth of her feelings."

With a bemused expression, Mr. Meagher watched them bat the theory of Bryn's homicidal tendencies back and forth.

"Or maybe she just got fed up with Nicole," A.J. said.

"A most annoying young woman," Elysia agreed. "I like it!"

Mr. Meagher said, "If Bryn Tierney had changed clothes midway through the morning, you can lay odds that someone would have noticed."

"But she was also best placed to change and shower if she had to." A.J. wondered what she was doing speculating on this stuff after she had firmly and forever sworn off sleuthing?

"Let's not dismiss her too hastily," Elysia said. "I think we've proven she had an excellent motive"

"You can't go by motive," Mr. Meagher objected. "Too

often motives don't come to light until the guilty party is revealed."

"True, true." Elysia looked reflective. "Besides, one person's motive is another person's madness."

"Let me guess. Shakespeare."

Elysia raised her eyebrows. "That was *me*, pumpkin. But thank you for the compliment. Anyway, there are people who will kill for a pair of shoes. And I don't mean Dolce & Gabbana, I mean ordinary trainers. You can't judge a motive by what you would be willing to kill for."

Was she willing to kill for anything? A.J. couldn't think of anything offhand. Those true crime shows on television about discarded wives and husbands committing murder? She might as well be watching the Sci Fi channel for all the sense it made to her.

They finished their meals in thoughtful silence. With the dishes cleared and dessert ordered, Mr. Meagher turned to A.J. once more. "Have you come to a decision about Lily Martin and the studio?"

A.J. shook her head. "As much as I'd love to get Lily out of there, I don't want to go to court. Even if we could be sure of winning, which we can't, I'm afraid of the effect it would have on the rest of the staff. I hate to admit it, but Lily is an integral part of the studio's success."

"If Lily's ever knocked off, we know who'll be the prime suspect," Elysia said cheerfully.

"Thanks, Mother. Hopefully you'll work as hard to save me as you're working to save Jane Peters."

"Harder, pumpkin. For you I shan't even stop for meals. Well, perhaps breakfast." She winked at Mr. Meagher.

Ignoring this heartwarming display of maternal devotion, A.J. said, "Anyway, as corny as it sounds, this is what Aunt Di wanted. Well, probably not me and Lily at each other's throats, but she did clearly want us to work together, and I can't find a way to justify getting Lily out of there. And believe me, I've racked my brain."

Elysia and Mr. Meagher exchanged looks, and watching them together, A.J. thought how—in an odd way—very well suited they were. It would be harder to find anyone more different from A.J.'s father than Mr. Meagher, but he had that same affectionate tolerance for Elysia's little foibles—little foibles like harboring fugitives from justice or crashing celebrity funerals or snooping in police business.

Dessert was delivered to their table, and between them they sampled and shared the raspberry white chocolate tiramisu, coconut pecan cream cake, and pistachio gelato.

"Speaking of dissolving partnerships," A.J. said, remembering. "When Mother and I were paying our condolences to J.W., he mentioned something about starting a partnership of some kind with Nicole. Had you heard anything about that?"

Mr. Meagher looked up from the cream cake, a speculative gleam in his eyes. "There was discussion of starting a film production company, but the plans were shelved."

"Who shelved them?"

"Now that I couldn't say."

"Couldn't or wouldn't?" Elysia asked shrewdly.

"Couldn't," Mr. Meagher assured her.

"Bryn might know," A.J. said.

Elysia met her gaze and smiled. "There's my girl," she purred.

Andy was still awake and listening to one of Gus Eriksson's jazz records when Elysia dropped A.J. off. She handed

over the disposable container of take out she had ordered
for him, guessing—correctly, it turned out—that he would
not bother to make dinner for himself.

"Beware of women bearing chicken cannelloni," he said.
"How was the funeral?"

"Oh . . . you know." She dropped down on the sofa beside him. "No one gave themselves away, if that's what
you're hoping."

"No ice cubes fell out of anyone's pants?"

"I'm not about to touch that line."

He chuckled.

Monster came over to the sofa and laid his heavy head
in her lap, gazing up at A.J. with soulful eyes. "Did you
feed him?"

"Every time he asks. I keep trying to win him over, but
he's a tough audience."

Neither of them spoke for a few minutes then casually,
she asked, "No messages?"

"No," Andy said. "No messages."

They smiled at each other in awkward understanding.

Andy said, "Give him a little time."

"The problem is, this was my second chance. We'd already argued over this after Aunt Di was murdered."

"It's mostly ego," Andy said. "He'll get over it."

"I don't know if it's really ego. He's right in one respect.
I did put him in an untenable position and maybe even compromised his investigation."

"Yeah, well . . . if he really cares about you, he'll see
you're worth it. He'll fight for you."

And suddenly A.J. knew they weren't talking about her
and Jake anymore.

She cleared her throat. "Speaking of egos, Lily wants to
revamp Sacred Balance. Starting with scrapping Aunt Di's
slogan."

"Why?"

She shook her head. "I'm trying to understand why. I guess it partly has to do with the fact that Aunt Di is gone now and Lily wants Sacred Balance to represent her. Us."

"Her," Andy said grimly.

"Maybe. I see where she's coming from. Sort of. She feels like it's time for a fresh start, a new beginning. Lily's point is that enough time has passed."

"Has enough time passed?"

A.J. swallowed hard. She said huskily, "I don't know if enough time will ever pass for me. I miss her every day."

No need to ask who "her" was.

"Sacred Balance belongs to you, A.J."

"But that's just it," she said. "Aunt Di didn't accidentally throw me and Lily together. She wanted us to work together, to find compromises, to . . ."

"Avoid killing each other."

"You're the second person to joke about that this evening."

"Third time's lucky."

A.J. tugged gently on Monster's silky ears. "Anyway, since Lily and I can't reach an agreement, she wants to have the rest of the staff vote on whether we change the slogan—and everything that goes with it."

Andy didn't say anything.

"It's just a slogan. Not even that original of a slogan. I don't know why it matters so much to me."

Andy gave her an affectionate look. "Because it was what Di really believed. She was a survivor. And an optimist. And despite the fact that she was also a hardass, she still believed in miracles."

"She did." A.J. smiled reminiscently. "She was a big believer in new beginnings and second chances. But I know there are more important things to spend my energy on.

And Lily—I hate to say this, but she's right. I've made a big point of wanting us all to work as a team. It's only fair that the rest of the staff have a say in this. It's not just advertising, it's our mission statement, it's our core value, it's our philosophy."

"You're not dealing with this well, are you?"

She laughed and shook her head. "No. But this is about more than winning out over Lily or getting my way. I want to believe I've learned something in eight months.

"Hey," Andy said. "It could happen."

Twenty-two

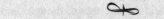

White-tailed deer were grazing in the meadow, delicately lipping wildflowers, their hides gleaming red-brown in the early morning sunlight.

"Morning, darlings!" fluted a voice down the hallway—and A.J. nearly jumped out of her skin, turning away from the window over the kitchen sink.

Elysia appeared in the kitchen doorway. "Something smells delicious. Blueberry muffins?"

"Mother! You could knock."

Elysia's pencil-thin brows arched. "Why, darling? There's nothing going on between you and Andrew—so you keep telling me." She added grimly, "More's the pity."

"There are other reasons why you shouldn't come barging in."

Elysia looked inquiring, and A.J. sighed, shaking her head.

Not bothering to conceal a tiny self-satisfied smirk, Elysia wandered over to the counter and A.J.'s breakfast preparations. "Where's Andrew?"

"Practicing yoga on the patio."

Elysia dipped one scarlet-tipped finger in the blue bowl. She tasted the batter and seemed to consider. "How is he?"

"He's . . . taking charge. Taking care of himself. Eating right, working out, getting enough rest." He needed to get himself under a physician's care again, though, and that was worrying A.J. She was glad his attitude was more positive, and that he felt yoga was helping, but she felt sure he also required traditional medical care.

Elysia sat down at the table, idly playing with a pack of cigarettes. "I heard something interesting on the way over."

"I really am done with sleuthing, Mother. I know I got a little carried away when we were talking last night—"

"Oh, I know that, pumpkin. No, I just thought it was . . . an amusing bit of local gossip. Oz Siragusa has fled the country."

"You're kidding!"

"They're not precisely calling it that," Elysia smiled at some inward thought. "No, the official story is he's left to compete in the French Open."

"Hasn't he?"

"I suppose he has, but he is a suspect in a murder investigation."

"But he has an alibi."

"Alibis are made to be broken."

"That one sounded pretty unshakeable. Is there any reason to think the police didn't give him permission to leave? They've got their prime suspect in jail now."

"I have my sources," Elysia said mysteriously.

A.J. put dollops of blueberry batter in paper cups in the muffin pan.

Elysia said absently, "I was thinking of asking J.W. to donate Nicole's clothes to the annual charity auction."

"That's not until December."

"December will be too late. Next week will be too late."

A.J. considered this. "You mean Bryn will be gone by then?"

"Exactly."

It wasn't a bad ploy. Bryn was the natural choice to help sort through Nicole's belongings, assuming that task hadn't already been completed. And now that Bryn had come up on Elysia's sleuth-o-meter it was inevitable she would want to question the young woman. Besides, Nicole's PA was bound to know all kinds of things about Nicole and J.W.'s relationship that might be worth knowing.

Elysia continued, "Assuming that Bryn really is leaving to get married."

"That should be evident fairly soon."

The doorbell rang, forestalling A.J.'s answer. Monster scrambled off the rug and loped down the hallway, barking.

A.J. followed the dog, pausing to glance out the window in the front room. There was an unfamiliar white car—a Porsche—parked in front of the house. She went to the door and looked out the peephole.

She had a quick impression of a tall, well-built man with dark hair. There was something vaguely familiar about him. . . .

Uh-oh.

She opened the door and Nick Grant, Andy's partner, stared somberly at her.

A.J. stared back. Nick was in his late thirties and craggily handsome. Right now he looked as grim as someone about to serve a search warrant.

"A.J., I need to talk to Andy."

A.J. opened her mouth but then closed it. Not only was this not her fight, this was not a fight anyone could win. Clearly Nick was going to have it out with Andy come hell or high water, and she respected him for that.

"He's on the back patio," she said, beckoning him to follow her. He did so in silence, and A.J. could imagine how very embarrassing this was for him, and how determined he must be if he was willing to track Andy down to his ex-wife's house.

They walked into the kitchen and Elysia looked up from the magazine she had been idly thumbing through and blinked.

"You remember Nick," A.J. said.

"Er . . . yes!" Elysia said, putting a hand to her upsweep of hair. "Nicholas. How lovely to see you again."

Nick said shortly, "I'm sorry to interrupt your Monday morning, but Andy and I need to straighten this mess out. Now."

Elysia looked like she wanted to object as A.J. led Nick to the back door, but she subsided at the look A.J. shot her.

Nick went straight through, opening the porch door and stepping outside. Looking past him, A.J. saw Andy, who was sitting at the wooden picnic table and staring at the meadow, glance around. He stiffened.

"What are you doing here?" he said without any indication of pleasure.

And Nick replied equally curt, "I came to bring you home."

"Then you wasted a trip."

Not a great beginning, but this was something they had

to work out on their own. A.J. let the screen door close and went back into the kitchen.

Elysia was nowhere to be seen.

Curious—uneasy, in fact—A.J. went looking for her. She found her mother in her own bedroom hovering next to the window that looked out onto the patio. A.J. could hear the murmur of Andy's voice through the open window.

"Mother!" she hissed. "What do you think you're doing?"

Not that it wasn't evident.

Elysia held up a hand like a stage manager cautioning the backstage crew. Then she nodded for A.J. to join her at the window. Unwillingly—though, in all honesty, she was every bit as curious—A.J. moved over to the window, staying to the side, well out of view of the men on the patio.

Andy was saying wearily, "We already had this out. You said your career was more important than spending time with me." A.J. risked a quick peek and saw Andy nervously massaging his knee with his hand. He was staring in the direction of the orchard, not looking at Nick. "This doesn't change that. I don't want you with me out of guilt or pity. I don't want you trying to glue this back together just because you feel sorry for me."

A.J. ducked back as Nick dragged one of the benches over, wood scraping loudly on bricks. She heard the squeak of wood as he sat down, heard him say calmly, "I don't feel sorry for you. I love you. What happens to you, happens to me."

"Look . . ."

"No, you look. I *love* you. That's what I came up here to tell you, okay? It was one thing when I thought you didn't want to be with me anymore. I'm not going to hold you hostage to commitment vows if you don't love me. But you do love me, Andy. I know you do."

With great difficulty, Andy said, "You don't understand. I'm . . . probably going to be . . . in a wheelchair."

"I don't care if you're in a damned iron lung. You're coming home. We'll work it out."

"I like him," Elysia whispered very softly. A.J. put a finger to her lips. Nick was still talking, still arguing but with a patience—a gentleness—that A.J. wouldn't have expected.

"Listen, when I said my career came first I was doing what people always do. I was assuming we had all the time in the world to spend together. I was thinking we could always take time off to play, but that for right now we had to put business first. You're just as driven and ambitious as me, Andy. Before this happened you were mostly pissed because you had to keep rearranging your schedule."

Andy said huskily, "You don't know what I felt because you never asked."

After a second or two Nick said, "You're right. I'm sorry for that. We should have talked more. I thought there was time for that, too."

Andy didn't say anything. Elysia opened her mouth as though she was going to chime in, and A.J. shook her head frantically. Elysia arched one brow but waited.

Nick said, "It never occurred to me that I was choosing between you and my job, because there is no choice there. Of course you come first."

A.J. stole another look. Andy was still staring away from Nick. His jaw worked, but he didn't say anything.

"Of course you do," Nick repeated softly, and he put his arm around Andy's shoulders, leaning his head against Andy's.

And A.J. realized that concern was one thing, but this was verging on voyeurism. She grabbed Elysia's wrist and dragged her away from the window.

"Blimey, pumpkin!" Elysia freed herself.

"This is indecent," A.J. said. "They deserve a little privacy."

"*This* is indecent?" Elysia looked sorrowful. "I knew you weren't getting out enough."

They returned to the kitchen and pretended to be busy.

"Do you think they'll feel like eating breakfast?" A.J. asked, sliding the pan of muffins in the oven.

Elysia raised her shoulders. She drifted toward the back door and A.J. said warningly, "Mother."

"I'm concerned, that's all. Andrew is like a son to me."

Minutes passed. A.J. checked the timer on the oven. Yep. Minutes.

"He's better looking than I remembered," Elysia whispered.

A.J. snorted.

The door to the patio opened and Nick and Andy came in. Andy looked like he had been crying. He also looked happier than A.J. had ever seen. Nick looked . . . well, less formidable. His hand rested possessively on the small of Andy's back, and there was a certain softness in his eyes when he glanced at Andy that reassured A.J.

Andy was going to be okay.

He said a little self-consciously, "It looks like I'll be leaving with Nick after all."

"Oh yes?"

"That is bloody brilliant!" Elysia said, and she moved to kiss them both. A.J. followed suit.

There were congratulations all around and then Andy said quietly to A.J., "I'm not sure what I would have done if you hadn't been here for me."

A.J. said, "I'm glad I was here. I'm glad I could help."

And she realized that this was the truth. Being forced to spend this time with Andy had taken her safely beyond her old hurt and resentment, and being able to forgive him had freed her once and all from the past. It was . . . a blessing. There was no other word for it.

While Nick went to help Andy pack, she rounded Lula Mae up.

"I'm going to miss you," she told the cat. "But I'll come and visit."

Lula Mae yawned widely in her face.

She put the cat in the carrier, and when Nick and Andy came out of the guest bedroom, Nick holding Andy's suitcase, she held the carrier up.

"Are you sure?" Andy said.

"Yes," Nick said. "Please be very sure, because if you have *any* desire—"

Andy nudged him in the ribs.

"I'm sure," A.J. said. "And Monster is counting the minutes. I think I heard him volunteer to pay her share of the gas."

"If you have any doubt that I love you," Nick told Andy, taking the carrier from A.J., "This ought to settle it once and for all."

Andy met A.J.'s eyes. He was smiling contentedly.

"I'll contact the rental company about Andy's car," Nick told A.J. "Somebody will be out in a day or two to pick it up."

"No problem."

"It's the end of The Three Investigators," Andy told her regretfully. "You'll have to carry on without me, Pete Crenshaw."

"Bob, I keep telling you I've hung up my magnifying glass."

Nick watched them, dark brows drawn together.

"I'll explain in the car," Andy said.

"This should be good."

Elysia and A.J. followed them out to the porch, watching

silently as Nick put Andy's bag in the trunk and the cat carrier in the back seat. He held the passenger door for Andy, waiting till Andy carefully lowered himself inside.

"Let me know when you crack the case," Andy called to A.J. and Elysia.

Nick stared at them. "Please tell me you aren't involved in another homicide investigation."

Not answering, Elysia wiggled her fingers in fond dismissal.

Shaking his head, Nick closed the door and went around to his side.

Andy grinned through the car window, then turned to Nick as the other man got behind the wheel.

A.J. felt the oddest sense of regret as she watched Nick's white Porsche drive sedately down the road. She was going to miss Andy.

Elysia watched the car out of sight. She sighed sentimentally. "If only you could find a man like that, pumpkin!"

Twenty-three

"These were her things," Bryn said quietly.

It was Monday afternoon and A.J. and Elysia stood before an enormous walk-in closet in the huge bedroom that had once been Nicole Manning's. The bedroom was nice, but the closet, in A.J.'s opinion, was to die for. She had dreams about closets with this much space and shelving.

Nicole's wardrobe—and that was the right word, this many garments could never simply be called "clothes"—was organized by type and color. On the left were silk T-shirts of the palest cream graduating to long-sleeved blouses in every shade of the rainbow, which then gave way to cashmere blazers and ended in black leather jackets. Sweaters were neatly stacked in plastic see-through containers. On the bottom rungs of the closet were pants—everything from summery capri's to leather jeans. And shoes . . . the shoes alone would make this year's charity auction.

The wardrobe carried the faint but distinct fragrance of Alfred Sung—ginger and bergamot—bringing Nicole vividly to life for a strange instant. A.J.'s throat tightened with unexpected emotion. She hadn't cared much for Nicole, but there was something moving about these tidy rows of clothes waiting for a woman who would never return.

"This is most generous of J.W.," Elysia said, fingertips brushing the beaded sleeve of a sage green Valentino gown. "These are worth a fortune."

Bryn said, "J.W. never wanted Nicole's money. Money isn't important to him."

That seemed a safe bet. J.W. made his living making conscientious and well-researched documentaries that mostly ran on public television.

"How is he doing?" A.J. asked.

Bryn's face was in profile, so A.J. couldn't read her expression. Bryn fingered the ruffle of a tangerine Versace pleated dress. "He's trying to get on with his life. What else can he do?"

"He's been a great friend to Jane Peters."

"He's a great friend to everyone," Bryn said. "He's a great guy."

"Did you ever meet Jane?"

Bryn shook her head.

"Do you remember seeing her here that day?"

Another shake of Bryn's head. It seemed for a moment that she would say something else, but then she moved away to Nicole's dressing table and studied the astronomically expensive array of bottles and jars.

"He's going to miss you, my dear," Elysia said.

Bryn blinked rapidly against the sudden moisture in her eyes.

"You must be leaving soon?"

"Yes." Her voice was husky. "Wednesday is my last day. It's going to be . . . strange."

"I imagine so. Will you work after you're married?"

Bryn smiled wryly. "Ross doesn't go in for working women."

"Ah, they still make that model, do they?" Elysia murmured. "I thought it was discontinued."

Bryn didn't seem to hear that. She was still examining Nicole's belongings, touching them gently; a kind of taking farewell, it seemed to A.J.

It struck her that this could very well be the first time Bryn had entered this room since Nicole's death. The bed was made, but garments were still laid out as though Nicole had yet to decide between them.

She said softly, "How did J.W. handle the news about the bracelet Oz Siragusa gave Nicole?"

A.J. had dropped the bracelet and note off at the police station the evening she and Bryn had discovered it in Nicole's locker. She remembered now that she never had heard from Jake about it. Perhaps he viewed it as another example of her failure to mind her own business?

Bryn stared at her for a long moment. "I don't know. I didn't tell him."

Somehow A.J. had not expected that. Granted, it would be an awkward conversation to have with the bereaved spouse of a murder victim. "The police must have asked him about it."

"I wouldn't know. J.W. isn't under suspicion."

"Will there be any final films?" Elysia inquired smoothly, changing the direction of the conversation as Bryn grew more and more stiff.

It did the trick. Bryn stared at Elysia, puzzled.

"Was she working on anything at the time of her death?"

"Oh. No. *Family Business* was the last thing Nikki worked on. She did a couple of public service announcements, but those have already aired. She was looking at different projects. She always got sent the same kinds of scripts. She was hoping for something a little more . . . meaty."

A.J. said, "She and J.W. were working on something weren't they? Or talking about doing something together?"

"They were, but then . . ." Bryn stopped. "I don't think anything was ever decided."

Elysia said brightly, "That's right. They were starting their own production company weren't they?" Then she frowned. "Or no. Come to think of it, I'd heard that had fallen through. J.W. changed his mind . . . was that it?"

Bryn opened her mouth but caught herself.

She must have been a good PA, A.J. thought. She hoped Nicole had rewarded her accordingly.

It was her turn to charge the drawbridge, A.J. said lightly, "That would have been an odd couple project, wouldn't it? Nicole and J.W.? I can see why he wouldn't want to jeopardize his credibility as a filmmaker."

"J.W. didn't pull the plug. That was Nicole." Bryn stopped, her mouth tightening.

"Nicole?" A.J. feigned surprise. "You're kidding. I'd have thought she'd have jumped at the chance to do something serious, to really test her acting chops."

Bryn said coolly, "Nicole was looking at a number of properties. J.W. supported her in all her creative efforts."

"He's heading back to Mexico quite soon, I expect," Elysia said.

Bryn turned to her. Elysia smiled. "He'll be wrapping up shooting on that documentary about the teacher's strike?"

"That's in the can," Bryn said shortly. "If you'll excuse me, I've got some last-minute packing. If you need any more boxes just ring housekeeping." She pointed to the phone on the nightstand next to the bed.

She left the room. A.J. listened for the sound of her footsteps retreating down the corridor.

"Not hard to tell where her loyalties lie," she whispered. "But you know . . . I think Bryn was fond of Nicole. Something about the way she was touching her things. It wasn't covetous, it was . . . like she was remembering her alive. And even though she's obviously fond of J.W., she avoided trashing Nicole. She avoided saying anything critical of her at all." She stopped at Elysia's expression.

Elysia was smiling—it reminded A.J. of a well-groomed lady crocodile.

"What?"

"Do you see one single article in this room that belongs to a man?"

A.J. stared around herself at the cream silk and ecru satin furnishings. It was certainly a feminine room. But more than that . . . there wasn't so much as a man's comb or handful of spare change anywhere.

"Maybe he moved his things out after . . ."

Elysia shook her head. "There are lots of photos but not a single one of him. There aren't any empty shelves or empty drawers. This was her room and hers alone."

It took several trips to empty the closet and drawers of Nicole's garments. In between one of their final treks to the Land Rover, J.W. looked in on them.

"How is it going, ladies?"

"Just about finished," Elysia said cheerfully. "We can't thank you enough for your generous donation."

J.W. smiled, but it didn't quite reach his eyes. "I'm glad these things will go to good use." He turned to A.J. "Are you still planning to do the documentary on the studio?"

For an instant she blanked. "Er . . . yes!" she said, recovering. "You mean you're interested?"

"Hey," J.W. said wryly. "I have to keep busy. And beggars can't be choosers."

"That's terrific. Why don't you come by Sacred Balance one night this week and I'll show you around."

"Any night in particular?"

"What is today? Monday? Really any weeknight."

"I'll check my calendar and give you a call."

"Great."

J.W. nodded pleasantly and departed.

"Brilliant," Elysia whispered jubilantly. "Well done, pumpkin!"

So much for A.J.'s decision to give up sleuthing. She'd let herself be roped into accompanying Elysia here today, and now she was going ahead with commissioning a documentary just so she could pump J.W. for information.

Granted, he did nice work, and a well-made documentary on Sacred Balance and Diantha might turn out to be a wonderful promotional tool.

Anyway, now that Jake was out of her life, she had to keep herself occupied somehow.

The next two days passed without incident. With no further breaks or developments, the Nicole Manning murder investigation slipped from the front pages, and slowly . . . slowly life returned to normal.

In fact, A.J. began to wonder if Nicole's death might go unsolved—assuming that the police did have the wrong woman in custody. That was debatable, although, a little irritatingly, Elysia's faith in Jane Peters never wavered.

The problem was . . . who else could have done it? One by one, all the possible suspects seemed to have fallen out of the race. Nicole's live-in lover had an alibi. And so did her part-time lover, Oz Siragusa. Elysia herself had knocked Barbie Siragusa out of the running with her own crack-of-dawn test drives to Nicole's mansion. And to put the seal on it, A.J. heard through the grapevine that Barbie was planning to divorce the Big Bopper and marry her personal trainer Corey Lovesy—now revealed to be the father of her unborn child.

It seemed that Barbie had lied about an affair with J.W. in an effort to get back at Nicole—an effort that had backfired badly when Nicole was murdered.

The last possible suspect—and that had been a stretch—was Bryn Tierney, and A.J. had ruled Bryn out. Not only had Bryn seemed genuinely grieved the afternoon A.J. had accompanied Elysia to collect Nicole's clothes for charity, but Bryn had left Nicole's mansion right on schedule, moving home to Virginia to begin planning her wedding.

So that was that.

A.J. went back to her comfortable and peaceful routine. Life was good. Except that she missed Andy and Lula Mae. She missed Jake even more—certainly more than he appeared to miss her—but apparently she was going to have to get used to it. She hadn't seen him since the evening of Nicole's funeral.

She toyed with the idea of calling him, but she wasn't sure she could take the pain of being brushed off. Jake had never struck her as someone prone to changing his mind once it was made up, and she'd had all the romantic rejection she could take for one lifetime. She would just have to hope that maybe time would soften his attitude, although it was more likely he had realized he just didn't care that much about her.

"You still love me, don't you?" she asked Monster when she got home Thursday night. Monster agreed, panting adoringly into her face as she ruffled his silky ears.

When the reunion of the mutual admiration society was

concluded, A.J. went into the kitchen to try and think of something quick she could make for supper. She wasn't very hungry these days, but she was determined not to give into the lure of Pop Tarts and Yoo-hoos.

She needed to go shopping, she decided as she checked the fridge's contents. A head of cabbage and half a head of lettuce. She inspected the pantry and found a can of salmon. Remembering the salmon salad Elysia had served the previous week, she decided to prepare one for herself.

She was on the patio eating her salad and admiring the sunset through the trees lining the meadow when she heard a car drive up. Monster got up and went trotting to the front, woofing in that undecided way.

A.J. rose and followed.

A heavy, plain, middle-aged woman with mousy brown hair was getting out of a Toyota.

"Hi." A.J. waved from the side of the house.

Spotting her, the woman left the front path and came toward her. "Alice Hart?"

"Who?" Recollection came belatedly to A.J. And then she had it: the night she and Andy had phoned Nicole's cyber enemy, Lydia Thorne.

Except . . . there was no Lydia Thorne. Just as there was no Alice Hart.

A.J. straightened her shoulders. She had put this ball in motion; she had to play it out. "Lydia Thorne, I presume?"

Lydia stopped short. "You're not Alice Hart. Alice Hart is a writer. She wrote a book about tea cups. She's never heard of you. She's never heard of Nicole Manning. I want to know what you think you're doing, harassing me?" Behind cute red spectacles, tiny, angry eyes blinked furiously at A.J.

"We're not harassing you. We—"

Lydia—or whatever her real name was—glanced at the house and repeated sharply, "*We?*"

A.J.'s embarrassment—there really *was* an Alice Hart somewhere?—gave way to unease. "Yes, my husband and I were concerned—"

"Where's your husband?" Lydia demanded. "I want to talk to him. I want to find out why you've been impersonating Alice Hart. That's against the law. You've broken the law. I could have you arrested. It's against the law to harass people."

Unwisely, A.J. said, "Then why were you harassing Nicole Manning?"

Lydia's pasty face went scarlet. She stepped right up to A.J., thrust her face into hers, and said venomously, "That woman was *scum*. She got everything she deserved. I was tired of reading about how everyone loved her, how adorable she was, how pretty she was. She was a third-rate actress and a first-rate *bitch*. She just used people. Used them and tricked them."

Monster, fangs barred, huff raised, began to bark in short, furious barks. A.J. took a step back, and said, "My dog thinks you're threatening me. You better calm down."

"I *am* threatening you! You can't treat people like this and think you're going to get away with it. You can't pretend to be someone else and harass them and try to turn everyone against them."

Somewhere a cuckoo clock was chiming the hour—warning A.J. it was time to get away from the increasingly virulent Ms. Thorne. Or whoever she really was.

She took another step back, saying, "I'm sorry if you think I invaded your privacy. We just wanted to know what you had against Nicole. We just wanted to ask you that one question. We're not harassing you, and we—"

"Oh no," Lydia said. "You don't get to decide when this

is over. I'm going to tell everyone about your studio, Ms. *A.J. Alexander*. I'm going to write every yoga site on the web and warn them about you. About how you've harassed me and tried to ruin me and what you're trying to do with that yoga studio. You're not even a real yoga teacher. You're a liar and a cheat and—"

She moved forward into A.J.'s space again, and A.J. put a hand up to ward her off. Lydia slapped her hand away and Monster lunged forward biting her.

It wasn't a hard bite—Monster wasn't really much of an attack dog. His sensibilities were outraged, but biting people was not his oeuvre. However, Lydia screamed as though the dog had removed one of her limbs, and began to kick and flail with the remaining ones, shrieking a stream of obscenities.

A.J. ran for the back porch and the broom that she had been using to chase spiders away during her yoga practice. Snatching it up, she returned to the scene of battle. Monster had one of Lydia's pant legs in his jaws, and he was growling and jerking on it while Lydia screamed and kicked at him the best she could.

"Let go of my dog!" A.J. commanded. She smacked the broom against the stone siding of the house. "Get off my property!"

Monster yanked tug-of-war style on Lydia's shredding pant leg, and A.J. grabbed for his collar with her free hand. Lydia slapped at her, but A.J. ducked, whacking awkwardly with the broom as she backed away, dragging the dog with her. She retreated quickly into the house.

Panting, she locked the back door behind her. Monster was still growling and barking, fur standing on end so that he looked about twice his usual size.

A second later one of the patio chairs hit the back door.

"Oh my God," A.J. gasped. "She's crazy."

No argument from Monster. He was now beside himself with rage. A.J. grabbed for the phone, dialed 911—then dropped it as it occurred to her that the windows all along the side of the house were open to let in the cool evening breeze.

On trembling legs, she raced from room to room, slamming windows and locking them, heart hammering in overdrive as Lydia threw something else—the picnic table?—at the back door. When she got back to the kitchen and picked up the phone, the 911 operator was placidly asking what her emergency was.

"Someone is trying to break into my house," she gulped.

"That happens to you a lot," the 911 operator said. And before A.J. could register her astonishment, he added, "Are you in a secure location, A.J.?"

Who *was* this guy?

"Doubtful," A.J. replied shakily. "She wants in here."

"Help is on the way. Stay on the line."

Well, on the bright side, she had plenty of weapons available with which to defend herself. Everything from knives to the heavy cutting block itself.

A flower pot came crashing through the window over the sink. A.J. screamed and the 911 operator began squawking questions.

"Are you still there? Can you describe your attacker?"

"Her name is Lydia Thorne. That's not her real name, though. I don't know her real name. But she's crazy. And not very attractive!"

Abruptly the silence from the back porch reached her. Monster was snuffling frantically at the base of the door. A.J. put the phone down, creeping to the broken window and trying to see out. There was no sign of Lydia Thorne on the empty patio.

Uneasily, A.J. crept to the front room. Lydia's car was still parked out front.

A.J. realized she had a clear view of the New York license plate number and she repeated it aloud. "AUU 2574."

The faraway wail of a police siren cut the tense silence.

There came a scrabbling, crunching sound from under the very window where A.J. stood, and to her horror, Lydia Thorne rose up. A.J. jumped back, nearly falling over a small footstool. Lydia banged, frustrated, on the window with her fists, then lumbered to her car, throwing herself in it and reversing in a wild arc.

AUU 2574 . . .

Shaking, heart thudding in a rush of adrenaline, A.J. watched the car retreat into the deepening twilight.

Lydia had been crouching under the window waiting . . . waiting for what? To attack A.J.? To kill her?

Whoever Lydia was, this changed everything because . . . that woman was nuts. A.J. had no trouble imagining her in a fury, grabbing the first available weapon and striking out.

The sound of sirens grew closer—and then faded away again, and A.J. guessed that the approaching police car had spotted Lydia's car racing down A.J.'s private road and given chase.

She made it to the phone, informed the 911 operator that help had arrived, then disconnected and tottered over to the nearest chair. She collapsed on the cushions, waiting numbly.

It wasn't a long wait. A second police car arrived and a pair of uniformed officers got out.

A.J. went to meet them, taking them around to see the damage. They took her statement and confirmed that the driver of a silver Toyota Camry had been arrested fleeing the scene. But more than that, they didn't vouchsafe, and A.J. could only imagine what kind of story Lydia Thorne (whoever she was—the police had presumably got a real name) told.

After the officers finally left, A.J. went outside once more to re-examine the damage to her property. Besides the broken window and battered door, flower pots had been broken or emptied, furniture tipped over, a statue of Kwan Yin, the Buddhist goddess of compassion, had been knocked down. Lydia had trampled through the flower and herb beds in her desire to peer through windows.

It was terrible—frightening. And yet it could have been so much worse.

A.J. went inside and fixed herself a calming cup of chamomile and lemon grass tea. It was too dark now to see to repot the flowers and plants. She would have to take care of that in the morning before leaving for work—right after she called someone to come and fix her window.

Luckily it was relatively warm at this time of year.

Monster sat beside her and rested his head on her lap, a sure sign that he was still upset. She stroked his head.

"Thank you for coming to my rescue," she said, and he licked his chops, giving her an expressive look. She chuckled. "You think you deserve a reward for that, do you?"

She rose and got Monster a dog biscuit and then settled with her tea in the old tree swing while the dog crunched away in the shadows. The quiet peace of the garden, the fragrance of the evening gradually calmed her shattered nerves although she was sure it would be a while before she was tranquil enough to sleep. Even the idea of her nighttime yoga routine seemed too . . . defenseless.

She thought of calling Elysia, but she wasn't ready to hear a dozen new theories about how Lydia Thorne was involved in Nicole's murder, and how they must continue to do everything in their power to get Jane Peters freed. She thought of phoning Andy to warn him about what had happened, but Andy was safe enough in New York under the protective eye of Nick Grant.

The shadows lengthened, the darkness now complete except for the stars overhead. A melancholy loneliness settled on her as she listened to the soft sounds of the world settling for another night.

And then from down the road she saw a pair of headlights gradually approaching, heard the rumble of a familiar engine.

She rose from the tree swing and went around to the front as Jake's SUV pulled into the front yard and parked. Jake got out.

Twenty-four

A.J.'s heart was beating nearly as fast as it had when Lydia Thorne had come after her. "I'm out here," she said over the wedge in her throat.

Jake turned, fast and easy. She must have startled him, but his voice was even as he said, "I heard what happened."

"Just don't say I told you so." She managed to say it lightly, although she felt anything but flippant.

Monster brushed past her, greeting Jake with snuffles and wagging tail—finally someone Monster was glad to see. Jake patted the dog and then came toward A.J., who still stood by the corner of the house.

"Are you okay?" he asked, and he took her into his arms. She hugged him back fiercely.

Maybe it was just a hug between friends, but it was a start. Jake's arms felt strong and warm and reassuring, and it was absurdly good to know that he cared. That if something bad had happened to her that evening, it would have mattered to him.

For some reason A.J.'s throat had closed up, so she couldn't answer without making a fool of herself. She settled for nodding, and Jake said softly, "Are you sure?"

Tears started to her eyes, she blinked them back fiercely. She nodded again, and got out a gruff, "Sure I'm sure."

He tilted her chin up, studying her face in the moonlight. His own silvered expression was inscrutable, but moonlight suited him. Then again, so did daylight. A.J. was once again painfully conscious of what she had lost by playing detective.

So it came as kind of a shock when Jake's mouth found hers. His lips were warm and surprisingly sensuous—he was so straightforward, so blunt, that his sexual expertise still caught her off guard. His mouth moved on hers, deepening the kiss, and A.J. felt a tingling shock of pleasure.

"I've missed you," he said softly against her, and he gave her another tiny kiss.

Neither of which felt like good-bye.

"I miss you, too," A.J. said. "I'm so sorry for what happened."

"I bet." He loosened his hold—a fraction—and his smile was one of not unfriendly mockery.

"That's not what I mean. Well, it's partly what I mean. I can't say I enjoy entertaining psychos on the patio, but what I meant was . . . I'm sorry, *really* sorry, for putting you in that position."

She could feel him studying her. "Which position are we talking about?"

A.J. drew a deep breath. "The position of you having to compromise your integrity in order to keep me—and my loved ones—from facing the consequences of our actions."

His brows drew together. "That sounds like you really *have* been thinking about it."

"And sorry for putting you in the position of having to do the right thing for the wrong reasons."

"Now that sounds more like you." But he was grinning. He glanced meaningfully at the house. "Is the ex still up?"

"Andy went back to New York."

"Oh yeah?"

There was a definite change in Jake's tone. Meeting his curious gaze, she said, "You do know I'm not in love with Andy, right? You do know that that's been over for me a long time?"

"Yeah, I know. It's just . . . you have a lot of family ties, A.J. You have a lot of commitments to other people. I like that about you, but it makes it hard sometimes."

His arm slid around her waist and they walked up the front porch together—only to realize the door was locked. They had to turn around and go back along the side of the house to the kitchen entrance, by which time they were mostly relaxed with each other again.

"I read the incident report," Jake said as they closed the kitchen door behind them. He automatically locked the door. "She tracked you down by the phone number here and then she started researching you. There's way too much information available on the Internet if you know where to look."

A.J. nodded. "I want you to know that it was just the one phone call, and really the single question we asked was whether we could talk to her about Nicole."

"I take it the answer was no?"

"It was a definite no. I can't believe we didn't pursue—" She caught Jake's expression and said, "I can't believe we forgot about Lydia as a possible suspect. It's just she seemed so . . . remote a possibility."

Literally and figuratively. That was the other danger of the Internet. It was easy to forget that there were real people on the other side of the intertube. And not all of them were sane and solid citizens.

"Her real name is Chris Summers," Jake told her. "She's a claims processor for an insurance company."

"Does she have an alibi for the day Nicole was killed?"

Jake grimaced. "There's something hinky there. She's refusing to say."

"Refusing to say what? Whether she has an alibi or not?"

He nodded.

"Well, she obviously doesn't have one then."

"I'm not so sure. There's something . . . smug about her. Like she thinks she's being clever. Laying some clever trap for us. Definitely an odd duck."

"I'd have phrased it a little differently."

Jake said, "I'm doing my best not to say *I told you so*. Don't push it."

A.J. made a face. "Okay, okay. So what does this mean for Jane? Surely it sheds some doubt on her guilt?"

"That's going to be up to the DA." At her expression, Jake sighed. "Look, A.J. I'm not happy with the collar either, but Peters was there, she had means, and a case could be made that she had motive. She ran—and kept running."

"There was no DNA evidence on her clothes."

"I don't think we're going to need corroborating DNA evidence to get a conviction on this. I'm sorry, but I think a jury will draw the obvious conclusion. But I'm not a lawyer. Maybe she'll squeak out of it."

"Jake, you questioned her. Does she really seem like a murderess?"

"There speaks a civilian. Listen, I'll give you this much. I'm personally not convinced of Peters's guilt, but we do have a problem in the fact that there's a shortage of other viable suspects. Maybe this Summers woman will turn out to have a rap sheet a mile long, but I don't think so. I think she *wants* us to charge her."

"And you've ruled out everyone else?"

"*Everyone* else? We've pretty much ruled out the principals. The narrow window of opportunity pretty much rules Barbie Siragusa out. No one could place her at the scene, and I personally never thought her motive was as strong as Peters's. Now if it was the kid—but we've tried. His alibi is good."

"What about Bryn Tierney and J.W. Young?"

"What about them?"

"Could they have worked it together? Maybe they were having an affair?"

Jake studied her for a moment. "I interviewed Bryn Tierney a couple of times. If she wasn't genuinely horrified and shocked by Manning's murder, then she was the real actress in that household. And at the moment she's five hundred miles away planning her wedding."

What better way to hide your guilty passion than behind marriage to another man? Then a year or two later, Bryn could go through the motions of falling out of love and divorcing her husband, meet up coincidentally with J.W. and . . . they all lived happily ever after?

Admittedly farfetched. Not to mention that it presupposed Nicole's murder had been planned and plotted from the first, and A.J. didn't believe that. She didn't believe Bryn and J.W. had conspired to kill Nicole. The whole method of Nicole's murder was too haphazard. Everything about it indicated that it had been a violent impulse.

Jake added, "And if Young is in love with anyone, it's his not-so-ex wife."

"Well, okay then. What about J.W.'s alibi?"

Jake said slowly, "Now that's something else. The fact is, we can't really verify Young's alibi."

"What?"

"It turns out that he arrived on an earlier flight—and before you get carried away, he volunteered this information early on in the investigation. There was a problem with some of his luggage getting lost, and he claims he was in the airport for a couple of hours trying to get that straightened out."

"That can either be proven or it can't, right?"

"Have you ever had your luggage lost?" Those ticket counter people don't remember you an hour later, let alone a week. Young did put in a luggage claim, but it was three hours after his plane landed."

A.J. stared at him. "He killed her."

"Whoa. We don't know that, and we sure as hell can't prove it."

"But you do know it," A.J. said. "I can see by your expression, you know it."

Jake said warningly, "I *don't* know it. Don't go off on this. As far as I can see, he had zero motive."

"Nicole was having an affair."

"He didn't know about it."

"Oh, give me a break! How could he not know about it?"

Jake said shortly, "I'm the one who had to question him about Manning's involvement with the Siragusa kid. Believe me, Young didn't know. Didn't have a clue. In fact, he didn't believe me at first."

"Okay, well . . . you said it yourself. He's still in love with Jane."

"Holy—! You're like a pit bull when you sink your teeth into something, aren't you? The fact that the guy still has feelings for his ex doesn't mean he would commit murder

for her. There was no reason to commit murder for her. He
wasn't married to Manning. He could have walked out anytime. He didn't inherit under the terms of Manning's
will . . . he had nothing to gain by her death."

"Murder isn't always about gain."

"Mostly it is. I don't mean financial gain . . . but gain.
Most people—sane people—kill other people because they
have something to gain from their death." Studying A.J.'s
mutinous expression, he said, "We're still investigating.
And we'll continue to investigate."

"Not once Jane has been convicted, you won't."

"We've got a ways to go before that happens. And if it
looks like Peters is going to be convicted . . . we might
catch a break."

"Like what?"

Jake said slowly, "A couple of things. The first forty-
eight hours are the most important in investigating a homicide, that's true. But just because we don't catch the bad
guys in forty-eight hours, doesn't mean we give up. And as
time passes people get careless, they start to relax, they
don't realize they're still being watched. A lot of times
that's when we catch a break."

"And meanwhile Jane Peters is rotting away in prison."

"Well, that's the other thing," Jake said. "If Young *is* still
in love with Peters, and he did kill Manning, then I don't
know that he'll stand by and let her take the rap if—*if*—he
did it."

"Yes, but what if he does? What if he just can't bring
himself to confess?"

"You're not listening to me. As of now we can't place him
on the scene, and we don't have a concrete motive for him.
He wasn't married to Manning, and he doesn't inherit her
property or money. They bought the house together. And he
was aware of the terms of Manning's will. And, yes, Man-

ning was having an affair, but since we're all agreed that
Young is probably still in love with his wife, we're going to
have trouble proving he did Manning in during a jealous
rage."

A.J. was silent. It was obvious to her that Jake instinctively felt something was wrong with J.W.'s story, even if
he wasn't openly acknowledging it. He had certainly done
a lot of checking and double-checking.

She said slowly, "No one would—or even *could*—plan
to kill someone with a piece of an ice sculpture. Not in
those circumstances. A house filled with all kinds of people
coming and going in preparation for the party? From the
very first Nicole's murder had to be one of impulse. Which
I think means that it had to be committed by someone who
had a lot of stored-up anger and resentment and aggression
against Nicole. And, as awful as it is to say, the most obvious suspect in such as case is a spouse or lover."

"You don't have to convince me."

"Which means—*hey*!"

He offered that lopsided smile that never failed to make
her heart flip over. "Just pointing out that cops tend to have
a jaded view of romance and matrimony."

"Well, but I mean . . ."

"Yes?" he teased.

"There are exceptions to every case."

"Uh-huh. Well, I'm tired of talking about *my* case. Let's
discuss the exceptions."

Jake turned out the kitchen light, took A.J.'s hand, and
drew her down the dark hallway.

Twenty-five

"I think it has something to do with that koala preserve," A.J. said.

It was early the following morning and she was on the phone—on hold—waiting to leave a message at Waldo's Home Window Repair. Not that the brisk morning breeze blowing in over the kitchen sink from the smashed window wasn't refreshing . . .

Jake was finishing the last swallows of his coffee. "Yeah? What is it you think Young has against koalas?"

"Probably nothing. But he and Nicole were supposed to start a film production company, and those plans were suddenly scrapped and Nicole threw herself into establishing this koala preserve. She was the kind of person who had . . . enthusiasms. She'd be totally into something like yoga one minute and then on to . . . kickboxing. I remember for a time she was really into dog breeding and dog shows, but as far as I can tell, when she died she didn't even own a dog. And she was the same way about gardening and flower shows. When she first moved out here she was very involved in the Garden Club, and then she just lost interest. Something else caught her attention."

Jake said, "I hadn't heard about the production company, but I can't see either of them wanting to work together."

"I don't know at what point in their relationship the idea first came up, but I can see that J.W.—the one with the talent and vision—would have jumped at the idea of Nicole's money funding his projects. He's always on the hunt for grants and financial backing. He's passionate about his work. You can tell. He really cares. So to have that money yanked out from under him—to have it go to a koala preserve."

"This is what a man likes to hear the morning after. His girlfriend speculating about koalas and murder. I'm assuming I had your attention at *some* point during last night's festivities?"

A.J. laughed. "Don't tell me you couldn't tell because I'm pretty sure . . ."

"Yeah, well." He ducked back behind his coffee cup.

The answering machine came on, and A.J. left her message for Waldo. Hanging up, she returned to the breakfast table and sat down across from Jake. He looked awfully good for a guy who'd had very little sleep the night before.

"Anyway, this is informed speculation. It's a fact that Nicole backed out of the production company, and it's a fact that it happened at the same time she came up with this brainstorm for a koala preserve—despite the fact that wildlife organizations were absolutely against it." A.J. added, "Right there, that was *classic* Nicole."

Jake shrugged, polishing off the last of his jam and toast.

"This is what I think happened," A.J. said. "I think J.W.

came back from Mexico exhausted, angry, and his luggage is lost. His relationship with Nicole is already on the rocks. They're not sleeping together anymore and she pulled the plug on this film company, which must have caused some major resentment. He gets home and everything is in turmoil because of this party for Nicole, and Nicole is in full ego-maniacal swing, she's going to make her big announcement about the koala preserve—that everyone in the world thinks is a mistake—and I think she must have said or did something that was simply the last straw. I think he walked out, saw the koala ice sculpture, which pretty much embodied everything he hated about her, and I think he turned around and slammed Nicole over the head with it."

"And nobody noticed?"

"The house was in chaos, and . . . if he hadn't been noticed coming in, well, he would certainly know how to get out without being seen."

"And then—spattered in blood—he drives back to the airport and makes a claim for his luggage?"

"Depending on which of his bags was lost, he could have easily had a change of clothes with him, and dumping the bloodstained garments wouldn't be hard. He could have stopped along the way or shoved them in one of the airport garage bins."

Jake rose from the table. He wasn't saying anything—which in itself was a comment.

"You could examine his phone records," A.J. suggested, raising her face to his.

He paused to deliver a quick kiss, which tasted a little like raspberry preserves. "And why would I want to do that?"

"Because there's just a chance you might find that he called Mother last Saturday night—threatening us if we didn't lay off the case." Catching his expression, she amended hastily, "Warning us to butt out of police business."

"That's what I thought you must mean." He eyed her grimly, thinking.

"It's just a chance."

"It wouldn't prove anything."

"No. But it would be a pretty good indication that we— you're on the right track."

Jake gazed down at her for what felt like a long time. Unexpectedly, he pulled out the chair next to A.J.'s, and sat down. Puzzled, she tried to read his expression. He picked up her hand in his, holding it lightly, staring out the window.

"Listen," he said finally.

She had a cold feeling in the pit of her stomach. Suddenly she was reminded of that awful day when Andy had finally told her the truth. She managed to say calmly, "I'm listening."

"I need to tell you something." He stopped.

A.J. waited. She wondered if her hand felt as icy to touch as she felt on the inside.

Jake said flatly, "I was engaged once. I won't bore you with the details. The bottom line is, everything I thought I knew about Jenny was a lie. And it destroyed us—destroyed our relationship. So . . . I don't know if you want to call it a hang-up or an insecurity or what-the-hell-ever, but it's important to me to be able to trust any woman I get involved with."

A.J. asked politely, "*Any* woman you get involved with?"

"The woman I fall in love with."

A.J. shut up.

"Maybe it seems silly to you or . . . I don't know. But if

you give me your word, I'm going to hold you to it. And if you lie to me, it's going to matter. A lot. Even if it's just over some stupid little thing. Maybe especially over some stupid little thing."

His gaze gravely held hers, waiting for her answer.

A.J. said slowly, "There's a lot you're not telling me."

Jake nodded. "Yes. One day I will tell you—when we're both ready. But in the meantime, if you do want something with us, between us, don't lie to me or pretend to me. If you're going to disregard my wishes, then do it to my face."

"Is that permission to—?"

"No."

"Just checking."

They continued to eye each other. Through the broken window floated the sweet song of a meadow lark.

A.J. smiled, though her eyes were serious. "Thank you for telling me. I won't lie to you. No lies of omission. Not even little white lies. I won't fudge the truth or claim ignorance or pretend I didn't understand. I won't fool around with something this important."

Jake leaned forward and kissed her—a long, sweet kiss.

They broke reluctantly, smiling into each other's eyes.

Jake pushed his chair back.

A.J. said, "But I do think you should check J.W. Young's phone records."

It was an ordinary Friday at Sacred Balance.

A.J. spent the morning interviewing receptionist candidates for the second receptionist position.

Candidate number one spent her interview texting messages in between distractedly answering A.J.'s questions.

Candidate number two asked to review her resume as she couldn't remember what answers she might have put down.

Candidate number three brought her crying baby in and midway through her interview began to breast feed.

Candidate number four was a no-show.

Jake called right before lunch.

"I thought you'd want to know. Summers finally coughed up her alibi for the night of Manning's murder. It's airtight."

"What is it?" A.J. couldn't help the note of disbelief. If ever anyone had struck her as a leading candidate for Psycho of the Year, it was Lydia—Chris.

"She was in the hospital having surgery."

"What kind of surgery?"

Jake sounded uncomfortable. "Some kind of feminine procedure. A laparoscopic hysterectomy."

"Then why didn't she just say so?"

"Apparently she was planning some grand lawsuit for false arrest. When we didn't cooperate by charging her right away in the Manning homicide, she got impatient and admitted where she was. We've already got confirmation from her doctor. There's no way Summers killed Manning. But so long as you're willing to prosecute we're still holding her on a variety of charges. Everything from trespassing to assault."

"Absolutely I'm willing to prosecute."

"Good girl. Another thing. We checked Young's phone records. There's no history of a call to Elysia's."

"He could have—"

"He could have made the call from elsewhere, yes. I know."

"So you're not ruling him out?"

"I'm not ruling him out. Yet."

They chatted amiably, made plans for the evening, and then Jake rang off. As A.J. replaced the receiver, she reflected how very glad she was that their relationship appeared to be well on the road to recovery.

She was on her way out the door to meet Elysia for lunch when Lily stopped her with a peremptory summons. "A.J.!"

A.J. tried not to wince. Possibly she didn't try hard enough. Reaching her, Lily said, "I realize you're in a hurry, but since you're taking off early again, I wanted to remind you about tomorrow's staff meeting."

"I haven't forgotten. And I'm not taking off. I'm going to lunch."

"Oh, and I'll bring the pastries for the meeting."

With superhuman strength A.J. managed to force back *That's a first!* She said with determined pleasantness, "Wonderful. Thanks for handling that."

Lily was smiling at her, but somehow that was even less appealing than her usual scowl. "Have a nice *lunch*."

What did that mean? What was Lily implying now? That A.J. wasn't carrying her weight? That she was sneaking off for noontime trysts? Who knew? And it was a waste of energy trying to understand the serpentine workings of Lily's mind.

Remembering the motto *smile, it makes people wonder what you're up to*, A.J. smiled graciously and waved bye-bye. But her stomach was churning as she walked to the parking lot. Lily was obviously confident of the outcome of the next day's meeting. Somehow A.J. was going to have to find the strength and the grace to accept the choice of her fellow team members.

Of course she could simply pull rank and refuse to consider any changes to Sacred Balance—cosmetic or philosophical. She and Lily were co-managers, true, but as the owner, A.J. controlled the purse strings, and ultimately had the final say.

She could do it—she *wanted* to do it—but she knew she wouldn't. Not only would she lose her self-respect if she proceeded to behave like a corporate overlord, she would lose the goodwill and team spirit that she had worked so hard to foster over the past year.

It was hard, though, sometimes very hard, to do the right thing when the right thing did not correspond with one's own wishes.

Elysia was flipping leisurely through a *People* magazine—shaking her head over the photogenic foibles of the next generation of thespians—when A.J. arrived at Patty's Pantry.

"Sorry I'm late." A.J. sat down on the gingham upholstered bench.

Elysia tossed the magazine aside. "Well, you certainly had an interesting evening by all accounts."

"You heard about that, did you?"

"Not from you." Elysia's tone was sweet, but it was obvious she was a little hurt.

A.J. brought her very quickly up to speed with the story of Lydia Thorne's visit and the fact that A.J. and Jake were once more "on."

Elysia's mouth pursed in a little moue of displeasure over the news that Jake was back in A.J.'s life, but she didn't say anything—for which A.J. was grateful.

"How did it go with Mr. Meagher?" A.J. asked.

"Not good. They've set Jane's trial date."

"Oh no."

Elysia nodded broodingly. She tapped a scarlet fingernail on the table cloth and said, "I'm considering hiring a private detective."

"Why?"

"Perhaps there was something in Nicole's past that contributed to her death."

"Well, before you spend any money on Sam Spade, it looks like J.W.'s alibi might not be as rock solid as we previously thought."

Elysia perked up considerably as A.J. filled her in on all she had learned from Jake the night before.

"But this proves—"

"It doesn't prove anything, Mother. Not in a legal sense."

"He was always the most obvious suspect. The only thing that kept the police investigating him too closely was that supposed alibi."

"According to Jake, he told the police early on that his alibi wasn't unbreakable. That seems either the action of an innocent man or a pretty gutsy move."

"Bryn knew," Elysia said, looking into some inner distance.

"I don't know. Maybe she suspected," A.J. conceded. "She would know better than anyone what their relationship dynamic was, what the tensions and frustrations were between them."

"I believe she's in love with J.W."

"Maybe. He obviously had her loyalty, no question of that. But she was fond of Nicole. Would she have stood by and let her murderer go free? I don't think J.W. is in love with *her*."

"It's all clear now. Of course he's guilty. If we were to work on her—"

A.J. nearly spilled her iced water. "Absolutely not! Did you miss that part about the crazy woman showing up at my house and trying to dismantle my patio—if not me? We can't continue poking our noses into crime and not expect to get punched in the schnoz."

"Very colorful, pumpkin, but meanwhile dear little Jane Peters who never did a wrong thing in her life is sitting in jail."

"Mother, the best way we can help now is to stay out from underfoot and make sure we don't do anything to compromise the investigation. I gave Jake everything we had—"

"Speak for yourself," Elysia murmured.

"Funny. I know him. He'll take that information and act on it, but he's going to do it by the book. Anything else is liable to make things worse for Jane," A.J. said.

"Pish and tosh! What could possibly be worse than being locked in prison accused of a murder you didn't commit?"

"Being killed by the real murderer."

Elysia blinked but recovered. "Well, why should that happen?"

"Why shouldn't it happen? If J.W.—or whoever the killer is—has committed murder once, he doesn't have a heck of a lot more to lose, does he?"

Elysia frowned. "The man has practically devoted his life to PBS. How ruthless could he be? If he did kill Nicole, it was obviously not a cold-blooded crime."

"If—if—he killed Nicole, he's letting Jane take the rap for him. Who knows how ruthless he might be about protecting himself? Fear drives people to do terrible things."

Elysia shrugged a bony shoulder. "At the very least this should throw enough doubt on Jane's guilt that we ought to be able to get her a bail hearing."

A.J. said wearily, "I think you should leave it alone. The last thing we want to do is tip J.W. to the fact that he's still under suspicion and being watched by the police."

Elysia gnawed her lip. "I need to speak to Bradley," she said abruptly, rising.

"Can't it wait till after lunch?"

"How can I possibly sit here gorging myself on pot pies while poor, dear Jane is sitting in a cell eating prison slop?" She began gathering her purse, magazine, and shopping bags.

"Whatever," A.J. said shortly, a little surprised at her own irritation. "Give my regards to poor, dear little Janie."

Elysia straightened, studying her. "I will, pumpkin," she said coolly. "Have a lovely lunch. I'll talk to you later."

"Ta-ta," A.J. bit out.

But Elysia was already out of earshot.

Twenty-six

❦

On Friday nights the studio always cleared out early.

A.J. was still working at her laptop as Suze, the last staff member to leave, called good night. A.J. called back, wishing her a good evening, and returned to her reports. Jake would not be getting off work until about nine, so there was no hurry to rush home.

During late nights and early mornings, A.J. was reminded of how far from town, how isolated, the studio really was. The woods seemed to close in when darkness fell—and the deep and peaceful silence grew strangely eerie.

For a time A.J. continued to work, but she began to feel restless—and a little uneasy. Every creak and squeak of the building was setting her nerves jumping. She signed out of her laptop, closed the lid, and considered whether she would take her work home with her. She decided against it.

Running upstairs, she quickly verified that the showers were turned off, lockers closed, no cell phones left behind. She walked briskly down the empty hallways, glancing into each room, making sure she was the only person left. Not that she really had to check. The studio had a hollow, empty feel to it.

Back in her own office, she slipped a sweater on over her sleeveless yellow T-shirt, gathered her things, and went to the front doors. She turned off the lights, set the alarm, unlocked the door, and stepped outside.

The evening was cool and the surrounding pine trees sighed overhead. A.J. locked the glass door and started down the curving walk, stopping dead at the sound of footsteps coming toward her.

A tall figure materialized out of the darkness, and A.J. went rigid as she recognized J.W. Young.

"Hi," he said. And then taking in her frozen figure, "Sorry. Didn't you say it would be okay to stop by any evening?"

"I . . . yes," she managed. In the excitement over Lydia Thorne and getting back together with Jake, A.J. had totally forgotten about telling J.W. to drop by anytime so that they could discuss making a documentary A.J. had no real intention of commissioning.

She continued standing there. She did not want to go into the studio with him—memories of her aunt's murder were still too vivid. And, knowing what she did about him, A.J. was afraid her doubts and suspicions would show.

She said, "I'm so sorry. Any other night would be perfect, but tonight something's come up and I can't stay."

"Oh."

After a moment he moved to the side, and A.J. understood that he expected her to precede him down the stone walk. And she couldn't do it. She simply could not turn her back on him and start walking into the darkness knowing he could stoop down, pick up one of the large stones lining the walk, and bash her over the head.

Not that he had any reason to do so. He couldn't know what she knew—suspected.

But suddenly she could see it all so vividly, see him walking up behind Nicole and raising his hand to smash her down with that stupid frozen koala sculpture. She could picture his pleasant face twisted with rage. . . .

But he had no reason to harm *her*, no reason to be in a rage with A.J. And he didn't *look* angry. He didn't look anything but puzzled . . . and she was to blame for that, standing here like a nitwit . . . unable to budge while he waited for her.

"Is something wrong?"

"No." She forced a smile and walked forward, muscles strung tense as though by wire as she passed him. He fell in step beside her.

"Quiet night," he said.

"Yes." Yes. Deadly quiet. The surrounding pines seemed to smother all sound.

No, that wasn't true. She was letting her nerves carry her away. If she listened beyond the pounding of her heartbeat, she could hear the pines whispering and crickets chirping and the persistent call of a hunting owl—and far down the road, the distant drone of a motor.

"How's the detecting going?"

She turned her head quickly, and J.W. was smiling, not looking at her.

He must have felt the startled look she threw him, though, for he said, "Was it supposed to be a secret? The whole town thinks you and your mother are a cross between *Cagney and Lacey* and *The Snoop Sisters*."

She said carefully, "We're all done detecting. The police made their arrest."

"I thought you didn't believe Jane did it? Your mother sure as hell doesn't believe it. She's going around telling everyone who will listen that Jane is innocent. That they have to find the real killer."

A.J. shrugged. "It doesn't matter. The police have made their arrest and we were told to butt out."

He gave a soft laugh. "And you always do what you're told?"

"When it makes sense."

He stopped walking. A.J. continued, but she turned around to watch him.

"What?" he asked.

She shook her head. There were now about two yards between them and it gave her a little confidence. She held her hand at her side, keys laced through her knuckles.

"Go ahead," J.W. said. "It's right there on your face. You're scared to death of me."

She couldn't read his face in the shadowy light, so she didn't see how he could read hers, but he was right all the same. She paused. "Okay," she said. "Since you asked, do you think we should stand aside and let Jane go to prison for something she didn't do?"

"She won't."

"Really? They've got her with motive, means, and opportunity. Plus she ran, and that always looks bad—even though everyone on TV does it."

J.W. said thickly, "She won't be convicted. I'm hiring the best defense lawyer I can afford. Everything will be okay if you people will just *stay out of it*!"

A.J. didn't move a muscle. It seemed to her that in that profound silence she could hear every invisible rustle in the bushes, every snap of twig, every spin of the stars over head—and coming up the deserted highway someone driving way too fast.

"We're staying out of it," she said. "We're not the problem."

He moved toward her, and A.J. jumped back, turning to run for her car.

Headlights bright as spotlights caught her and J.W.—a few steps behind—in their beams as a big Land Rover tore into the parking lot.

As A.J. ran to the safety of her own car, J.W. also started running—in the opposite direction. The Land Rover wasn't slowing, wasn't swerving; it was bearing straight down on him. He threw a panicked look over his shoulder and nearly fell.

A.J. covered her mouth in horror, but J.W. caught himself and stumbled onward, the glare of the Rover's high beams pinning him in the light as he ran, crossing the parking lot and heading across the clearing toward the trees—the Land Rover roaring in pursuit.

"Mother!" shrieked A.J. afraid that Elysia would actually mow him down.

J.W. disappeared into the woods. The Land Rover lurched to a stop at the woodline, exhaust drifting into the night, engine rumbling in what seemed to be frustration.

A.J. fished around in her purse and found her cell. She began to dial.

She was braced to leave Jake a message, so his voice took her by surprise.

"Hey."

"J.W. Young just . . ." she gulped and had to try again. "I think J.W. may have tried to kill me."

"*What?* Where the hell are you?"

"At Sacred Balance. Mother's got him pinned down in the woods."

"Dear. God."

She laughed shakily at his tone. The Land Rover was reversing, the red taillights coming slowly toward her.

"I'm on my way. Grab your mother and get out of there now."

"I think we're okay. I don't think he's coming after us. I think Mother scared him."

"I have zero doubt she scared the living hell out of him. I don't care. I don't want the two of you anywhere near him."

The Land Rover pulled neatly up beside A.J.

"Roger," A.J. said to Jake. "Over and out."

He disconnected.

Inside the Land Rover, Elysia leaned over and pushed open the passenger side door. She was smiling, her eyes glittering ferally in the pallid glow of the cab light. "Going my way, pumpkin?"

It was nearly two o'clock in the morning when Jake arrived at Deer Hollow. A.J. and Elysia were still wide awake, high on caffeine and nerves after hours of drinking coffee and talking.

While they had not actually fled Sacred Balance, they had retreated to the safety of the open road so that they could keep an eye out in case J.W. made an attempt to reach his car. There had been no sign of him, but in any case, the state troopers had arrived within minutes of A.J.'s phone call to Jake.

Shortly after the studio parking lot had filled with cop cars, J.W. had walked out of the woods, hands behind his head, and surrendered himself. He had been taken into custody for attempted assault while A.J. and Elysia made their statements.

Of course if anyone should have been arrested for attempted assault—never mind assault with a deadly weapon and a host of other charges—it was Elysia. But none of the officers on hand seemed to want to touch *that* one with a ten foot pole.

J.W. had been driven away in the back of a police car and finally A.J. and her mother had been allowed to leave the scene. They had headed straight for Taco Bell.

Two seven-layer burritos, two Chalupa Supremes, eight crunchy Taco Supremes, and an alarming number of cinnamon twists later, they had managed to regain their composure—beyond a hysterical tendency toward giggles.

"What made you drive out to the studio?" A.J. had asked finally, sweeping the last of the empty food wrappers off the table—much to Monster's keen disappointment.

Elysia shoved at her slightly off-kilter upsweep. "Bradley and I had an early dinner and I passed J.W. as I was leaving Stillbrook. I didn't make the connection immediately, but then I remembered you'd invited him to the studio one night, and I knew. I *knew*."

There was nothing funny about it, but for some reason that started them tittering again. Jake had called not too long after that to say that J.W. Young had confessed to killing Nicole Manning, and that he figured he would be in interrogation most of the night.

"I have tomorrow morning off," A.J. told him. "Shall I leave a light burning in the window?"

There was a pause. "I may cost you a fortune in candles."

"It's worth it."

"I'll see you in a bit then."

Jake had probably not been expecting to see Elysia as well, but he took it calmly, settling at the table and taking the coffee A.J. handed him.

"Thanks." He swallowed hot coffee and said, "He says it was an accident."

"They always say that." Elysia spoke dismissively.

Jake's green gaze rested on her thoughtfully.

A.J. said, "I don't think he could have planned it, but he didn't accidentally hit her."

"True. And he had presence of mind to get out of Dodge and begin concocting the best alibi he could given the situation."

"So was it all true? Had he really been in Mexico filming a documentary?"

"Yep. Absolutely. He flew back just as he said—even his luggage really was lost."

"What happened?"

Jake swallowed more coffee. "Well, Miss Marple, what happened is pretty much what you theorized happened."

"You're kidding."

Jake laughed tiredly. "Nothing like having confidence in yourself."

"Well, but I mean . . ."

Elysia put in, "I keep telling you, you've inherited my knack, pumpkin. You have the sleuth gene."

"If we're lucky it'll skip the next generation," Jake said, yawning.

Elysia's eyes met A.J.'s. Neither of them said a word. After a beat, A.J. said carefully, "So . . . J.W. came back from Mexico and arrived at the house, and Nicole . . . ?"

"It's not totally clear. Apparently she tied into him for nearly being late to her party because of his loser preoccupation with Third World countries and ugly poor people." He added dryly, "I guess she liked her causes cute and fluffy and four footed."

"He really didn't know about her affair with Oz Siragusa?"

"He really didn't. To tell you the truth, I don't think he really cared about that, but when she denigrated his work, his professional competence as well as his purpose in life . . . that seems to have been the breaking point. I mean, it sounds to me like he'd barely restrained himself from strangling her any number of times over the past six months."

"He probably couldn't get over the fact that he'd wrecked his relationship with Jane for *that*," Elysia remarked.

"Poor Nicole," A.J. said. "She wasn't evil, she was just . . ."

"She was the kind of person you want to strangle," Jake agreed calmly. "Or hit over the head. And this time someone did."

"What made him confess?" A.J. asked.

Elysia said loftily, "Fear of divine retribution—and a mother's wrath."

"Uh . . ." Jake controlled himself. "Two things, I think. The guilt of his wife being arrested for his crime was eating at him—Young really does still love Jane Peters. And . . . just the fear of being caught. It's a helluva strain living under suspicion." His eyes met A.J.'s. "The two of you poking into things didn't help settle his nerves any."

"Was he the one who placed the threatening phone call?"

Jake nodded. "He was trying to scare you off. But that's about as much intimidation as he had the stomach for."

A.J. looked guiltily at her mother, but Elysia looked serene. In fact, she looked smug. Smug as the kind of person other people sometimes wanted to strangle.

Reluctantly, Jake added, "He's not a bad guy, really. He reacted violently and in anger, but . . . people do."

"He tried to kill A.J.," Elysia said bleakly.

A.J. shook her head. "I don't know that for sure. I mean I know for sure he didn't actually try. I don't know that he *wouldn't* have tried, he was working himself up to something, but I'm not sure he wanted anything more than to insist that I hear him out."

Elysia looked unconvinced, but the night was taking its toll on them both. Suddenly A.J. could barely keep her eyes open. She wanted nothing more than to cuddle up with Jake in the big bed beneath the tender gaze of the Kwan Yin statue that had guarded Aunt Diantha's dreams for so many years.

The three of them talked a little more and then Elysia insisted on going home to Starlight Farm.

As the Land Rover disappeared into the night, A.J. switched off the porch light and closed the door, leaning back against it, sighing wearily. She opened her eyes. Jake was smiling down at her.

"So today's the big day?"

Jake sat on the side of the bed fastening his watch as A.J. examined herself in the dressing table mirror. His reflected gaze met hers.

She said, carefully neutral, "The day the staff votes on the new slogan? Yes."

"It's just a slogan, right?"

Right. And wrong. It was a slogan and it looked good on coffee mugs and bumper stickers. But it was also their philosophy, it was their public commitment to their students. "Maybe. I think it'll be symbolic of whether everyone feels Sacred Balance needs to move in a new direction." She tried to infuse a little brightness into her tone. "But that could be good. Change is good they tell me."

Apparently she didn't fool him. He was watching her, his alert gaze a little sympathetic. "Well, it's part of the process, right? I mean, part of the natural flow of things. Isn't that sort of what yoga is about?"

A.J. resisted the temptation to say, *you stick to solving crimes and let me handle the traffic jam on the eightfold path*. She nodded. "Yes. I'm all primed to embrace change."

She held up her MAC lipstick. "See, I'm applying the primer right now."

Jake rose, joining her at the mirror, turning her to face him. "My favorite color. You." He kissed her.

It was four thirty. The doughnuts had been eaten, the tea and coffee drunk, and Lily had made her case for a new and improved Sacred Balance—starting with a slogan that would really capture the fresh direction they would be moving in.

The last thirty minutes had been spent debating just what such a slogan might be. Lily was still strongly in favor of The Time Is Right although she had expressed a willingness to consider Now Is the Hour.

Whether her staff would be able to agree on any one slogan remained to be seen, but A.J. was now resigned to the fact that the old motto was history.

Well, perhaps "resigned" was not the word for her feelings, but she had managed to control herself, and for that she was proud. Regardless of the slogan painted on the wall, she was happy with all they had achieved together this year—and all they would continue to achieve. Hopefully one of those things would include finding a backup receptionist—and maybe an attitude adjustment for Lily—but either way, they were doing good work at Sacred Balance.

"All in favor of changing the slogan of Sacred Balance, raise your hand," Lily said.

She had made her pitch, and A.J. had to admit that much of what Lily had said made sense. And just because they changed the slogan didn't mean they were rejecting Aunt Di's work or her legacy. And if she was going to cry because she lost this vote, she might as well pack it in now. *Yogis don't cry!* How was that for a slogan?

No one moved for a moment after Lily's call for a vote. Then Simon raised his hand.

Lily smiled and threw A.J. a quick look before saying, "That's two of us."

"Sorry," Simon said. "I just wanted to say something."

Lily looked inquiring. She was smiling patiently; this was her meeting now and she knew it.

"I don't talk about my past much." Simon looked down at the conference room table as though considering the wisdom of what he was about to say. "Fifteen years ago . . . fifteen years ago to this very day . . ." He glanced up at the clock on the wall. "Just about to this hour . . . I was driving home from work—down a quiet residential street that I had driven a million times before—and a dog and a kid ran out from between a couple of cars. I saw the dog. I didn't see the kid. I hit him. I killed him." Simon's face twisted up, tears filled his eyes, and he struggled for control while the others sat in shocked silence.

"I . . . can't tell you what that did to me. How that changed my life. It wasn't my fault. The police . . . court . . . even the kid's parents . . . everyone said . . . not my fault." Simon sucked in a harsh breath. "But . . . I couldn't forgive myself. Couldn't get past it. Couldn't let it go. I lost my friends, wife, my job; I lost just about everything because I could *not* forgive myself, couldn't forget even for a minute what I'd done."

A.J. wiped hastily at her wet face, glanced up, and to her astonishment saw that Lily's eyes were suspiciously bright as she watched Simon struggle for the words.

"Di . . . was the one friend who wouldn't leave. Wouldn't let me drive her away. Wouldn't let me go when I thought letting go was all that I wanted. Well, you know Di. When did she take no for an answer?" Simon managed a half-smile at some long-ago memory. "She said, insisted, that it would get better. That one day I would be glad to be alive again. I told her my life was over, and she said . . . *that* life was over, and a new life had begun. I told her I didn't want it. And she said . . . one day you will. One day it could happen."

Simon fell silent.

No one spoke.

No one moved.

At last Denise expelled a long shaky sigh, and said, "Well, frankly, I hate change anyway."

Unsteadily at first, everyone began to laugh.

A FEW WORDS ABOUT
SUN SALUTATION

Sun Salutes (Salutations) are a series of flowing poses or asanas designed to wake up and energize the body through the integration of body, mind, and breath. There are many, many variations. Traditionally the sun salutation is performed at dawn facing the rising sun, but do what works for you!

Step One: Let's start by sitting on your heels (legs tucked under). Sit up straight, place palms together in prayer position, thumbs grazing your sternum (breast bone).

Step Two: Inhale slowly and steadily (breath control is crucial in yoga if you want to reap full benefits), opening palms and raising arms over head. As you sweep your arms up you should be rising off your heels, arching your back and tilting your chin skywards.

Step Three: Exhaling, stretch forward from the hips, sliding palms, forearms along the floor until your forehead is at rest on the ground.

Remember to keep smoothly sliding through one asana into the next.

Step Four: Slide your palms along the floor until your body is fully stretched out, arms are fully extended before you. Brace your elbows and raise your chest—think of a cobra raising sinuously up to strike.

Are you remembering to breathe evenly? Are you remembering to breathe at all?

Step Five: As you exhale, turn your toes under and lift your hips up. Extend your legs while lowering chest and flexing arms. You're forming a human V. It's not dignified, but it feels very good on your spine!

Step Six: Inhale, dropping knees to the floor. Head facing forward. Again, focus on breathing and awareness of your body.

Step Seven: Exhale and sit back on your knees, returning to start position.

Repeat the routine five to ten times.

Recipe

Salmon Salad

A.J. is trying to eat more healthily these days. This is one of her favorite recipes (and mine). It's fast, easy, and especially tasty in the summer when you can barbecue the salmon!

Ingredients

2 fresh salmon filets
Olive oil
Head of leafy green or red lettuce
1 bag of organic baby spinach
2 green onions
2 hardboiled eggs
1 small can of sliced black olives

1 small bag of grated parmesan or mixed Italian cheese
Your favorite Caesar salad dressing (I'm partial to Girard's)

Directions

1) Rub salmon filets with olive oil so they don't stick to the pan or grill. Cook for 5–7 minutes.

2) Wash lettuce, spinach, green onions—and dry. Tear into little bite-sized pieces.

3) Slice the hardboiled eggs and set aside.

4) In a large bowl toss the greens with the olives and cheese. Dish out onto two plates.

5) Add the egg and salmon, toss lightly.

6) Add dressing—sparingly.